Catherine Ryan Hyde is th  acclaimed novels including made into a feature film Helen Hunt), *Love in the Pre* Book Club bestseller), *Cha* *Found You*.

Catherine lives in a very small town in California. She also writes novels for young adults.

For more information on Catherine Ryan Hyde and her books, see her website at www.catherineryanhyde.co.uk

PRAISE FOR CATHERINE RYAN HYDE

'This gritty love story is compelling reading'
Sun

'Surprisingly wonderful'
Mirror

'A remarkable story of the magic of love'
Daily Express

'This novel has a steely core of gritty reality
beneath its optimism'
Amazon.com

'A quick read, told with lean sentences and an edge'
Los Angeles Times

'A sweet and honest look at the pains and pleasures of love'
JANE GREEN

'A work of art . . . enchanting'
San Francisco Chronicle

www.rbooks.co.uk

Also by Catherine Ryan Hyde
and published by Black Swan

WHEN I FOUND YOU
CHASING WINDMILLS
PAY IT FORWARD
LOVE IN THE PRESENT TENSE

Other books by Catherine Ryan Hyde

JUMPSTART THE WORLD
DIARY OF A WITNESS
THE DAY I KILLED JAMES
THE YEAR OF MY MIRACULOUS REAPPEARANCE
BECOMING CHLOE
WALTER'S PURPLE HEART
ELECTRIC GOD
EARTHQUAKE WEATHER
FUNERALS FOR HORSES

Second Hand Heart

Catherine Ryan Hyde

BLACK SWAN

TRANSWORLD PUBLISHERS
61–63 Uxbridge Road, London W5 5SA
A Random House Group Company
www.rbooks.co.uk

SECOND HAND HEART
A BLACK SWAN BOOK: 9780552776622

First publication in Great Britain
Black Swan edition published 2010

Printed and bound in Great Britain by Clays Ltd, St Ives plc

Typeset in 11/15pt Giovanni Book by
Kestrel Data, Exeter, Devon.

2 4 6 8 10 9 7 5 3 1

In memory of my niece Emily, whose heart gave out on her, and in honor of my niece Sara, · who survived with distinctive grace.

Acknowledgments

First and foremost, I want to thank a wonderful local team of cardiac and cardiothoracic surgeons, Drs Stephen Freyaldenhoven, David Canvasser and Luke Faber, for their generous contributions to this work, which included not only reviewing the manuscript for medical accuracy, but allowing me to observe an actual 'open heart' surgery first-hand. Such opportunities do not come along every day in the life of an author, and I'm deeply grateful.

Many thanks also to John Zinke MD, and Nancy Vincent Zinke RN, BSN, for reviewing the early manuscript and referring me to the surgeons mentioned above.

I also want to note that the aforementioned details of cardiac surgery are quite removed from the fictional scientific opinions of my researcher character, Connie

Matsuko. I have read and studied extensively the writings of the neuroscientist Candace Pert and the psycho-neuroimmunologist Paul Pearsall, and their research was helpful to me while creating the purely fictional Connie Matsuko and her views. I do want to be clear, however, that Connie Matsuko is neither Candace Pert nor Paul Pearsall, and that I created her myself through my own interpretations of such studies. Those who argue with her theories on cellular memory should definitely see them as coming from me and no one else.

Finally, I want to thank my friend Lee Zamloch for allowing me to borrow a small but rich detail of her life, taken from a story she once told me of waiting with her daughter for a donor heart that never came. It's these small truths that bring fiction to life. I'm sorry you had to live it, but appreciate your generosity in allowing it to be used.

VIDA

On My Upcoming Death

I'm probably going to die really soon. Maybe in my sleep tonight. Maybe next week. Maybe three weeks from Thursday. It's kind of hard to tell.

I guess that'll sound like a big deal to you. Whoever you are. Whoever will read this someday. It doesn't sound like such a big deal to me. I'm pretty used to it.

I've been practicing for almost twenty years. Ever since the night I was born.

Not to rock your world too completely, but you're going to die, too. Probably not as soon as I am, but you never know. See, that's the thing. We don't know. None of us. I could get a donor heart and live happily ever after, and you could walk out in front of a bus tomorrow. Hell, today.

Here's the difference between you and me: you think

you're not going to die anytime soon. Even though you could be wrong. I know I probably will.

Sometimes I wonder what it feels like to go to bed every night figuring you'll definitely wake up. Lots of people do, I guess. Every day. But I have no idea what it would feel like to be them.

I only know how it feels to be me.

On My Mother

My mother named me Vida.

I think it's the stupidest name in the world. But I have to try to be patient with my mother. She has issues.

First of all, I'm an only child. And also, even though she's had just as much practice as I have getting used to the idea of losing me, she hasn't made much headway so far. She says it's because she's a mother, and I really have no choice but to believe her. For myself I wouldn't know. I'm not a mother and I never will be, unless I adopt. My heart could never take childbirth.

I'm lucky it got me through today.

In case you don't know any Spanish at all, 'Vida' means 'life'. Get it yet? You know. Like, make sure this kid stays alive. Not that we're Spanish. We're not. But I guess naming your only daughter 'Life' or 'Alive' might be a little weird. Even for her.

My mother has control issues, but I honestly don't think she knows. I haven't told her yet because she has a lot going on, and I'm not sure I want to stack that on top of everything else.

She rules our little world very tightly.

It's funny, too, because . . . Well, it's hard to explain why it's funny. But if you saw her, you'd get it. She's about four foot ten (she says five feet but she's totally lying), and has apple-red cheeks and a big smile, and looks like one of Santa's elves. If Santa had girl elves. She doesn't look like the dominatrix type.

But man, can she hold on.

On My Really Good Friend Esther

Esther used to be in a concentration camp.

Buchenwald.

When I say Buchenwald it comes out sounding different than when Esther says it. Even though she's been in this country for more than sixty years, she still has a very thick German accent. Most people drop the accent after a few years, but Esther hasn't dropped it yet. So she must still need it for something. When she says Buchenwald, the 'ch' sound does this very complicated hissy thing in her throat (which I could not do if I tried, and I've tried), and the 'w' sounds like a 'v'.

When Esther was my age, she was in Buchenwald.

She's very old now. I don't know how old. She won't tell me. But you can figure the years based on when the Allies liberated the camps (I'm very good on the Internet, because I spend so much time indoors, and it's something I can do without anybody getting worried and telling me to take it easy), and then do some simple math and figure she must be at least ninety.

She actually looks older. So I'm thinking maybe she lied a little about how young she was when her whole family got rounded up and put on the train.

I guess it's like my mother saying she's five feet tall when she's only four ten. I guess people do that a lot.

I don't. I tell the truth. I'm not even sure why.

Esther gave me this blank book. The one I'm writing this all down in, right now. The one you must be holding if you're reading this.

She said it's a journal, but it looks like a book. A regular bound book. Just with nothing on any of the pages. I was very excited when she gave it to me, because I figured it was a real book. I like books a lot. I rely on them.

This is true of most people who can't do much of anything without dying.

Esther said if I wanted it to be a real book I'd have to write in it myself. I'd have to write my own. Sounded like a tall order, especially for someone who might be a little short on time. I guess in a weird sort of way that was part of the idea of the thing.

Esther says nobody can tell you when you're going to die.

She says a few days before the Allies came and liberated Buchenwald, one of the camp guards laughed at her and taunted her in German. When she tells me this story – which she does a lot – she repeats what he said in German. I can't do that. But anyway, what he said translates to mean something like, 'You will die here, little Jewess.'

Esther figures that guard is dead now. I figure she's probably right, which is a satisfying thought.

She's our upstairs neighbor and she's my best friend.

She also gave me the worry stone.

On the Worry Stone

The very first day I was in the hospital (and by that I mean this time around – there have been lots of hospitals and lots of times), Esther came to see me and brought me the worry stone.

It's some kind of quartz, and it's very smooth. About the size of a walnut, but flatter. Esther said she brought it all the way from Germany with her. I think that means she must have gotten it after she was liberated. Because I don't think they let you keep any of your stuff when they put you on the train.

I guess it makes sense that when you've spent years in a concentration camp, and you are the only member of your very large extended family to walk out alive, and you're about to go all by yourself to a new country on the other side of the world, you might want something that could possibly absorb your worry.

What I don't get is why she gave it to me. I love it. I just don't get why she gave it up.

She came in that very first morning. As soon as visiting hours started. She was wearing a scarf on her head, and a coat with a big fur collar. And, honestly, it wasn't very cold outside, so far as I knew.

She showed me how she had worried a slightly smoother spot on to the stone by rubbing it with her thumb all the way to America.

She went on a boat and it took weeks.

She told me I could put all my worry into the stone. And maybe it would even wear a groove into solid rock.

I said something like, 'You're kidding. This is only skin.' And I held up my thumb so she could see what was only skin.

'Water is only water,' Esther said. 'But water can wear away stone.'

I took the stone in my hand and held it. I liked the weight of it, and the warmth of it, from being gripped so tightly in Esther's palm.

I said, 'Maybe I won't have time.'

'Or maybe you will,' she said. 'No one can tell you when you are going to die. You die when you are done. Not a moment before. Not a moment after. No matter what anyone says. No matter what anyone wishes for you.'

'Thank you for the worry stone,' I said. 'But I actually don't think I'm very worried.'

'Really?' she said.

'I don't think so.'

'Most people in your situation would be worried.'

'Maybe because they were never in my situation before. I've always been in my situation.'

Esther shook her head and clucked with her tongue.

'Maybe you have worry and you don't know. Just like you have air all around you, but you don't know. If sometimes you had air and sometimes not, then you would know.'

'Maybe,' I said.

'It really doesn't matter what you have,' she said. 'Whatever it is, give it to the worry stone all the same.'

So I've been rubbing it smooth(er) ever since.

On Lying in the Hospital Waiting for a Heart

I'm number one on the list for a heart. That's sort of the good news and the bad news all mixed up into one. Short version, it means I'm more likely to die than anybody else on the list, as best they can figure these things. So it's one of those contests nobody's dying to win. No pun intended. Then again, if there's a heart, it's nice to be number one on the list for it.

It's all very emotionally complicated.

Here's the bad news: there isn't any heart right now for anybody on the list. Not even number one. That could change at any time, I suppose. But this is now. And there isn't a heart.

Ready for the statistics that go with the 'urgent' category? The majority of patients on that list will either die or be transplanted within two weeks.

So this life of mine is coming down to the wire. One way or the other.

Last weekend was a late-spring holiday. One of those ones nobody really cares about. Just a stupid excuse to give everybody Monday off.

My mother was nervous and guilty all weekend long.

She just kept moving. All weekend. She moved into my hospital room. She moved out of it. She walked from my bed to the window. She walked back. She dusted the food tray. (Right, like dust is always a problem in hospital rooms.) Pulled dead petals off the flowers. Went out for a walk in the hall. Came back.

If I'd had more energy I'd have screamed. But I can't even breathe well enough to breathe, not to mention to scream.

Not that I don't get where she's coming from. But when you're nervous and somebody else is nervous, too, you feel like you want them to help you stay calm. Maybe it's not a reasonable request, but you do. Otherwise their nervous kind of stands on the shoulders of your nervous, and then the whole nervous thing is so big and tall that it gets to be too much nervous for anybody to bear. Especially anybody with a bad heart. And then the whole shaky system wants to come crashing down.

So, even though I know it's probably not really fair, it was hard not to blame *her* nervousness. If for no other reason than the sheer volume of it. Figuratively speaking. It didn't literally make any noise. But in another way it drowned out everything else in the room. Hell, everything else in the *world*.

Now. In fairness to my mom, here's what was so hard about this weekend in particular: there are more traffic fatalities on a holiday weekend. Really, if you know the statistics, you know the chances are very good that someone will die.

This is why she was nervous: because maybe nobody would. Or, worse yet, maybe somebody would, but they wouldn't have a donor sticker on their license. Or their family would get squeamish, and decide to bury them all in one piece.

That drives her out of her mind.

Also, this is the part probably nobody knows but me. This is the secret part about why she was feeling guilty: because maybe somebody would. Because part of her was wishing somebody would.

Nobody did.

On Dying

I think I look at it differently than other people do. And I think the way I look at it is right, and the way other people look at it is wrong.

I don't say that about too many things. I'm not vain. I'm not one of those people who always thinks I'm right about everything. I'm just one of those people who always thinks I'm right about this.

Here's why, and I think it's a very good reason: let's say the subject is something else besides death. Say it's a mountain. Or a tree.

Yeah. Let's say it's a tree.

I'm standing under the branches of it. Close enough to reach out and feel the texture of the bark against my palm. The rest of you are two or three miles back, peering through binoculars with foggy lenses.

Now. I ask you. Who knows more about the tree?

Here's what I think about dying: I think it's not so much about being and then not being. I think it's more about *where* you are. Not *whether* you are.

Take me. I'm lying on this hospital bed. Dying. Unless someone dies suddenly in an accident while they're still young and healthy and gives me a heart, and they die in a way that it can be harvested in time, and it gets to me really fast. But let me tell you, there's not much time left for all that stuff to fall into place. Meanwhile, here I am getting weaker and weaker. Like this light that just dims and dims. Until after a while you can't see it at all. Maybe it gives a little flicker. And then nothing. Out.

My mother cries and says, 'That's it, she's gone. No more Vida.'

But somewhere else, in some other place – some very different place – there's this little flicker of light, and somebody is saying, 'Look. What's that? Someone new is here.' And I think they're very happy about that.

And maybe the someone new isn't *exactly* Vida. Definitely not in every earthly sense of the word. And definitely she doesn't have my skinny body. But it's me.

I still *am*. I'm just not what you expected me to be, from experience.

You can live with that. Right?

Not if you're my mother you can't.

On the Heart

It wasn't even a holiday. Just a regular weekday night. And some woman skidded off the road in her car.

I don't know too much about her. Just what my mother told me. That her name was Lorraine Buckner Bailey, and that she went by Lorrie. And that she was thirty-three years old.

And the accident was pretty close by, too. San Jose. Maybe an hour by car, though I doubt that's the way they'll send the heart.

I wanted to know if she had any kids, but I was afraid to ask. My mom gets very emotional around stuff like that. Even though when she was telling me about the heart she was very, very happy. Like, if you didn't know better, you would think it was too much happy to ever knock her out of.

But I know her pretty well. And it was too much happy, really.

It's like when you're a kid and your mom sees you roughhousing with your cousins and screaming with laughter, and she says something like, 'You're laughing now, but in a minute somebody's going to be crying.' Because you're overexcited.

It's like there's a fine line between hyper-happy and falling apart.

Actually, I only know that from watching my cousins play. I could never afford to get overexcited. I wonder if I'll be able to get overexcited when I get the heart. Or whether I'll stay mostly pretty quiet out of habit.

Either way, I don't have it yet, and I definitely can't afford too much excitement right now. And my mother was sort of wearing me down. Actually, my mother was definitely wearing me down. After a while my cardiac surgeon, Dr Vasquez, came in and congratulated me, and said how happy she was for me, and told my mom I needed rest.

So I actually got a little time alone. As you can tell, I'm using the time to write in my journal.

While I'm writing, I'm picturing my mother out in the hallway, jumping up and down as quietly as possible.

On My Mother and the Heart

My mother feels guilty.

She won't say so. But I know. I know her pretty well.

She feels guilty because she's so happy. And she knows she shouldn't be happy when a woman just died. She keeps saying she's sad that the woman died, but happy that her husband was willing to donate the heart.

That's not entirely true, which is why she feels guilty.

She didn't know Lorrie Buckner Bailey. And she knows me.

Probably we should feel bad when anybody dies. I mean, if you're not into my flickering-out theory. If we're going to feel bad about anybody, then we should feel bad about everybody. Even if we don't know them, we should still feel bad.

But we never do.

On How Much I Have to Hurry

The heart is going to be on its way to us soon. Right now it's still in this poor donor, who's being kept alive on machines. But still, I think I might only have around an hour and a half, maybe two hours if I'm lucky, before they come prep me for surgery. They like to get a good head start on that, and once the heart is out and on its way to us, believe me, nobody wastes any time.

And there's all this stuff I want to write down before that happens, because I won't be writing for a few days, if not longer, and there'll be all the painkillers, and all the pain, and I'll be in the intensive-care unit for three or four days at least, and there's really no privacy at all in the ICU, and besides, maybe afterwards it'll feel like everything's different. Maybe everything I was thinking before the surgery will seem really far away, if I even remember what it was. I probably won't, though.

I'll probably have forgotten all the things I wanted to write by then.

The stuff I'm going to write is mostly not about the heart, and it'll seem like I'm getting off track, but I still need to write it. I'm going to get down as much as I can as fast as I can, and if my writing is messy, it'll just have to be messy.

That's just the way things are sometimes. First the days go by so slowly in the hospital, and every minute seems like an hour. Then they find you a heart, and everything happens all at once. Everything happens really fast.

More on My Friend Esther, So the Next Thing I Write Will Make More Sense

When I was five (nearly six) Esther moved in upstairs. She was an old lady even then. 'Then' was about fourteen years ago now. That's how long I've known her. About fourteen years. When you're nineteen, that's a long time to have known somebody.

My mother sent me up the outdoor stairs all by myself (looking back, I'm guessing she watched me out the window the whole way), with a little basket of muffins and a note to welcome Esther to the neighborhood.

I always liked it when I got to go anywhere by myself, which I think is part of why the whole Esther thing worked so well, right from the beginning. Because, you know, I'm thinking about it now, and I can't think of any other times when I got to walk out of the house on my own two feet without my mother right there with me. When I was well enough to go to school, she'd walk me there and pick me up. When I wasn't well enough, we were together all day long because she had to help me with my schoolwork. At least, until I was a whole bunch older, and by then I was so sick that I really couldn't go out much anyway.

So, at that point in my life, walking up the stairs was pretty much my far-flung frontier, and it was completely thrilling, not to mention making me feel very self-sufficient and proud.

I had to stop twice on the one flight of stairs. To breathe. Just for a minute, though.

I knocked on Esther's door, but she didn't answer, which seemed weird, because we'd noticed she didn't go out much. She had groceries delivered twice a week. Sometimes, later, she'd have a doctor's appointment or something, but just in those first couple of weeks we really hadn't seen her go out.

To this day I don't know if she was home or not. I always had a feeling that probably she was, only maybe she didn't answer the door for just anybody. That's only a gut feeling, though. I never asked her, so I can't say for sure.

After a while I gave up and left the basket in front of her door, and about two days later we got a little note from her saying thank you, but not too much more.

My mom was right on the borderline of thinking she was weird, or that there was something wrong with her, but I could tell she still wanted to give Esther the benefit of the doubt, at least for a while longer.

So then about a week or so later it was my birthday, the day I turned six. My cousins Max and Eva were there, making a lot of noise and being difficult, and two friends from the first grade, Pauline and Janna. And my mom, of course, and my grandmother and Aunt Betty, who was Max and Eva's mom. That was it. For us, that was a big party.

We were having hot dogs and pork and beans and birthday cake, and I know my mom wanted to try one more time with Esther, so she made her up a little plate.

'I'll take it up to her!' I said – screamed, actually, very desperate – because I was terribly hurt when I saw my mom was halfway out the door with the food.

Didn't she know the thrill of freedom I got from walking up those stairs all by myself? How could she take an important moment like that away from me, when I had so few? I felt hugely misunderstood in that moment.

'No, that's OK, honey,' she said. 'It's your party. You stay and enjoy your party.'

But the thing is, I wasn't enjoying my party. Not at all. The kids were too loud, they were all hyped up on sugar, and they wanted to play.

I didn't mind playing if it was something like a board game or dressing up dolls. And I liked card games a lot, Go Fish and Old Maid especially. But they wanted to play in that running/wrestling sort of way. And I not only couldn't do that, I hated to be reminded that everybody else could.

So I was just desperate to get out of there.

I pleaded with her. I actually got down on my knees and held on to her legs so she couldn't go. I was wearing a short skirt, and the rug made little indentations in my knees. They were red, and they stayed indented that way for a long time, because I remember looking down and seeing the red indentations while I was waiting for Esther to answer the door.

So, I guess I've let on that my mom gave in. Eventually. It took some heavy kneeling and begging, but she let me be the one who got to go.

This time I sort of knew, almost by the feel of the thing, that maybe Esther didn't answer the door for just everybody. So I talked to her through the door.

I said, 'Mrs Schimberg? It's only me. Vida. From downstairs. You know. The girl who left you those muffins.'

Esther is one of those elderly women who makes a big groaning, complaining noise when she pulls herself up from a sit, and I could hear that noise come right through the door.

After a minute the door opened, and she looked down at me. Not really smiling. Not making me feel bad, like I shouldn't be there, but not really smiling, either.

And she said, 'Yes, little girl? What can I do for you?'

I'd never heard a heavy accent like hers before, at least not that I could remember, and I wasn't quite sure what to make of it.

I looked down at the tray of food I was holding, so she would look there, too.

'We're having a birthday party downstairs, and my mother said to bring you this.'

'Whose birthday is it?' she asked.

I said it was mine.

'Well. Happy birthday to you, young lady. Would you like to come in?'

I was very happy and excited about that, because I'd never been to visit anybody all by myself, and I'd never known anybody that my mother didn't also know, except the kids from school, but they all knew each other, so that's not quite the same.

'Yes, ma'am,' I said, and I started to walk in.

But she stopped me gently with one hand on my shoulder.

'What I'm about to say may sound very strange to you,' she said. 'But I need to say it, and I hope you will do your best to understand it. You are welcome inside, and you may please bring that nice piece of cake. But the hot dog, which I'm guessing is a pork hot dog, and the beans, which I can see are pork and beans, will have to stay outside.'

It did sound a little strange, but I put the cake on the napkin and left the rest outside on her little stoop.

When I got inside, I was surprised by how bare every-thing was. My mother was really big on *things*. Filling up our living space with all kinds of things. Esther didn't seem too wrapped up in things. Back then I thought it was because she'd just moved in. But that never changed. I just had to change my theories on why.

The window was open, and there were two pigeons and lots of little black birds on the windowsill, eating crumbs she'd put out for them. I liked the way the breeze came in, and the way you could hear the city sounds. My mother never left windows open. It's like she was scared of air.

Esther explained to me what it meant to keep kosher. I didn't completely understand. But I did get the connection between that and why the pork had to stay out on the stoop. I tried to follow it as best I could. I understood everything except why, but I figured it would be rude to ask too many questions about a thing like that. Especially questions that have a 'why' in them, because that might make it sound like you're judging.

'Do you have room for one more piece of cake?' she asked.

'I can always eat cake,' I said. That was back when I used to eat.

'Then you eat that piece, the one in your hand. And we can let your mother think that I at least enjoyed the cake, even if I couldn't have the franks and the beans.'

So I sat with her, feeling more grown-up than I ever had, eating my third piece of cake in one day.

I looked on her counter and saw that most of the muffins we'd given her were still there, getting all old and stale, and then I looked at the windowsill again and I knew that's what the birds were eating. I could see the yellow with black dots of the lemon-with-poppy-seeds one.

I guess I knew, somewhere inside me, that my mom would be hurt and offended if she saw what had happened to the muffins, but I thought feeding birds was actually a pretty nice thing to do with them. Maybe they weren't kosher, either. I still wasn't sure how you would tell, outside of pork, which is the easy part.

After we'd talked a little, just about the usual stuff like how old I was and where I went to school (which in my case was complicated because of how sometimes I wasn't well enough and had to go to school at home), she said something nice to me.

She said, 'You are a pleasant child to have for a visitor. Normally I am not so fond of being around children, but you are welcome to visit me anytime you please. Most children are very noisy, and they never stop moving. They make me feel too weary. You don't tire me out. You hold still, like you were a grown-up, and you seem very quiet and contained.'

I guess I could accidentally be changing a couple of words in the remembering, since this all happened so long ago, but for days afterwards I kept replaying those words again and again in my head, which is why I think I'm still getting them pretty right.

I told her it was because I had a bad heart. I told her the doctors said I might only live to be a teenager, and maybe not even that long. Maybe only that long if I was lucky.

She sat back in her chair, and sighed. Then she said, 'Sometimes people will tell you things, but then those things turn out to be wrong. No matter how much they think they know.'

'That's what my mom says.'

'I've cheated death once already, for the privilege to grow old. And because I'm old, I now cheat death every day that I wake up and breathe air.'

'How did you cheat death?'

'Well, that's a long, involved story,' she said, 'and maybe one best left to another day. Maybe your guests will like to have you back at the party now. After all, it is in your honor.'

I was disappointed, but I just said, 'OK, but I want to come back and visit you again.'

And she said, 'Any time at all.'

I felt very honored, because I knew nobody else came and visited her – at least no one had up till then – and that made me feel special.

When I got outside, the beans were gone and there was an orange cat eating the hot dog. He (or she) had dragged it away from Esther's door and was chewing on it and looking very defensively over his shoulder, and then when he saw me he carried it away. That only left the bun, so I broke it up in pieces and sat down on the stairs, and then birds came close to me, because I guess it was worth it to them, for the bread.

I looked up at the window and saw Esther looking out, and she waved to me. That's how I knew I had a new friend, one I'd made all on my own.

So after that I went up and sat and talked with her nearly every day. Even on the days when I wasn't feeling my very best.

I could tell that my mom was a little concerned about the whole deal. Not like she thought there was anything bad about my visiting Esther. More like she could see I had a whole new area of my life, and it was a place she didn't get to share. I remember she asked a lot of questions about what sort of things we discussed on our visits. And she made me a little mad once, because she went up and talked to Esther behind my back.

I only found out because later Esther said, 'Your mother came up to see me. To express some concern about whether or not a six-year-old needs to be hearing stories about a concentration camp. I assured her I was not relating horrors that would give you bad dreams at night. Even so, I think she feels that all should be made to sound pleasant and happy to you. As if life is quite benign.'

I didn't know the word benign when I was six, but I didn't want to waste time asking.

'What did you tell her?'

'I told her that I sincerely felt someone needed to discuss the topics of living and dying with you, so that you would feel free to discuss these things as well. I said I believed that was why you sought out my company. Because we talk about subjects that you are not allowed to discuss in your home.'

'What did she say?'

'Not much. And she did not look completely convinced. But she went home. And you are still here visiting. So that says a lot.'

So Esther and I have been talking ever since.

So, now that I've got all that scribbled down, hopefully the next things I say won't seem so weird and out of place.

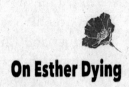

On Esther Dying

Like I said, I guess all this Esther stuff seems like a weird thing to sandwich in here. While everybody else is thinking and talking about the heart. About nothing but the heart. But I'm really not getting so far off track here as you might think.

This morning I was reading back in this blank book (OK, right, time to call it a journal because it isn't blank any more), and I was reading the part on dying. And I realized I shouldn't have called it 'On Dying'. I should have called it 'On Me Dying'.

Esther dying is a whole different ball game.

I wanted to change it, but then I would've had to squeeze a word in-between the two other words, or cross it out and write it again, and either way it would have been messy. I couldn't bring myself to make this book messy. Even though it's kind of messy now anyway because I'm in a hurry and writing really fast.

I guess I'm getting a little off track here after all.

Here's the thing: I was supposed to die before Esther. This is more or less why we're friends. Most people who are not quite twenty don't have a really good friend who is over ninety. What would they have in common? But Esther and I have something in common. We are wrapping up here.

Oops. Look what I just wrote. A mistake. Something that might not be true any more. Esther and I *had* something in common, because we were both people who were going to die pretty soon. But I just got a heart. Let's say I survive the operation. What if it works, and I just keep being OK? We won't have anything in common any more. Plus, then I'll have to deal with losing Esther. I'm not sure how I would do with that.

This is why I don't have what you might call tons and tons of friends. Because nobody really wants to get close to someone when they are just on their way out the door. I did have one nice friend named Janie, from about the third grade to halfway through sixth, but then she moved away. We still write. Now and then.

Sometimes I wonder if the reason I didn't make lots more friends was because they stayed away from me, or because I stayed away from them. When you've been doing something for so long, it gets harder to dissect it and figure it out. But it's possible that I was the one who didn't want to risk my heart too much.

Oh, interesting. That's interesting what I just wrote, and I didn't realize it until after I wrote it.

But I did with Esther (risk my heart, that is), because I was so sure I would die first. And then I would never have to deal with my friend flickering out.

See, all that stuff I said about the light flickering off and flickering on again somewhere else? There is a very definite difference that depends on whether or not you are the person doing the flickering, or the one who gets left behind. I don't want to be here when Esther flickers out. I don't want to get left behind.

Maybe it should make me more patient with my mom. In fact, I'm sure it should. But, truthfully, I don't make Esther's life miserable just because I don't want to lose her. I let her be. All the same.

Listen to me go on and on about my mom. I should get off her case. I'm sure she's doing the best she can, even if it *is* a little shaky.

Anyway. Everybody thinks getting a heart for me is all good. And it's good, don't get me wrong. It's more good than it's not good. But nothing is really all good. Everything always looks all good from the outside, but then when it finally lets you in it's more complex and layered inside than you ever would have guessed.

Don't ever try to explain that to anybody. They are outside. It will never work.

I guess it really should make me understand my mother better. Like I said.

But, really, if you knew her, I think you'd want to scream, too.

About My Father

My mom just brought me in an email from him.

She was holding it like it might have some kind of a disease.

I think she never forgave my father for leaving. But it's not like he left because he was disinterested or something. I don't think there was another woman or anything like that. I think it just got too hard to stay.

I wish she could cut him a little more slack. But I know better than to say so.

'Did you tell him about the heart?' I asked.

And she said, 'Of course I did.'

'Did you call him?'

'Yes.'

'You always say that's too pricey.'

'This seemed too important not to.'

Usually I don't really ask much about how often she talks to him, or what she says.

He used to come see me every weekend. Until I was seven. Then he moved to Sweden. So after that he just sends me a card and a present every birthday and every Christmas. Mostly they're good presents, except for a while they got a little too girly for me, because he wasn't here to see me grow up, in which case he would've known I was going toward the tomboy side.

Can't really fault him for that.

I write him letters three or four times a year, because it's too 'pricey' to call (I would say expensive, but you-know-who calls it 'pricey'), and he always writes back, but his letters are about ten times shorter than mine. He has a new family with four kids, so I guess that's why. Four kids will keep a guy busy. But at least he always answers.

I took the email and she left me alone for a minute to read it. Almost like my father was in the room for real and she didn't want to see him. Also, like she hadn't already read it and then printed it out. Like retroactive privacy.

Sometimes I wonder if all families are this weird, or if it's only mine.

He always calls me Kiddo. It's a sign of affection. I like it a lot.

From: Paul James
To: Vida Angstrom

Hi Kiddo,

An email doesn't seem quite right, but your mom just now told me the good news, and I guess she hasn't known for much more than an hour herself. I guess when a thing like this finally happens, it happens all at once. No time to really think. I wanted to talk to you on the phone, but she was calling from the lobby, and we thought maybe you were asleep. And I figured God knows you need your rest and your strength. But I did want to talk to you. I was disappointed that I couldn't, but your rest comes first.

And I'm sure you can figure out that if I sent you a nice card or something, it wouldn't get to you until about two weeks too late. So, email for now. Proper card and letter later.

I'm so glad there's a later for you, Kiddo. I think in my gut I always knew there would be. Everybody said otherwise, but I never believed them. I didn't say so, because they would've thought I was delusional. Now I wish I had. I could say I told you so. Oh, well.

I'll be thinking about you all day today. That's as close to being there as I can get, under the circumstances.

More to follow.

Love, Your Dad

I waited a few minutes. To see if my mom was coming back on her own. Then I called for her, in case she was right out in the hall. Which I was about ninety-nine per cent sure was the case.

I said, 'OK. Thanks. You can come back in now. He's gone.'

And she stuck her head back in, sort of tentative, like he really had just left the building. Like she had to look first. Make sure the coast was clear.

It's funny how we give some people so much power over us. Not funny funny. Strange. At least, I think it's strange. Everybody else acts like it's the most normal thing in the world.

What I Remember Best About My Dad

I didn't know I was about to take time to write this, but here I go. This memory is from back when we were all living together.

It's the one when he took me for a ride on his motor-cycle.

You see, I would always sit in the window and watch him drive up and watch him drive away. Partly because I was sad to see him go, and excited to see him come back. Partly because I just loved to watch him ride the thing. I liked the way the wind caught up in the back of his shirt in the summer (in the winter he wore a leather jacket and it didn't look the same), and blew it all around. It looked like some kind of freedom I'd only seen from a distance.

It was summer when this happened. I think I was four.

It was dusk, kind of a warm night. He came up the stairs, and I was still sitting in the window, staring at his motorcycle, where it was parked down at the curb. I spent a lot of time looking out the window, because my health wasn't too good when I was four. That was right before the third heart surgery, my Phase III Norwood procedure, and I was flagging big time. So I didn't get much time out of doors.

My mom rushed out as soon as he came in, because she'd been waiting to go someplace, but she couldn't go until he got home to take care of me. I don't remember where she was going. But I think she was mad at him for keeping her waiting.

After she left, he looked at me. I guess I looked really sad. I didn't know I looked sad. I knew I felt sad, but I didn't know it showed. But I could see it on his face.

'Poor kid,' he said. 'Poor Vida. It breaks my heart to see you staring out the window like we we're keeping you in a cage or something. Come on. Let's get you some air.'

He put me on his shoulders and we walked around the block, and people smiled at me when they walked past.

Then we got back to the front of the house, and he lifted me down from his shoulders, and I looked at the motorcycle and so did he. Then he looked at me. Then back to the bike.

'Do *not* tell your mother,' he said.

I nodded in triple-time. I felt like I was about to explode.

I got to sit on the gas tank, kind of wedged between his thighs, so I couldn't possibly fall off. Of course he didn't have a helmet my size, so he just went slow. But it felt fast to me. It blew my hair around, and I got to laughing so hard I couldn't stop, so then he turned back for home, like he was afraid I was going to laugh myself to death.

I remember how I was holding one of his sleeves in each hand, and how I had to reach up and out to do it.

Then he put me to bed, and I lay there feeling exhausted from the excitement, like he'd taken me to Disneyland and the circus all in one evening. My nerves were all jangly, and it's like I was so tired I couldn't sleep.

After a while my mom got home and they had a really bad fight. I have no idea how she found out. One of the neighbors, maybe? I just know she was pissed.

I don't remember too much of what they said, specifically, which is strange, because they were yelling the same stuff over and over, just in slightly different words each time. You'd think I'd have had plenty of time to memorize it. Maybe I don't remember because I don't want to.

I just remember how my dad said somebody needed to take care of other parts of me, besides my heart. My other needs, too. Not just the physical stuff.

Of course, that just made my mom even madder. If there's one thing you don't want to do to my mom, it's suggest she isn't taking care of me exactly the right way. That's her specialty in the world, so you're taking your life in your hands to question that in any way.

They screamed at each other for most of the night, and then the next day he packed up a few of his shirts and things and went to stay with his friend Moe from work, and then a few weeks later he moved the rest of the way out.

Two things I want to say about divorce.

One. They say kids tend to blame themselves. But I always have to be different, I guess. I sort of blamed my mother. It was just a motorcycle ride. I was fine. She could've let it go by.

Looking back, I'm sure it was much more complicated than all that. But I was four. And it seemed simple.

Also, this. Two. I read somewhere about how they've done studies of families after a child dies. And this huge percentage of couples get divorced. I forget the percentage, but it's really big.

But, so far as I can tell, nobody studies the families who know they're probably about to lose a child pretty soon.

I bet the statistics are not so hot for that, either.

On Dr Vasquez

She came into my room just now, to talk to me one more time before the big event. Fortunately I'd gotten all caught up with my writing by then.

When I saw her, I knew it was getting to be time. And I felt this jump in my chest. Well, I guess I shouldn't say my chest. That's a little euphemistic. It was my heart that jumped. Maybe it knows its days are numbered. But really, I think it was just a simple fear reaction. You know how your heart beats faster when you get scared? Like that.

So all of a sudden I could *feel* my heart, and I thought, Oh my God. You can't just cut it out and throw it away. It's my heart! Granted, it's not much of a heart, but it's mine. I've had it all my life. It's me. After all.

Who will I be without it?

But I didn't say any of that to Dr Vasquez, because she has an important job ahead of her, and I didn't want what she was about to do to seem any weirder or more complicated than necessary. To her, I mean. Even though I knew somewhere in the back of my mind that this was probably a lot weirder for me than it was for her. She does heart transplants all the time. This is my first.

She stood by my bed and reached out for my hand and I gave it to her.

She asked me how I was doing.

Probably seems like a simple enough question. At least from the outside of me.

I said I figured I was as close to OK as anybody could be in my position, and she smiled in a way that made me think she was actually listening. (Lots of people will ask you how you're doing, but usually when you answer, if you pay close attention, you'll see they're not really listening.)

She asked me if there was anything I wanted to know about the surgery. You know. Any final questions.

I said at this point I was thinking maybe the less I knew about it the better, and she laughed a little.

'Really?' she wanted to know.

'No, I'm kidding,' I said. 'You can tell me.'

'Well. You know an awful lot about heart surgery already. Too much for a girl your age, really . . . I wish you didn't have to be such an expert. This probably seems like a really unique surgery, and it is in some regards, but the basic sequence of events isn't all that different from the procedures you've had in the past. In some ways it's simpler. We make the same size incision. Saw through the sternum the same way, except this time we have to go through more of the wire sutures left from the last couple of procedures. And you probably know about how we use a cauterizing tip to keep the bleeding down—'

'Yeah,' I said. 'I hate that thing. It smells really bad.'

She looked at me, kind of curious.

'Who told you that?'

Then I knew I'd made a mistake by talking about something I promised myself a long time ago I would never talk about.

'Oh,' I said. 'That's a long story. Never mind about that.'

See, back when I had that third procedure, when I was four, I either saw or dreamed part of what happened. I have no idea which, and I probably never will.

I just know I saw myself on the table, except I couldn't see my head at all because it was behind these blue drapes. My chest wall was pried open with that big metal separator, and Dr Vasquez was standing there, along with one other surgeon and three nurses and the anesthesia guy and the heart-lung machine guy. Staring down at my heart. Watching it stop. She'd put a bunch of ice in there, on my heart. To slow it down and stop it. I could see the wet chunks of it filling up that cavity in my chest.

Actually, the heart-lung machine guy and the anesthesia guy weren't looking down into my chest. They were too far away from the table for that. They were watching the monitors. But it amounts to more or less the same thing, because they were still watching my heart stop. Even a four-year-old knows what it means when that red line goes flat. At least, this four-year-old did.

After a minute she lifted out the bulk of the ice and suctioned out the rest, and I could see the two thick tubes of blood going from me to the heart-lung machine, and how the blood was a different shade of red coming and going.

While she worked, Dr Vasquez kept stopping to use that cauterizing tip on anything that was still bleeding, and when it touched the bloody live tissue it made this little wisp of smoke or steam, and the smell was bad.

Do you dream a smell? Maybe. But probably not.

I watched her for a minute or two, from high up, and I could see really well. I could see straight down. It's almost like I was watching from up where the lights were.

Oh, and just one other weird little detail. The radio was playing. Some kind of semi-mellow classic rock.

The thing I remember best was the weird thin medical drape they had on my body, actually stuck on to my skin. It has iodine in it, so it's kind of reddish-yellowish, and I thought it was my skin at first, and it made me look like a corpse. It made my skin look papery and weird, like I was a hundred years old, or even like I was decomposing. It was shocking to me.

That and the cauterizing smell. It's really hard to forget that smell.

I never checked the details with anybody after I came out of surgery, and I never told anybody what I either dreamed or saw. Because I knew it would freak my mother out. Because, if it wasn't a dream, then it was something like being dead for a minute. I mean, if your heart isn't beating, what's that? Under the circumstances, hard to say.

But I've learned in my life that not everything that happens needs to be talked about. Some things are better left alone.

Anyway, back to my talk with Dr Vasquez.

While I was thinking about all that stuff, she was telling me more details of the surgery, and what to expect, but I was only half-listening and I don't remember enough to write them down now. I think a lot of it was about the heart-lung machine, though. How it'll circulate my blood while nothing else can. As if I didn't know *that* already.

'Anything else you want to know?'

'Is the heart here yet?'

'No, but it's being harvested. Right now. They had an

option on when to harvest, because the donor was being kept alive artificially. But it'll be on its way soon.'

And I thought, Good. Maybe more time to write.

'Are you going to take me into the operating room and take out my heart while you're waiting for it?'

'We're going to take you into the OR while we're waiting, yes. But we won't take you past what we call the point of no return. I think you know what I mean by that. Not until we see that donor heart walk through the door. Not that there's likely to be any trouble. But you just never know. What if the helicopter crashed?'

'What difference does it make? I'll die without it either way.'

'It makes a difference,' she said.

I figured she meant to her. I'm not sure how much difference it makes to me.

'Can I ask you a favor?' I said.

'Sure. Anything.'

'I know the last two times you operated on me you used those defibrillator paddles on my heart. To get it to start again.' I hadn't actually seen that. I just knew from being told. 'And that's OK, because it was my old heart. But I read that sometimes a transplanted heart will start beating on its own. Not always, but sometimes. Sometimes you can just warm it up and it'll start to beat. So maybe you could give this one a chance. You know. To beat on its own. Because I feel like it's sort of a guest. In a weird sort of way. I'll just be getting to know it, and vice versa. And I want to get off on the right foot with it. You know. Be welcoming. Treat it as politely as we can.'

She smiled, but I couldn't tell what she was thinking. I was hoping she was listening to me with the right side of her brain, or with both sides at least, and not entirely from the professional side on the left.

'Circumstances will have to dictate that,' she said. 'But I'll keep your request in the back of my mind. We'll be as welcoming as we can.'

'Thanks,' I said. 'One more thing. It's about my journal.'

'OK. What about your journal?'

'I want to write something about my transplant surgery in my journal. But I won't be able to. Because I'll miss the whole thing. So I was hoping *you* would.'

'You want *me* to write in your journal?'

'About the surgery. Yeah.'

'What do you want me to write?'

'I don't know. Anything that seems important. Anything you want. It'll be at the nurse's station. I can't give it to you now because I need to work on it some more before they come prep me. But I always leave it at the nurse's station unless I'm awake and using it, because I don't want my mother to read it. And I think she would, too, if I gave her half a chance. So just leave it back at the nurse's station when you're done, OK?'

There was a silence at that point. And she scratched her head once.

'It's a bit of an unusual request,' she said. 'Can't say I've had one like it before. But I guess I can manage something.'

'Thanks,' I said.

Then she wished me the best, and all the usual stuff you say to someone in my position, and as soon as she left I scribbled down everything I could remember about my talk with her in this journal. In a big hurry.

Dreaming About the Heart, Unless I Wasn't Dreaming

So, here's another thing that was maybe a dream and maybe not. I'm not even sure how I'm supposed to tell things like that apart.

I thought I'd written everything I wanted to write, so I drifted off into a little short nap, maybe just ten or fifteen minutes. The kind where you're only about three-quarters asleep.

And I kept having these dreams where I saw the heart.

I mean, not the actual heart. Not the bare, finely-veined muscle of it.

More like the movement of it. The journey.

I kept dreaming I saw this medical cooler. Dangling at the end of someone's hand. Moving fast across a parking lot. Sitting in a helicopter, holding perfectly still while the copter lifted off and sped in this direction. It was bright orange. The cooler, I mean. Sort of that highway-safety orange. And it had the words 'Transplant' and 'Organ' stenciled on it. It might've said 'Organ Transplant' or it might've said 'Organ for Transplantation'. I'm not sure because I couldn't really see the whole side of the cooler because of the way they had it strapped in. But other than that I could see it really well. I could even see a little wisp of steam from the dry ice.

Then I woke up, and my mother was still gone, and I wondered if what just happened to me had been all dream or partly real. Maybe part of my spirit was so involved with the journey of the heart to this hospital, to me, that I got to meet it and travel along.

Only, I don't think there would be a wisp of steam from the dry ice. I think there would be nothing until they opened it, which I guess they wouldn't do until it was in the operating room with me, and then I guess it would be a big cloud of steam. But while they're closed, I think those medical coolers are too perfectly sealed for that.

But I was asleep, mostly, and maybe my dreaming self could have been partly dreaming and added that little part in a dreamy sort of way.

And maybe the rest of it was some form of real.

I wish I'd had that dream before Dr Vasquez came in and talked to me, and then I could have asked her about the medical cooler, what color it is and all, but maybe she wouldn't know anyway, because it isn't even here yet.

Besides, maybe the whole thing was just a dream and nothing else.

But, really, I don't think so. I'm pretty good at feeling things. And that's not the way it felt.

A Secret About Me and the Heart

You know that thing I keep talking about? About changing form? Changing locations? Just flickering off here and flickering on somewhere else?

So, on the one hand, it's dying. So, really not preferable.

On the other hand, even though it's not the kind of outcome you purposely choose, it was starting to sound kind of . . . peaceful. Compared to the alternative.

Pretty much the polar opposite of having your cardiac surgeon cut you open from your collarbone to the bottom of your ribs, power-saw through your sternum, pry open your ribcage with this big metal separator (until your thoracic cavity is open so wide a surgeon can get two gloved hands in there, and everybody else in the OR can see your weak, defective heart doing its best but failing miserably), cut out this poor heart, which is the most primary organ of your survival, even though that's not saying much, throw it away, replace it by sewing in a big chunk of somebody else entirely, then wheel you into the ICU, where you'll wake up later feeling like you'd been kneeling in the street and a speeding car hit you right in the middle of your chest. (Despite being on enough IV morphine to lay out a small horse.)

Not that I'm not glad she can. I don't mean to sound ungrateful. Not that I won't be really happy about it when it's over. But right now it isn't over. Right now I'm looking it in the eye, and I'm writing the damn truth about how I feel. I'm just trying to describe how it feels to have to reset my internal clock to suddenly gear up for more pain and struggle.

So, that's my huge secret about me and the heart. I have a very small pocket of mixed feelings about it showing up when it did.

Please, whoever is going to be reading this, please, please, don't ever tell my mother what I just wrote.

Dear Vida,

I'm sitting in the doctor's lounge with the two surgeons who assisted me on your transplant. Talking over what we think you might want me to write. I wasn't really sure I was clear on that, and although these two are tremendously helpful in the OR with surgery, they're not too much help in the lounge with journaling. So I'm just going to do my best here.

I'm guessing you don't want to know too much about the bare medical details, things like whether or not I had to order another unit of blood sent, and how the ICU nurses were concerned about the amount of fluid in your drains, and how long we monitored that before we decided you were doing OK and we could go have a soda. That's all in my paperwork if you care, but I'm guessing that's not why you gave me your journal. So I'll tell you a few more personal things, things that come more from my heart. How appropriate is that?

I've known you for a long time, Vida. We go way back, don't we? This was the third time I'd opened your thoracic cavity and watched your poor beleaguered heart doing its best to circulate your blood. The first two times, of course, being the second and third phases of your Norwood procedures.

A couple of things I'll note.

One, every time I close up a patient's sternum I

have a little wish, or hope, or even prayer as the case may be, that this will be the last time any human will witness the beating of that heart. I'd wished that for you twice already, and I remember feeling that your poor heart has had far too much exposure and supervision in its short life. But this time I got to wish it with more conviction. When you're doing the Phase II Norwood, that's hard. It's unrealistic. You know there will probably have to be a third, especially in your case. Then after the third, you just don't know.

But this time, maybe we really are done.

I hope so.

Secondly, I also want to say that, even though it's not medically logical to feel this way, I felt a little guilty toward your old heart. For giving up on it. It was still living, still trying. I had to remind myself it was also failing, and would have ended your life soon. But it seemed, each time I saw it, so valiant in its efforts.

Lastly, and this is something that both of my colleagues agree with one hundred per cent: we have looked into many thoracic cavities, and seen many different conditions. We've seen old hearts, loose and oversized and covered in fat deposits. We've seen neonatal hearts barely the size of a walnut. We've seen newly transplanted hearts, small and fit, beating in old bodies, looking too young and enthusiastic for their surroundings. We've seen single-ventricle hearts like yours, struggling to do their work against overpowering odds. But there is one thing we never get used to seeing, and that is an empty thoracic cavity, one containing no heart at all. No matter how many transplants we perform, we never really get used to the strange shock of that sight.

One more thing I'm sure you'll want to know: I didn't use the paddles on your new heart. I would have if I'd had to. If it had fibrillated even a few seconds longer. But I remembered what you said, and I gave it just a tiny bit more time. Just warmed it and trusted it for a split second or two longer, and it started beating on its own. I remember you told me that was important to you. To get it off to a welcoming start.

Have a good life, Vida. Of course I'll see you again, but I hope to begin to see far less of you as these next few years go by. Go slow, take good care, but don't neglect the business of living, now that you can have a chance to get on with that.

With affection and no small measure of admiration,

Juanita Vasquez

RICHARD

Dear Myra,

The purpose of this email is to let you know I'm OK. I've been meaning to write to you for days. Ever since you more or less held me up graveside. To let you know I'm OK.

Now if I were only OK.

Truth be told, I'm still fogged in. I'm still pretty fully enmeshed in that no-man's-land, the one I think I tried to explain to you at the time. No doubt I failed. Worse yet, maybe I only thought it. Never actually said it out loud at all. It's been harder, lately, to tell the two apart.

The land I'm referring to is that numb, foggy shock that follows one around in the wake of a traumatic event. Only, not for long enough it doesn't.

It's a blessing in its own way. It really is. You wake in the morning with no orientation. No memory of what was lost. Then it comes back on you like a sleeper wave, followed by the numbing shock. It's horrible, but it's easy. All you have to do is get up and wash your face. Then you call a friend and say you got up and washed your face, and your friend says, 'Fabulous, Richard. You *will* survive.' No mention is made of the finer details: the day's work ignored, the unbalanced checkbook, the stacks of bills and messages.

No one would dare suggest what I'm sure they will later tirelessly insist, that life goes on from here. For the moment, simply putting one of your feet in front of the other is a source of pride.

I've been talking about myself in the second person a lot lately. I'm not sure what that means.

Anyway, my point is that later, I suspect, the bar will not be set so low on my life. But I'd rather not think about that right now.

I almost went to see Vida in the hospital today. Even though I know you think it's a bad idea. Even though, when we talked it over, you made that very clear. But I think I will, sooner or later. It's one of those things that burns a hole at the back of your mind, where you store it every minute of every day. You can't stop feeling for the way it's resting – or more likely not resting – there in its makeshift storage. It becomes an irritation, and you find yourself working with that, like an oyster making a pearl out of a speck of foreign object, in self-defense.

I'm just so sure I'm going to break down and see her, against advice, someday. Today began to look like as good a day as any to mess things up. But I was saved by an odd sort of a bell. Because first I have to have that small oil leak fixed on my car. I called the mechanic, but he needed a couple of days to schedule it in.

That is one detail I was not about to numb away for later. If some innocent soul were to skid off the road in a fine late-spring rain, the mist of water sitting on a wash of filmy crankcase oil, unable to soak into the pavement, just pooling there where the rubber meets the road, it was important that none of the oil be mine. That this new disaster not be any of my leaving. The fact that no rain is predicted didn't seem to influence the matter.

Come to think, no rain was predicted on the evening Lorrie left us.

Sorry to be euphemistic, but I'm so tender that the truth feels like a type of violence to me just now.

Anyway. I put off my visit until I can honestly know I'm not leaking oil on to the road, and making it the problem of some innocent soul driving behind me, or driving that same road at a later point in time. Possibly someone's irreplaceable loved one. I guess, on some level, everyone is irreplaceable to someone.

Don't you think it's strange how we're all driving everywhere, dropping little bits of ourselves along the road? Oil, transmission fluid, antifreeze. Old tire rubber. Leaving trails of discarded us wherever we go. Well, OK, I guess you'll say our cars are not us. But I'm not so sure. It's like they say about dogs, how they grow to resemble their owners after a while. Only, the dogs and the cars, both, I think it's more that we've created them in our image.

Why am I talking so much? I never used to be a man who did that.

I don't know why you put up with me, Myra. Assuming of course that you do. Maybe because you loved Lorrie as much as I did. Maybe because we are the only two people in the world who lost so much that night. People bond over all sorts of things. Why not that?

Maybe I'll write again when I've been to see Vida. We can compare notes. Undoubtedly see how right you were.

My best to you,

Richard

From: Richard Bailey
To: Myra Buckner

Dear Myra,

I haven't been to see Vida yet. I'm cheating. Writing early.

I have something to confess.

I'm mildly lactose intolerant. And of course you know Lorrie wasn't. So we always kept both kinds of milk in the house. Only that night we were out of my kind. It's silly when you think about it, because I'm a grown man. I'm thirty-six years old. I'm not ten. Why do I need to drink milk with my dinner? It's just one of those habit things.

All I had to do was to break the pattern. To say, 'Never mind. I'll drink water.'

That was all I had to do, Myra.

All I had to do.

Can you imagine what that leaves behind for me to live with?

I've said it about three hundred times since. I wake up in the night saying it. Before I wake up I'm pretty sure I was saying it in my dreams.

'I'll just drink water.'

I could have just drunk water.

Or, at very least, why didn't I go out and get milk myself? It was me who wanted it. I'd brought some work home. I was sitting in the living room working on my laptop, and Lorrie just took it upon herself to slip out and get my kind of milk.

I never knew it had rained. It wasn't even enough rain to hear on the roof. I guess it just sprinkled for a few minutes. Late-spring rain. First rain in a long time. There's some physics thing to that. Later, after it's rained hard for ten or fifteen minutes, the oil washes off the road. But at first . . . No, how could that be? You can't just hose oil off the driveway. I've tried. But it's something about the first minutes of that first rain. The water sits on top of the oil. Or something. I had it explained once. But I haven't asked since, because I couldn't bear to hear it again.

A bit of a disjointed confession. But now that I've told one other human being, maybe I can finally get to sleep.

Then again, maybe not.

My best to you,

Your son-in-law (am I still?),

Richard

The Worry Stone

When I arrived at the hospital, Vida's mother, Abigail, was nowhere to be found.

I'm not sure why, but somehow it felt important to find her.

Maybe because I felt as if I knew Abigail, having received a letter from her, thanking me profusely and discussing the prospect of our all meeting in person just as soon as Vida got out of ICU. Tossing it about as if it were the most normal thing in the world. Something that could never destroy an already tenuous life. Keep anyone from moving on. As if it were something that couldn't even cause pain.

Notice I talk about it as if I'm in no way responsible for it. But I have to report the truth, which is this: If I'd wanted to remain anonymous, so that Abigail had never known how to reach me, I could have. In fact, anonymity would have been the default setting for this donor arrangement. The donor program encourages her to write to me. But they don't give away my address. I invited further contact. Then, the moment said contact accepted my invitation, I backed up and began to feel imposed upon.

And yet, there I was in the hospital, ready for the drama to begin.

Why? Hard to say. I'm halfway guessing.

I suppose we wanted to think of it as one of those happy human interest stories on the evening news. Life springs from death, and even the deepest tragedy can open up to reveal a miracle in its wake. And here is the gratified young woman, lying in a hospital bed, breathing. Living! Living proof.

What a tribute to the deceased woman and her grieving family!

As I stood in that stark hospital hallway, I believe it was dawning on me that there would be more to it than that. It would be real.

Maybe this is why it was so important for me to find Abigail. She was my partner in denial, and I needed her. Perhaps, with her help, I could still find my way back.

I even asked at the nurse's station on Vida's floor, but as far as they knew she had gone home for a nap.

I had two choices. Come back later. As if one drive to the hospital hadn't used up a week's worth of my scant supply of energy already. Or let myself into the girl's room alone, without introduction.

I suppose there was a third choice of forgetting the whole questionable idea. Accepting that I had hit a logistical and emotional red light, perhaps for a reason.

But I dismissed that idea, having passed a point of no return within myself on this Vida issue.

I decided that seeing her alone at first was preferable anyway. With no one taking notice, able to observe that I'd come with an agenda, some indistinct expectation for gain. Especially if that expectation turned out to be misguided. Especially if I was about to fall on my ass.

I steeled myself outside her door for so long that two nurses came by and gave me questioning glances. One with raised eyebrows. As if I must need something. And I did. But nothing they would likely have on hand.

I walked through the door.

I expected her to be asleep, but she sat half-propped-up, her dark eyes wide open and staring at me. There was some startling element to them, something wild and intense. I'd expected at least to see her groggy and half-conscious. Just a handful of days after such a traumatic surgery, wasn't she still on some kind of heavy painkiller? If so, what must her eyes look like naturally?

I couldn't imagine she was nineteen, though I knew from her mother's letter that she was. She seemed high-school age, underweight and frail. Perhaps borderline anorexic, with dirty-blonde hair which might actually have been dirty, or just looked it. She had dark circles under her eyes, a body strangely slack and at rest, only her eyes fully alive. Only her right thumb was in motion, rubbing an obsessive, repetitive pattern over a small oval object.

Above the neckline of her hospital gown I could see the top of the scar, shockingly unbandaged and still stapled. It caught and tingled in my stomach and made me feel squeamish, as though I should sit down.

'You're the guy,' she said. 'Huh?'

I never bothered to ask how she knew. I figured I must be wearing it on my face, entering her room with an expression that only one person in her world could possibly fit.

'Yes,' I said. 'I am the guy.'

I walked over closer, and sat down on a hard plastic chair. I remember a vague sense of disappointment. I'm not sure what I thought I might see. Whatever it was, I didn't see it. Just a stranger, a girl I'd never met before.

She turned her head to follow me with the stare. Her assessment of me made me uncomfortable, a role reversal I hadn't meant to allow. I found myself wondering what her stare did while I was elsewhere. It was all part of that disconnectedness, that sense that only I existed in the world, because everything else felt like a dream.

'My mom wasn't kidding in her letter,' she said. 'It really was a matter of probably days. I was going to die that soon. You really get a chance to look death right in the face. You know?'

'Is that what the worry stone is about? That *is* a worry stone you've got there in your hand. Isn't it?'

She held it up under the lamp, as if to scrutinize it more closely. Or to allow me to. Or both.

'Come here,' she said. 'I want to show you this.'

I moved closer, not sure what I was trying to see.

'See how it's smoother right there?' She indicated the spot with her thumb. Then she held the stone by the edges.

I looked closely, but I wasn't sure if I could see or not. Maybe it was a little smoother. The difference wasn't all that clear.

'I actually did that with my thumb,' she said. 'Wore away stone.'

I touched her thumb. I wanted to feel it, to see if she had a callous. To see what had worn away more of what. Who was really winning.

The sudden touch electrified us. Or, actually, maybe it only electrified me. How would I know about her? She did have a heavy callous on that thumb, the kind guitar players have on the tips of their fingers.

'It's like water,' she said. And I had no idea what was like water. Certainly nothing I could see. 'You wouldn't think water could wear away stone. But it does. It just takes its time. I want to see if I can wear a little groove right into the center of this rock. It may take a while. But I've got time. Now I do.'

'I should go,' I said.

'Do you believe in love at first sight?'

Without hesitation I said, 'No.'

'No? *No?* I didn't think anybody would be cynical enough to say no.'

Her thumb returned to its almost circular pattern over the worry stone. I guess if your goal is to wear a groove into solid rock it doesn't pay to take vacations.

'Well, I stand by my answer,' I said. 'But it's not cynicism. Just the opposite. I have too much respect for love to believe that. I don't even believe in the concept of falling in love. The falling part, I mean. We should all be so lucky that love is something you just fall into. Like, "A funny thing happened to me today. I was walking down the street and I tripped and fell into some love." You don't fall down to love, you climb up to it. There's hard work involved. That's why I believe you can't love someone you don't know. Loving someone *is* knowing them.'

Then I stopped myself, breathed. Felt half-dizzy, as though I weren't in the room at all, which I've been feeling a lot these past few days. And I realized I'd said a great deal more than necessary.

I've been talking too much lately. On the rare occasions when there is anyone around to talk to. I never used to be a man who talked too much.

Everything is changing.

'Then I need to know you,' she said.

The door to her room swung open, and a woman came in. I knew it was Abigail, Vida's mother. I could tell. I'd known it would be.

I jumped to my feet, defensive somehow, as though I'd been caught doing something wrong.

Her head tilted, questioningly, probably hoping I would identify myself without forcing her to be so rude as to ask.

'Richard Bailey,' I said.

Her face softened, and she hurried across the room and threw her arms around me. And did not let go. I stood awkwardly, not quite embracing her in return. In time I managed to put one hand on her back, a sort of brotherly pat, and she turned me loose.

I realized I'd been forgetting to breathe.

She was small and short and had to crane her neck back to look up into my face. And I'm hardly a giant. Her eyes held too much, and too much of it was for me. I didn't want all that, so I looked away.

'You got my letter,' she said.

'Yes. Thank you for that.'

'I meant what I said, Mr Bailey, I want you to know that. We are so, so sorry for your loss. We wouldn't want you to think that because we gained from it we're not just as full of empathy for you.'

'I don't,' I said.

I could feel myself needing to get away. Needing to go back into my shut-down mode. Needing to be home, with the covers over me, and no one watching. I felt unable to carry that moment.

I had run out of gas.

'I wouldn't think that,' I said. 'As close as you just came to losing a loved one, you probably understand better than anybody.'

I edged for the door.

'You're not leaving?' she said.

'I have to. I'll be back. I'll come back when I'm . . . I just have to get some fresh air,' I said. 'Or something.'

At the door I looked back at Vida, and of course she was still staring at me. Her eyes were still the only part of her fully alive, her thumb still the only moveable piece.

'Thanks for the heart,' she said.

It was a surprisingly simple statement in the midst of all that life and death and indebtedness.

'You're welcome.'

I turned to leave. But then, for reasons hard to explain, I looked back over my shoulder one more time.

Vida had taken a bound book with a blank cover off the table and picked up a pen. I was slightly curious. Was she journaling her life? Was she anxious to write down the details of our encounter before they faded away?

I didn't stay around to find out.

I drove the forty miles home and went to bed for two days.

While I was in bed, I thought about journals. I'd never kept one. I'd never given them much thought. Was there a comfort in them? There must be, or people wouldn't bother with them. Still, I wasn't sure I could imagine where such comfort would be hiding.

Then again, how often can one really stand outside comfort and correctly imagine it, especially if it's in an entirely new and unexplored realm?

Even though I still don't know for sure if that was a journal I'd seen in Vida's hands or not, I finally got up out of bed this morning, two days later, ventured out of the house, bought this journal, and wrote down this account of my meeting with Vida and Abigail.

I can't honestly say whether I found the journaling comforting or not. Definitely compelling. There *is* something about telling a story, even to ourselves, that makes us want to continue with the telling.

But comfort . . . I think it would take more comfort than this to break through my walls.

Will there be more to my story with Vida and Abigail? I not only don't know, I don't even know my preference in the matter.

Just in case, though, I bought a nice thick journal.

From: Myra Buckner
To: Richard Bailey

Dear Richard,

I'm wondering if I might try one more time to talk you out of going to meet the girl.

Here's my concern: you asked me if I believe that the heart really is the seat of all human emotion. I'm not sure if you remember, but when I was down for the funeral, you asked me that. Just out of nowhere.

I'm not sure if I do believe that. I'm not sure it was something I'd ever thought about before.

At first I thought nothing of the question. Or little of it, anyway. I thought it was a more general curiosity.

But last night as I was going to sleep, I put it together with something else you said to me when I was down for the funeral. Were they meant to be together? I still don't know. But, if so, I'm troubled by what they add up to.

You said you'd watched a program once, a year or so ago. A handful of people with transplanted organs. They seemed to feel some connection with their donors, the people they carried a small part of, inside. A trace memory here, a favorite food there.

Do you remember saying that to me?

It crossed my mind that possibly, just possibly, you might attach too much emotional significance to Lorrie's heart. As if it can still love as she did. As if it were a valentine heart, and not a real one. But it's an organ, Richard. Just an organ. It pumps blood, and that's all.

I apologize for putting that so bluntly. I remember how you said the truth is a type of violence to you now. But really, that's why I'm saying this. I thought it might be better to hear it from me than to cut open a vein with it in the real world.

You're tender now, Richard. We've suffered a terrible loss. Don't go.

It's just an organ, Richard. It doesn't carry anything but blood. Someone else's now.

With love and apologies,

Your mother-in-law (yes, still),

Myra

From: Richard Bailey
To: Myra Buckner

Dear Myra,

Are you sure?

Is there even a very small chance you could be wrong?

Also, it's too late. Sorry.

Can't tell you who was right and who was wrong about going because the jury is still out on that.

My best to you,

Richard

The Rubber and the Road

Vida called me from the hospital. It was late, nearly 1 a.m.

'Did I wake you?' she said.

Of course she had.

'How did you get this number?'

'It's . . . *listed*?'

'Oh. Right. It is. Isn't it? What's on your mind, Vida?'

'I was just thinking about that expression, "Where the rubber meets the road". I think it used to be from a tire commercial. But I had this pen pal once who used to use it, like . . . You know. Like an expression. She would say, "Yeah, that's where the rubber meets the road." She meant, like, the bottom line. Like that's what's really the heart of the matter, you know? And that's another expression I've been thinking about. The heart of the matter. They're both ways of saying what's really important. I just thought that rubber one was interesting, because of what happened to your wife.'

We both allowed a long silence to fall.

'Well, it certainly is the bottom line at my house,' I said.

That proved to be a definite conversation-stopper.

Then, determined to start off in a cleaner direction, I said, 'I was meaning to ask you if you keep a journal.'

'Yeah, I do. I sort of call it a blank book, though. But I shouldn't. Because it isn't blank any more. Esther gave it to me. Do *you*?'

As if I would automatically know who Esther is. As if all details of her life were self-explanatory.

'Actually,' I said, 'yes. I do.'

I was just about to admit that it was very recent, and that I had picked up the habit from her. I think I was seeking some sort of instructions. As if there must be more to it than what I've been doing. As if I needed an expert to show me the way.

Before I could launch into any of that, she said, 'Oh, wow! That's really cool. We have something in common.'

And then I couldn't bring myself to disappoint her.

'Will you come visit me again?' she asked when I didn't say anything.

'Yes. But right now I'm going to go back to sleep.'

'Promise you'll come?'

'Yes.'

It was a promise made to end the conversation. Maybe I would go or maybe not. But I was acutely aware that the option was mine. I could promise, yet not go. I could simply break a promise. People do it all the time. They are not usually me. Still, a broken promise is a common enough occurrence.

It was a comfort to me, knowing I could lie if I ever chose to. An odd refuge in the otherwise unfriendly reality of everything changing.

Vida called me from the hospital. It was late. After two.

It was five days later. Five. Exactly. I counted.

'You promised,' she said.

'I didn't promise I'd come in five days or less. Just that I would.'

'Well you said you'd come see me in the hospital. And if you wait much longer I'll be home.'

'No. That's not what I said. You said, "Will you come visit me again?" And I said, "Yes."'

I wondered if I was parsing promises too tellingly. And, speaking of telling, if I was tipping my hand on the attention I paid each and every word of our interaction. Maybe she would think I merely had a photographic memory. Maybe she would not imagine that I recreated conversations in lieu of sleep.

'I'm bored *now*,' she said. 'It's *boring* in the hospital. Do you have any idea how long I've been here already?'

'Um. No. I'm not very good with time.'

'Well, I've been here for ever. Almost a month before I even had the surgery. Please come visit me tomorrow.'

'Maybe,' I said.

'Not good enough. Promise.'

'No. I can't promise.'

'But you already did. You promised me already. You can't just take it back. It's not fair.'

'I can do my best. I'm doing my best, Vida. And that's all I can do.'

'Why is this so hard for you?' she asked.

It rankled me. More so than I could have imagined. Something about having to explain myself. So much energy.

'You don't know much about grief,' I said. 'Do you?'

Quick silence on the line. Then, 'I don't know much about grief? Is that what you just said to me? *I* don't know much about grief? *Me?* That's *all* I know. I don't know just about anything *else*.'

'That explains a lot, then,' I said.

'What does it explain?'

'Maybe why you have trouble recognizing grief when you see it.'

'Promise me you'll come.'

'All right,' I said. 'I promise.'

I'm such a fool. I didn't used to be. Or at least I'm pretty sure I didn't used to be. But now I am. That's one of the very few things I know for sure.

*   *   *

The following night I drove to the hospital and parked in the parking lot.

And got no farther.

It was fairly late in the evening, which was rather telling in itself, because visiting hours were about to end. I'd left only about fifteen minutes to spare.

The sun was not exactly still up, but it was not exactly done going down, either. It glared over the hospital roof, blazing into my eyes. I shaded them with one hand, which didn't help much, if at all.

I knew I wasn't going in.

I looked up at a bank of windows, any one of a number of which could have been hers.

I was in the act of conscious breathing. Reminding myself of each breath, concentrating as if the whole system could fall apart otherwise – which I can't swear was not the truth – and longing for the days when I'd breathed quite expertly without so much as a thought.

There was a small figure framed in one window. Patient, visitor. How could I know? I wasn't close enough to see. It could even have been Vida; I can't swear it wasn't. But the odds seemed to be against that.

But then it struck me that the figure could see me far better than I could see her, what with the sun shining on me and obscuring my vision. Assuming it was a her. Vida or no, it made me feel vulnerable. Fated to be at a disadvantage. It made me feel, suddenly, as if I were walking on a partially frozen lake. Feeling the ice shift. Wondering if the next step would be the one to break me through. Plunge me down.

I got back in the car and drove home.

I'm either a terrible coward or I finally wised up. Depending on whether one put Vida or Myra in charge of the assessment. And if it were me in charge? I either have no opinion of my own, or I'm torn. Or my own opinion is torn.

I don't guess that counts as a visit.

I don't suppose that qualifies as a promise kept.

Vida called me from the hospital. It was early, for her. Before nine.

I hadn't been home all that long.

'I saw you,' she said.

'You could be wrong.'

'I'm not. I'm not wrong. I was looking out the window. I'm always looking out the window. It's the only place I can stand to look. I can't even look at these awful hospital walls any more. They're driving me crazy. They're killing me.'

'You'll get to go home soon.'

'I saw you in the parking lot. Why didn't you come in?'

'It's hard to know what you're seeing from so far away.'

'How do you know how far away I saw you from?'

'I'm tired, Vida. I'm going to go to bed.'

'Why didn't you come in?'

'I don't need to explain myself to you.'

'But you promised you'd come.'

'Next time I'll know better.'

'It isn't fair. And if you say life isn't fair I'll scream.'

'I wasn't going to say that.'

'Then what were you going to say?'

'I was going to say, "Goodnight, Vida."'

'You know I'll just call you again.'

'Yes,' I said. 'I do know that.'

From: Richard Bailey

To: Myra Buckner

Dear Myra,

I think I should have listened to you. I think you were right.

Love,

Richard

PS: I don't really think, though, that it's so much about that question I asked you at the funeral. I don't think I've completely lost it and started believing that all the love Lorrie amassed in her lifetime, particularly for me, still resides there in the heart. I think it's a simpler trap than that. Vida has a piece of Lorrie. An actual part of the woman I love. Inside. Alive. Beating. Carried with her. Wouldn't that make a difference to anybody?

I hope so. I'd like to believe that, even though I've completely lost it, I'm not completely losing it.

By the way. What I just said about my connection to the heart is true. So far as I know. At least, there is definitely a level at which it is true. Except to the extent that it isn't true. Except in light of that peculiar phenomenon in which something can be true and not true at the same time.

Good God. Listen to me. I've become an attorney for conflicting realities. Or maybe that's redundant. Maybe that's the only kind of attorney there is.

God help us all.

PPS: I boxed up Lorrie's clothes today. That's all. I hope you weren't expecting more from me. Just put them in boxes. Taped up their tops. I didn't move them out of the house or anything. I may never do that.

Let's be reasonable.

From: Myra Buckner
To: Richard Bailey

Dear Richard,

Please know it gives me no joy or satisfaction to have been right in this case.

It all makes sense, what you explained. Even the part of it that's true.

But I'm still troubled by one question: What about the old woman who received Lorrie's corneas? Why aren't you off somewhere gazing into her eyes?

Love in return,

Myra

PS: Interesting coincidence. You were packing boxes and taping them up. I was cutting the tape on boxes and emptying them out. Well, one box, anyway. I went through the attic today and found a whole carton of photos of the girls as children. I'd guess more than half include Lorrie as a child. Of course they mean a great deal to me and I could never part with them in their entirety. But I would share them with you.

From: Richard Bailey
To: Myra Buckner

Myra,

Oh, yes, please. Please, anything you can spare me. As many as you can bring yourself to let go of, thank you. It would mean so much to me.

You see, I'm slowing down on my wall. I went to a garage sale day before yesterday and bought a whole box of photo frames, all different sizes. Mostly 8×10, but a little of everything, really. A great assortment, and I picked it up for almost nothing. Classic garage-sale pricing. Which is a consideration, because of course I haven't been working. As I carried them home, for that moment, I was almost happy. Relatively speaking.

But then I got home and discovered that I only have a few photos left unframed. I'd been careful not to check. I wanted to think of my photo stash as infinite. Bottomless. Almost to the point of pretending that more photos could appear, as if by magic, at the bottom of a dark drawer or in an electronic image file.

Almost. I'm not quite that bad. Silly, huh?

I've been slowing down on adding photos to the wall. I'm down to about one a day. And I know this will sound insane, but I'm terrified of the day I have to stop. The day I see I have no more photos left to frame and hang.

I feel like that crazy Sarah Winchester, who built her crazy Winchester Mystery House (uncomfortably close to where I live), to appease the ghosts of all the souls who died of bullets fired from Winchester rifles. Adding to it and adding to it and never wanting to finish it, for fear of what would happen if she ever stopped building.

I don't know what she thought would happen. I mean, not really I don't. I should know as well as anybody, having been a guide there in grad school. (Did I ever tell you that,

Myra?) I can still recite the entire memorized tour speech.
But I can't tell you what she actually thought would happen
if she ever stopped. I only know I'd really appreciate more
photos of Lorrie. What would I do without you, Myra?

Many thanks and much love to you,

Richard

PS: Roger phoned today. From the university. He seems to
want this leave of absence to have an end date already.
As if I could simply look forward through my grief to the day
it will ease to the point of allowing me to function again.
And then I guess he wanted me to just read him off that
date. The whole thing was so completely ridiculous but also
totally overwhelming. My ending to the conversation was a
step or two short of hanging up on him. I might need a new
position when I'm ready to teach again. Or maybe he'll be
understanding. Right now I can't find a place in me that
cares.

PPS: Thanks again for the photos. Whatever you can bring
yourself to spare.

Power Cords

I was still in my pajamas and robe when I stumbled out to get the mail. In my bare feet. With my hair un-combed.

This would be an easier confession if my mail were delivered in the morning. Let's just pretend for the moment that it is.

I opened the mailbox slowly. As if it might contain poison or explosives or, worse yet, something requiring action, like a bill.

Inside I found a newsprint flyer of missing children. 'Have you seen me?' I had not, but it stretched some-thing in my chest. All that loss. Then I remembered that every one of those parents could at least hold hope of seeing their children again, and a measure of my empathy was lost. Or at least dulled. Ignoble but true.

Under that was a catalogue, and a thick, large-format Priority Mail envelope that I knew was from Myra. It didn't actually have her name on the return address, but I recognized her street name, and I don't know anyone else in Portland.

It made my heart beat too fast. Painfully so.

I took it inside, and opened it, still standing in my living room. Pulled out the thick mass of snapshots.

I couldn't really fan them out and look at them, not without a surface. I tried, but only ended up spilling some. So I dropped to my knees. Literally dropped; there was pain involved. But then, there's pain involved in everything.

I spread them out in front of me.

I didn't even exactly look at them one after another. I just left them spilled there before me like some false idol, and I just stayed there on my knees and . . .

And nothing.

I just stayed there. On my knees. In front of them.

How I would prefer to report that I sobbed like a baby. In truth I never do. How I would love to describe a feeling. But I think I have none left. Except emptiness. Just a blank slate of nothingness that seemed to swell in my chest, causing pressure. Such a large mass of nothingness needs room to operate.

Lately I've been feeling as though Lorrie's death jolted me in such a way as to pull my plug out of the wall. So now there is nothing. No power source.

Or maybe she was the entity I was plugged into. Except I walked and talked before I met her.

But maybe meeting her changed everything.

I can't tell you how much time went by before I was able to gather up the photos again. It felt like an hour, but it could have been a minute. I have no idea. If I can't even name or isolate what's going on in my own chest, how can you trust me with a thing like time?

In time, though I have no idea how much, I separated out four photos. Not for any special reason. In fact, I chose four that had been lying on the rug face down.

The rest I carefully scooped up and slid back into their cardboard envelope, more or less unseen. At least, unexamined. Not singled out with my eyes and fully taken in.

There is a method to my madness. Which, of course, does not make it anything less than madness. It just keeps it methodical, which is better than nothing.

When you look at a photo too many times, or for too long, or both, you lose it. It becomes memorized. Whatever impact of emotion it used to produce in you will be dulled to the point of nonexistence. After that you can stare at it for hours trying to recreate its original effect, but it will only dig you deeper into the hole.

Also, the experience of receiving new photos, photos of Lorrie I had never once seen before, was such a monumental one that I couldn't bear to see it end. I wanted to recreate it, over and over. Every week for months. Three or four photos at a time.

Or maybe I'd even have to whittle it down further than that. To two at a time, or even one. But I chose not to think about that in this otherwise satisfying moment. I would enjoy my generous helping of four without worry.

I turned them over in my hands.

The first was a photo of Lorrie at about the age of five or six. She was captured with her two sisters, and a litter of fairly new kittens. I studied the perfectly matched color of the sisters' hair. The three children looked so much alike that only their size seemed to distinguish them, and I studied the dark-honey color of their hair, bobbed into matching short haircuts. Lorrie's hand reached out to touch the back of a fuzzily striped kitten.

I pulled up the next one.

Lorrie at age two or three, all by herself in the photo, wearing a patterned dress that came only about half-way down her amazingly skinny little thighs. Smiling shyly, her eyes cast down. Behind her, the door of what appeared to be a fort or a castle. A vacation shot of some sort.

The third. Lorrie at age thirteen, or maybe fifteen, or maybe somewhere in-between, standing beside her parents, wearing some sort of chiffon dress which didn't suit her in the slightest. And she seemed to know it, too. She was obviously dressed for some special occasion, and it must have made her feel like a fish out of water, and it showed. Again, her eyes were cast down, refusing to meet the camera.

I hesitated briefly before turning over the fourth. Wondering if it would show her looking directly into the camera. Brimming with confidence.

I turned it over.

Lorrie with her two sisters, apparently on their way out the door for a Halloween party, or to go trick-or-treating. Lorrie's sisters were dressed as a ghost and a witch. Lorrie was the only sibling who chose a non-macabre costume. A pirate. Lorrie was a pirate. I could picture that for her. I could see her as a pirate, confident, swaggering. Ready to win the day. But in the photo, her eyes (well, her eye – one was covered with a black eyepatch) gazed at the floor.

Lorrie had been a shy girl? She'd had trouble with her confidence?

The first true hit to my gut in a long time. I mean, one I could actually feel. She'd been so sure of herself when I met her, a pathetically short nine years ago. That's one of the things that drew me to her. That comfortable sense that she knew which way to go, almost always, almost instinctively, even if I didn't.

If she'd been a shy young girl, I should have known that. Why didn't I know that? Why didn't I ask?

Why hadn't I met her sooner?

I went back to bed and took a long nap in preparation

for framing the four photos and hanging them on my wall.

I sat with my back pressed uncomfortably against the uncomfortable back of an uncomfortable chair, gazing out the window as a way of avoiding Abigail's face. The tables were the type that sat high enough over the coffee-house floor that one could use them while standing. Which made the chairs oddly high, with rails to rest your feet. But Abigail's feet did not reach the rails, so they dangled like the feet of a kindergartner. She tugged at her dress and shifted her weight often, tipping her hand on the fact that she couldn't focus off that discomfort.

'Thank you for agreeing to see me,' she said.

'It's all right.'

'I know from what you said in your email that it must be hard to get out and do much of anything.'

'Yes,' I said. 'It is.'

'Well . . . So thank you for meeting me here.'

But I had already absolved her once, and it seemed too tiring to do it again. People should consolidate their requests of me. Not use up any more of my resources than necessary. I looked out the window again.

'Do you have children, Mr Bailey?'

'Richard,' I said.

Another example. It was the third time I'd asked her to call me Richard.

'Richard.'

'No. I don't.'

'Your wife didn't want children?'

'She worked with them. She taught the fourth grade. So she loved kids.'

'She must have.' An interjection. An interruption, really.

'But sometimes we wondered if the reason she loved them so much was because she got to spend just the right amount of time with them. If you know what I mean. She got to know them, and enjoy them, but she also got to send them home. I'm not saying she was dead set against it. We discussed the idea. I guess it was one of those things we thought we still had time to decide.'

Abigail looked down into her tea and allowed a silence. A sort of forced – or at least mandatory – reverence.

Then she said, 'This next thing I'm going to say might be hard to understand if you never had a child. Or even if you had children, really, but if you never had a critically ill child. Which most people never do. So this might be hard to understand. But ever since the first night Vida was born, I've been told to prepare myself to lose her. But when you're a mother, there's just this part of you that can't accept that. Even when you know there's nothing you can do. You just can't let it be that way. You can't. So you put every ounce of energy you have into keeping your child alive, and then after a while you start to feel that it really is you keeping her alive. You know. With the sheer force of your will.'

'So, what you're saying is, you slip into the trap of magical thinking.'

'I guess that's as a good way to put it as any.'

I felt the tug of home, and tried to ignore it. But I think it spurred me to honesty.

'I'm not at all clear on what you're trying to tell me.'

'I feel guilty.'

'About what?'

'I feel like I was wishing for somebody to die in time to save Vida. Some nameless, faceless person. Only she wasn't. She was your wife and you loved her.'

I breathed deeply. It didn't really feel fair that I had been called here to save Abigail, rather than the other way around. I thought carefully, spoke carefully. Slowly, too, I noticed. As if I must be precise.

'Lorrie died because the road was slick and she skidded off it. And because the place she skidded off happened to be on the saddle of a hill, at the edge of a sharp drop. Not because of anything you wished. No offense, Abigail, but you're not that powerful.'

I waited to see if she would look offended. Instead she looked hopeful.

'So what you're saying is that I shouldn't feel guilty.'

'I can't tell you how to feel. But I can tell you there's nothing real there to feel guilty about.'

She pulled in a deep breath and smiled. I knew then that she had gotten what she'd come for.

'So that's why you wanted to see me,' I said.

'Part of it. I wanted to ask you a question, too.'

I steeled myself. Prayed this would not be tiring. 'OK.'

'Why did you decide to donate?'

'Wouldn't anybody?'

'Oh, my goodness, no! Oh, you have no idea, Mr Bailey. Richard. You have no idea how many people bury perfectly good organs when someone in their family dies. Sometimes even against the wishes of the person. When you have a child lying in a hospital bed, with only maybe a few days to live, it's unbelievably frustrating. I can't even tell you how frustrating it is. It kept me up for days at a time, because I'd get so angry I couldn't sleep.'

'I guess it's a form of not being able to let go,' I said.

'Why did you decide to donate?'

I sipped my coffee. Made a show of buying time to think. Truthfully, I'd never had to put it into words before.

'I guess so the whole thing wouldn't be so damned futile.'

Abigail nodded and said nothing.

'No, wait,' I said. 'I know. I just got it now. I know why I donated. I wanted people to never forget her. As many as possible. This way I knew you would never forget her, and neither would Vida. And anybody who loved Vida. And the woman in Tiburon who got her corneas, she'll never forget Lorrie, and neither will her family and everybody who loves her. And I could go on with the other organs, but . . . I wanted as big a group of people as possible to think about Lorrie on an ongoing basis. Not just get over it and forget.'

Abigail squirmed in her tall chair.

'I'll certainly never forget her,' she said.

'Is that a bad reason?'

'There is no bad reason. Whatever gets people to donate is great.'

Then we fell into an awkward silence. Abigail was finished with her tea, and I was just about to make noises about moving on.

'Vida would really love to see you again,' she said. 'I don't know how you feel about another visit.'

'I don't know how I feel about another visit, either.'

'She may come home as soon as tomorrow afternoon.'

'Maybe I'll visit in the morning. On one condition. If you'll be there the whole time.'

She tried to look into my face for answers, but I refused to give any away. You don't want to know, I was thinking.

'Sometimes I find her challenging,' I said.

To my surprise, Abigail burst out laughing.

'Most people do,' she said.

'Oh. OK. She just has an energy that's . . . sort of . . .'

'She's very intense.'

'Yes. I guess that's it. Intense.'

'I'll be there the whole time.'

I agreed that I would make an effort to visit.

I definitely didn't promise.

From: Richard Bailey

To: Myra Buckner

Dear Myra,

Was Lorrie a shy child? Why is she looking down at the floor in so many of these photos? She was so confident when I knew her. So calm. And steady. So the opposite of me. I was all over the map and she always brought me home safely.

I think that's part of what I loved so much about her. I think I felt welcome to relax in her presence, because she had everything so under control.

That's a bit of a role reversal, I guess. But I don't really care. I'm not hung up on gender stereotypes.

Speaking of role reversals, here's another one.

I never told this to anybody before. Not for any special reason. There's nothing wrong with it. It's just not one of those things you talk about. It's one of those things you just do.

Lorrie was a very heavy sleeper, and she always slept straight through the night. I woke up at regular intervals, but even if I got up to go to the bathroom or get a glass of water or milk, it never woke her.

So sometimes I used to lie with my head on her chest and listen to her heart beating. She always slept on her back, and the weight of my head never seemed to cause problems for her. So I would just listen.

I'm not even really sure why. There was just something comforting about it.

Now that I think about it, I don't even think Lorrie knew I used to do that.

Anyway, I guess what I'm saying is . . . What am I saying?

I guess I'm saying I had a long-standing personal relationship with Lorrie's heart.

Does that help explain any of this? I hope so.

Something has to.

Much love,

Richard

PS: I was rereading our old emails today. And I realized I'd ducked a question. I didn't do it on purpose, I don't think. Oh, hell, of course I did. I just didn't do it consciously. You asked me why I wasn't off gazing into the eyes of that old woman in Tiburon. But then you told me about the photos, and that pulled me all off track. But I guess I wanted it to.

There's really no answer, anyway. I really have no idea. If I hadn't gotten distracted, all I could have said was something like, 'Good question, damn you.'

Maybe it's because I never shared any personal visits with Lorrie's eyes while she was asleep.

From: Myra Buckner
To: Richard Bailey

Dear Richard,

I think college made a huge difference for Lorrie. When she was living at home, her sisters seemed always to overshadow her. They both had strong personalities. And I guess Lorrie did, too. But by the time she came along, they'd had so much practice. It's almost like she couldn't compete with them.

But at the same time she had that strength modeled for her.

It felt like the minute she stepped out of the house and started living on her own, she became the strongest of the lot. It's as if she'd been saving it. Like it was there all along, just waiting to be activated.

I always forget you didn't know her until she was in her twenties.

I wish I could give you what you missed.

Love,

Myra

PS: Take care of yourself, Richard. I'm worried about you.

From: Richard Bailey
To: Myra Buckner

Dear Myra,

What if Vida smokes?

I was up almost all night last night. I dozed off for about an hour or so, and then I woke up, and I started thinking there's no way to assure that Vida is taking good care of that heart. What if she smokes, or eats nothing but deep-fried foods?

I didn't give her the heart to abuse.

But then I lay awake the whole rest of the night because I knew that even if she were taking very bad care of the heart there would be nothing I could do about it.

Does that sound like a normal concern to you? Or am I really swan-diving into the deep end here? I swear I can't even tell any more.

It's scary.

With love,

Richard

PS: I'm worried about me, too.

The Maybe Place

Vida called me from home. I could see the difference in the number on the caller ID. It was late. After 1 a.m.

'I'm home now,' she said.

'So I gathered,' I said.

'You never came to see me in the hospital again. You told my mother you'd come.'

'Actually, I didn't promise. I said I'd make an effort.'

'So?'

I was sleepy, and it sounded like a hard question.

'So . . . what?'

'So, did you make an effort?'

A long pause while I decided whether to be irritated, intimidated, or guilty. Or some part of each.

'There's a question I've been meaning to ask you, Vida.'

'OK. Ask.'

'Do you smoke?'

'No. I don't smoke.'

'Did you ever smoke?'

'Not once. Not one cigarette. Can't really afford it, you know? Have enough problems with the system as it is. Besides, I've never been out from under my mother's thumb long enough to sneak anything.'

That was a good point. One I'd never thought of before. I lay in bed with the phone in one hand and the other hand behind my head. Staring at the ceiling and feeling oddly relieved. Almost satisfied.

But then it hit me that I was only taking her word. And it was the type of issue a person would lie about. Especially someone who smokes when she can't afford it.

'Let me ask you another question, then. Do you ever lie?'

'No. Never. I always tell the truth.'

'Nobody always tells the truth.'

'I've definitely gotten the sense that it's unusual,' she said. 'But I always tell the truth. I don't know why I'm different from just about everybody else that way. But I always tell the truth.'

A break. A silence. During which I pondered the idiocy of asking someone if they lie. And assuming their answer will be the truth.

'OK,' she said out of nowhere, startling me. 'Maybe not every bit of the whole truth every time. I can think of one thing, but it's pretty small. That day you came to the hospital. And I was showing you the worry stone. I said I wore that smooth spot on it with my thumb. But that was only partly true. Esther wore most of the smooth spot when she was on the boat to America. But I've been rubbing ever since I went into the hospital this last time. So some part of that smooth spot was me. It must be at least a little smoother because of me. But maybe if I really always told the truth I would have mentioned Esther's part in that. In the smooth spot.'

I still had no idea who this Esther was.

'You're right,' I said. 'That's pretty small.'

'I can't believe you thought I would smoke. I have a heart condition. I mean, I had a heart condition. But then, I guess that was the old heart, wasn't it? I guess now I have a different kind of heart condition. The kind where it's somebody else's entirely. Anyway, I wouldn't smoke.'

'I have a nephew who has asthma. And he's a chain-smoker.'

'Wow,' Vida said. 'That's amazingly stupid. Anyway, this is a weird conversation. Why are we talking about this again?'

'OK, never mind. We'll talk about something else. Let me ask you another question. What did you have for breakfast this morning?'

A long pause on the line.

'This is weirder than the last thing we were talking about.'

'It's just a simple question,' I said. Though it wasn't.

'I didn't have any breakfast.'

'OK. What did you have for lunch?'

'Chicken soup. With one matzo ball. Esther made it for me.'

I suppose I could have stopped the line of questioning long enough to find out who this Esther is, since she kept coming up, but I didn't care enough to pursue it.

'How about dinner?'

'I had a carrot and a hardboiled egg. I wasn't hungry. But my mother won't let me off with eating any less than that for dinner.'

I was thinking that explained a lot about her abnormally low weight.

'Oh, my God,' she said, 'I just got it. You're trying to figure out if I'm taking good care of the heart.'

My brain flew in a dozen directions, nearly at once, like a wild animal suddenly trapped in a cage. I was all prepared to say I was doing no such thing. How ridiculous of her to think so. My real point was . . . I thought I'd get a perfect idea any second. A perfect finish for that sentence. My mouth completely betrayed me.

It said, 'Well . . . do you blame me?'

'Oh, no,' Vida said. 'Of course not. I don't blame you for anything. I love you.'

I squeezed my eyes shut.

'Never say that to me, Vida. That is the one thing you must never, never say to me.'

Without so much as a beat of silence she said, 'OK, fine. I just won't say it, then.' Then the expected pause. Then, 'But it'll still be true.'

'That's just another way of saying it.'

'OK. You know what? You seem a little upset tonight. So I'll just call you some other time.'

I pulled a deep breath and steeled myself as best I could. I'm low on steel these days.

'No, Vida. I really think . . . Maybe . . . Maybe . . . it would be best if you didn't call here any more.'

'OK, talk to you later,' she said.

And then I heard the click.

I lay staring into the receiver for several seconds. Until the dial tone startled me out of my coma.

I hung up the phone and tried to get back to sleep. I suppose it goes without saying that I had very little success. If any.

Vida called again from home. Two nights later.

It was a little earlier than her usual. Eleven-something.

It still woke me up.

'I know what you're thinking,' she said.

'Do you?'

'You think I don't listen to you. That I didn't hear

what you said at the end of our last talk. And that I'm going against what you asked.'

'That actually sums it up pretty well, yes.'

'What would you say if I told you I listen to you better than you listen to yourself?'

'Sounds a little off the wall so far, but go ahead and make your point.'

'You think you told me you never wanted me to call you again.'

'That's what I said. Yes.'

'No. It isn't. You didn't say that. You didn't say you never wanted me to call. You said "Maybe" it would be best. You said the "maybe" twice. And you never said whether you *wanted* me to or not. You said "maybe" it would be best if I didn't. So I'm calling you again. To see if you ever made up your mind for real about that. Or if we're still in the maybe place.'

A silence fell.

It was my job to fill it.

I failed miserably.

It was a long, long silence. I'm not going to say it was minutes or any ridiculous exaggeration like that. I wasn't really counting, but if I had been, I expect I would have made it all the way to ten. Doesn't sound like much, but try counting out ten beats of silence sometime in a phone conversation. Particularly when there's a lot riding on your prompt response.

'OK,' she said. 'I'll see you, then.'

Click.
This time I didn't wait for the dial tone.
I also didn't pretend I would get back to sleep.

From: Myra Buckner
To: Richard Bailey

Dear Richard,

I think the care she's taking of the heart is a normal thing to wonder about. I'm not sure it's normal to lose sleep obsessing about it. Then again, to judge what's normal for a person assumes that the person is in normal circumstances. I would tend to give you a lot of extra slack for what you're going through right now.

I certainly do that for myself these days. I'm not sure how I'd survive otherwise. And I would hope you would do the same for yourself.

It does seem, however, that the situation inside your world might be getting worse rather than better. While I wouldn't expect it to get better very quickly, I would hope that if you really feel yourself falling into a hole, you might want to talk to somebody.

I don't mean somebody like me, although you're welcome to anytime. I think you know that. I also think you know what I mean.

You might want to talk to a professional.

But maybe first you could try being more patient with yourself. You seem to expect yourself to be functioning normally, and I think you're the only one who does.

Only, if you're going to wait and watch before seeing a professional, promise me you'll say something if things seem to be spinning out of control.

I do worry about you.

Much love,

Myra

PS: Is this about Vida?

From: Richard Bailey
To: Myra Buckner

Dear Myra,

No. Not really. At least, I don't think so. It's really about me. I think. But Vida isn't exactly helping.

Love,

Richard

Green

Vida showed up at my house without notice. I hadn't heard from her for ages. I hadn't expected to ever see her again.

I'm not sure why not. She hadn't shown any special evidence of letting go, and clearly letting go was not her strong suit. But it seemed, in some odd way, final. As if she'd simply moved on. Reached the end of her likely short attention-span and just kept moving.

Now that I really stop to think about it, I was practically delusional to think so. But that's what I'd managed to believe.

And I was OK with that. So far as I could tell.

Then there was the knock on the door. And the way it filled me with dread. Not because I thought it would be Vida, or any other variety of tragedy. Just because it represented a situation. Something I'd probably have to deal with.

I opened it anyway. I'm making progress.

She stood in my doorway in a shabby, oversized trench coat, her feet bare, her bright-red toenail polish half-chipped away, the worry stone in her right hand, her thumb working it – theoretically – smooth. Behind her I watched a cab draw away. I wondered if Vida even drove. If she'd ever had a chance to learn, like a healthy teen.

'Does your mother know you're here?'

'I'm almost twenty years old. You act like I'm a child. Can't I even come in?'

I stepped back away from the door and she did.

She cut a straight path to the opposite wall, where the pictures of Lorrie loomed like a shrine. I think I'd been adding nearly one a day, purposely not counting the balance of Myra's new additions as I wore the pile down.

'Wow,' she said. 'That's weird. She doesn't look at all like I expected. I thought I knew just what she would look like. I guess I thought she'd look familiar. Not like a stranger, you know?'

I wanted to say, 'Now you know how I felt when I first saw you.'

I didn't.

She went on. 'Lorrie, right? My mom told me her name was Lorrie. That's an OK name. I hate my name. It's weird.'

'You know what Vida means, don't you?'

'Of course I do,' she said.

'Then I would think you would like it.'

'Know why she gave me that name? Cause I tried to die the first night I was born. From all my heart stuff. She was trying to make sure I never pulled anything like that again.'

Transplant statistics rattled around in my brain. How many patients, by ratio, would still be alive in five years. How many in ten. Quite possibly I was remembering the numbers all wrong. But the message in my brain felt clear.

'Tell me something about her,' she said.

'Like what?'

'I don't care. Anything.'

'That doesn't help me narrow it down much. She was a whole person. A fairly complex person, at that. There were a lot of "things" about her, and I have no idea how to separate out which one you want to hear.'

'What was her favorite color?'

I paused briefly in that odd moment. Felt it. Which was odd in itself. Just to feel a moment, right there in the moment.

'I don't know,' I said.

Her mouth fell open. Almost laughably so.

'How can you not know your own wife's favorite color?'

'It's just not the sort of question I would ask her. This

is not high school, Vida. That's more like a teenager's dating question. It's like asking someone, "What's your sign?" It's not an important detail about someone. It's not significant.'

We stood awkwardly for a moment. I was becoming more aware of the fact that we were both still standing, and had been for a long time. It was growing more awkward by the moment, but I didn't want to ask her to sit. I didn't want to issue any invitations.

She pulled her coat more tightly around herself, which I took as a sign – the only sign she betrayed – that I had hurt her slightly. Or maybe more than slightly.

'But you know her sign,' she said. 'Right?'

'Yes. I know Lorrie was an Aries.'

'Well, good. Then you're not totally hopeless.'

She began to wander around my living room, looking a bit aimless. Gazing up at each wall and window treatment. Running her hand over the back of the couch and the two big recliners.

'Did she decorate this place?'

'Yes.'

'Then her favorite color was green.'

I looked around at my own living room as if for the first time. The rugs and the furniture all carried a color theme of deep hunter green. It seemed absurd that someone from outside the house, outside the marriage, needed to point that out to me.

I didn't answer. All answers felt like snares.

'That's weird,' Vida said. 'Green. I wouldn't have thought green. I would've guessed blue. My favorite color is blue.'

'Not surprising,' I said.

'Meaning what?'

But I just shook my head. Never answered.

I knew what I meant, but I couldn't put my finger on it. Couldn't put it into words. There's a big grouping of people who like blue, and they have something in common, but I couldn't get a verbal bead on what that was.

'OK,' Vida said. 'So colors aren't important to you. They're not significant. Fine. Tell me something about her that's significant. Just one thing. Tell me the one thing about her that you think is the very most important thing.'

I didn't even have to take time to consider the question.

'She was calm,' I said.

'Calm?'

'Yes. Calm. Peaceful. Serene.'

'That's important?'

'It was to me. Because I don't have that. I would get all spun out on the smallest details. The most insignificant complications of my day. But then when I got home and we had dinner, I could borrow some of her calm. She actually had enough to spare. I could breathe it in. Drink it. And then I'd be grounded again.'

'OK,' she said. 'That'll do.'

I felt vaguely insulted, as if my most important memories shouldn't have to pass muster for her purposes.

Vida turned off the light. I thought maybe she just didn't want to see the pictures of my late stranger-wife any more. The only light left in the room was the lamp in the corner, more of a glow than a light.

Vida let her coat drop to the floor.

She was naked underneath.

I wasn't entirely surprised. Part of me was. The part of me that was surprised seemed to be under scrutiny by the part of me that wasn't. I registered no genuine feeling about it. One way or the other. I think it mostly just bumped me back into a state of numb.

I just want to clarify that it was unwelcome. But I'm not sure I registered that as a genuine feeling, either.

She looked painfully thin. Her breasts were small and hard, like unripe fruit. So different from Lorrie, whose breasts had been full and soft, a little drooped, like over-ripe fruit, sweeter and more promising.

After that comparative observation all I could see was the scar.

I walked to where she was standing, picked up the coat, handed it back.

'Cover yourself,' I said. My voice sounded authoritarian. I noticed that. As if I had unexpectedly slipped back into my professorial mode.

'I'm not going home.'

'Put on your coat, Vida.'

She did. Blinking back what I think might have been tears. But blinking a lot, in any case. She flew off into my bedroom, which seemed odd. I thought I'd made myself so clear on that point.

Then I heard the bathroom door slam shut, and the deadbolt click into place.

That clarified a lot.

When she ventured out again, it was nearly two hours later.

I was sitting under the glow of the corner lamp, reading a novel. I tried to show no special reaction to her presence.

She stood over me, all full to exploding with her own deficiencies, whatever they may have been. I could feel energy pouring off her in waves. Intensity. But she didn't speak.

With a flip of my head I indicated the couch, where I'd laid out a pair of Lorrie's old pajamas.

Ah. I just wrote down a secret in black and white. I told Myra I'd boxed up all of Lorrie's clothes. And yet somehow I'd been allowing the dresser drawers full of underwear and pajamas to fall into a different, non-clothes category. I'd pretended they didn't count.

Vida threw off her coat and threw it on the back of the couch. In my peripheral vision I could see her look back to catch if I was watching. I didn't watch. She put my wife's pajamas on and tucked in under the blanket I'd left for her.

By this time it was close to midnight.

'Why are you being so cold to me?' she said.

I put my book down, took off my glasses. Pressed my eyes shut and squeezed the bridge of my nose, the way I always do when I'm trying too hard at thinking. It's as if I'm trying to focus all my confusion into the bridge of my nose, but I don't know why.

'I can't afford to lose anything else right now. Can you understand that?'

'No,' she said.

And I found myself thinking, No? No? I didn't expect that anyone would say no. But I said nothing.

'I set myself up for loss all the time,' she said. 'Over and over.'

I wanted to say, 'Yes. I know. I know lots of people who do. And I do not aspire to join their ranks.'

Instead I said, 'Well. Women have a higher pain threshold. About nine times higher. I think. I think I read that somewhere. It's for the purpose of childbirth, but I suppose it comes in handy for all kinds of things. I just lost my wife, Vida. Can't you show any respect for that at all?'

'What if I waited?'

'It takes years to get over a thing like that.'

'What if I waited years? What if a couple years down

the road I was still right here, waiting? A couple years is a long time.' She held up her right hand, stone and all, her thumb still smoothing. 'Maybe I could even wear down *you*. You think I don't know that you really wanted me here? All you had to do was tell me you never wanted me to call again.'

'I was just afraid of hurting your feelings.'

'You're a lousy liar.'

'Well,' I said. 'I guess I haven't had enough practice.'

And then I picked up my book again.

About an hour later I knew she was asleep, because her thumb stopped moving, and the stone slid from her hand. I stole over to the couch and sat on the edge without disturbing her.

I pulled her blanket down a little. Stopped to see if she would wake up. She didn't. Then I placed my ear lightly against Lorrie's old flannel pajamas. Again waited to be sure I wouldn't wake her. But she just kept sleeping.

So I put my ear down and listened.

I closed my eyes, to block out everything that wasn't right. All that remained was the feel of the flannel on my face and the sound of the heart beating against my ear. But it still wasn't quite the same. I knew how it was supposed to sound. Slow and confident and healthy. This beat was quicker, as if unsure of itself. As if needing to remind me that even the most minute details had undergone change.

Even the heart was not exactly the same.

After a few minutes of that I felt around for the worry stone. I found it half-fallen behind the cushions at the back of the couch. I placed it in the pocket of Lorrie's pajama top.

I wondered, if I'd taken Vida up on her offer and made love to her, would she have taken a few minutes off from her battle against rock? Or would she have held and worried that stone the entire time?

Of all the things I should have been wondering, I question why that was so high on the list. But that's what I was thinking, all the same.

I rose and called Abigail. Even though it was very late.

'Oh,' she said. Obviously quite worried. 'Mr Bailey. I mean, Richard. You wouldn't happen to know where Vida is?'

'Yes,' I said. 'That's what I'm calling about. She's sleeping on my couch. And I'd really appreciate it if you'd please come collect her and take her away.'

We stood over her, watching her sleep. We still had only the glow of the corner lamp, but I didn't want to turn on a light for fear we'd wake Vida. Whatever she was about to say as her mother led her away, I wasn't anxious to hear it.

'Who belongs to the pajamas?' Abigail asked. Sounding – understandably – a bit off balance.

'She can just keep them,' I said.

A strained minute, then Abigail said, 'Where are her clothes?'

'I'm not sure that's a story you'd enjoy hearing.'

Abigail wandered over to the Lorrie wall, and stood with her back to me.

'I guess she thinks she loves me,' I told Abigail's back. 'Maybe it's not so strange. When you consider all the circumstances.'

'Don't take this the wrong way, Mr Bailey. Richard. Not to diminish you one bit as a man, or as a human being. But my daughter has a lot of emotional problems. Always has. She thinks she loves a lot of men. Every couple of months she meets a man and decides it's love at first sight.'

I felt a pang of loss when she said that. Just what I swore I could not afford. But it moved through me and I was left standing, so I suppose I could have been wrong.

I guess – I realized with no small surprise – I might have believed for just a moment what Myra was so afraid I believed. That Vida had seen something special in me, loved me the way Lorrie had, through her eyes or with her exact same heart.

Maybe I thought Vida would be there, years from

now, waiting for me to come around. So there was the loss, and I felt it.

That's when I knew I'd moved beyond the numbing shock.

'Usually the man is ten or twenty years older,' Abigail said. I wondered if she'd said other things in-between, and maybe I'd missed them. 'Maybe if her father was around, but I don't know. I'm not a psychiatrist. I just know it's like she has some big empty hole inside. She's always grabbing on to something or someone to try to fill it up. Most men are all too happy to take advantage.'

She just kept staring at the photos of Lorrie, all through this speech. I couldn't tell if she was talking without thinking, or looking without seeing, or both.

'I guess I'm not most men,' I said.

She turned halfway back to me. Smiled a little. 'Then I owe you two debts of gratitude.'

'Just take her home, and I'm willing to call it even.'

'Can you carry her to the car? She only weighs a little under a hundred.'

'She won't wake up?'

Abigail laughed. 'Nothing wakes Vida. She's just like a child that way. You can carry her snoring over your shoulder like a six-year-old. It's a part of childhood she never outgrew.'

One of many, I wanted to say. But it seemed cruel. Also unnecessary.

*   *   *

I placed one arm behind Vida's shoulder blades, one behind her knees.

She wasn't heavy.

She didn't wake up.

Abigail threw the coat over her like a blanket.

On the way from my front door to the car I heard a small tap, something hitting the driveway. I started to point it out to Abigail, knowing it was the stone. I almost said, 'Get that'. It seemed a shame to let all that hard work go to waste. To spoil Vida's chance to triumph over solid rock.

But my mouth froze up on me, and didn't work.

I picked it up on the way back to my porch, knowing full well what I had done. I wasn't stealing it. I would never do that. No, it was even worse. I was holding on to something of Vida's, something important. Something that she would later come after, or that I would later have to return.

And I knew I was doing it all the time.

Just not how to stop.

As soon as I got back into the house, I pulled it out of my pocket and began rubbing it smooth with my thumb.

From: Richard Bailey
To: Myra Buckner

Myra,

Vida was here last night. It was all very strange. I had to call her mother to come take her away. I stood in the street and watched them drive off, and in that moment, in that watching, I felt something pull out of me. It was as if something was being pulled from the center of my gut, following them away down the street. The way someone can take up a loose thread of your sweater and pull, and theoretically you could be left with no sweater.

Whether it was Lorrie's heart I felt leaving, or the girl wrapped around it, I can't say.

So what was I supposed to do, Myra? To deal with feelings like that?

I guess in the morning I could have called a friend and said, 'I washed my face just now and yesterday night I let myself feel.'

But I didn't. And do you know why not? You're smart, so you probably do.

Because my friend would have said, 'Marvelous, Richard. You *will* survive. Oh, and by the way, Richard. Life goes on from here.'

You see what I'm trying to tell you. Don't you, Myra? I will now be expected to get on with it. It's over. I don't have the numbing shock any more. And I'm no longer entitled to it. That fog has lifted, and now I can feel everything.

Everything is spinning out of control.

Richard

From: Myra Buckner
To: Richard Bailey

Richard,

I'll be out the door in less than an hour. The drive will take me almost twelve. And even that is assuming I miss the rush hour going through San Francisco.

Just don't do anything, Richard.

I'll be there as fast as I can.

Love,

Myra

From: Vida Angstrom
To: Richard Bailey

Dear Richard,

PLEASE DON'T HIT DELETE.

Just listen for just a second, OK?

First of all, I apologize for getting your email address off my mom's computer, and I hope you're not mad about that, but I've called you a lot, and you don't seem to like it much, and I was afraid you would yell.

It's not that I don't get it that you don't want me getting any closer. I mean, for a while I guess we were in that maybe place, but I tested it pretty hard and it got real definite real fast. And I'm not such a freak that I don't get that. I'm also not such a freak that I don't even know to be ashamed that I did what I did when you didn't want me to.

I'm put together pretty much like everybody. Except my heart.

I mean my old one. I keep forgetting.

Still, I guess the fact that I have this heart that used to be your wife's makes me different than everybody else, and I guess the fact that I lived every day of my life getting ready to die might make some differences.

But I'm more like everybody else than you probably think.

I'm only bugging you again because I lost my worry stone and I have to get it back. I have to. I have to find it. Esther brought it all the way over from Germany more than sixty years ago, and she put all her worry into it on the boat, and since she just barely got liberated from a concentration camp, and since nobody else in her family made it out, I think that adds up to a boatload of worry. (Pardon my pun. I didn't actually do it on purpose.)

Anyway, so it was absolutely amazing that she would give it to me, and I can't lose it. I can't.

The last time I had it was on your couch, and then I fell asleep, so I'm thinking if you pick up the couch cushions you'll find it. I definitely think it will be right there. I know it, in fact. I have to. I have to know that. Otherwise it will be gone, and it can't be. Gone, I mean. It can't be gone. It has to go like this.

Thanks for not hitting delete. Which, if you read this far, you didn't do.

Love (not the scary kind),

Vida

From: Richard Bailey
To: Vida Angstrom

Vida,

I have your worry stone.

I also have a confession to make.

I'm not sure why, as I'm usually not a big fan of the confession. I have to feel my back pretty firmly up against the wall before I'll spit something like this out. Maybe it's because you always tell the truth. I never met anybody before who always tells the truth. At least, not as far as I know.

Maybe you inspired me.

I picked up your stone from behind the couch cushions and put it in the pocket of your pajamas. Which I guess was stupid, because that's not a very secure place. I heard it hit the driveway as I was carrying you out to the car. I could have said something to Abigail. I almost did. Instead I just picked it up later and held on to it for you.

I guess I feel a little better after confessing that. I'm not sure. My own feelings have gotten so muddled these days. It's like I need a map to navigate around in them, but all the maps are outdated and wrong.

I'll give it back to you, of course, but right now Myra is here, which makes it a bad time for a visit. Myra is my mother-in-law. Lorrie's mother. She came down to help me with some things. Like staying alive and not flying apart into millions of little pieces.

See? You did it again. Inspired me to tell the truth. I'm not sure if this is a good thing or not.

Anyway, if you can be patient for just a little while, I'll make sure your stone gets home safely to you.

My best to you,

Richard

PS: Maybe I wanted to see if it would hold some of my worry, too. Maybe I wanted to see if there was anything to it. I do have some worry I'd like to be rid of. I guess we all do. But I might be a little accelerated in that department lately.

I'm sorry I didn't give it back to you that night. I was wrong.

I think I just wanted to spend a little time with it, alone.

From: Vida Angstrom
To: Richard Bailey

Dear Richard,

You carried me out to the car? That's so sweet and strong and brave and romantic and sweet. Oh. I guess I said sweet already.

I wish I'd been awake for that. It seems sad that I had to miss it.

How long will Myra be there? Why can't I meet her?

I won't pull anything weird. You can trust me.

Love,

Vida

PS: Maybe you just wanted to be sure you would see me again.

From: Richard Bailey
To: Vida Angstrom

Vida,

Myra is a very strong, very practical woman. And she advised me not to meet with you. Right from the beginning. She felt it would be opening up a can of worms, emotionally. And that I would be better off if I just stayed away. Maybe that we all would, but definitely that I would.

So that's why I think it would be better if you could just wait a few days, until she goes back to Portland. And then I'll make sure you get our worry stone back.

I'd be afraid to mail it. If it was lost in transit I'd never forgive myself.

Don't worry about losing time wearing it down, because I'm wearing it down on your behalf. I hope that's OK.

Actually, it probably isn't OK, seeing as I didn't ask your permission first. But that's what I'm doing, and I hope it's OK after the fact.

Best,

Richard

PS: I just gave this a quick read-over. Even though I have my email set to do automatic spell-checks.

Force of habit.

And I noticed I dropped the 'y' at the beginning of 'your worry stone'. So it came out 'our worry stone'. Maybe I didn't hit the key hard enough. Anyway, I'm not trying to claim it. I know it's yours.

I left that little typo in place. Thinking Freud would want me to own up to it. Or you would. Or both.

From: Vida Angstrom
To: Richard Bailey

Dear Richard,

Best? What does that even mean? Best what?

Is it so important to you not to love me that you can't even use the word to close an email? That seems weird.

And here's the other thing that seems weird: you say I inspire you to tell the truth. But you're keeping it a secret from Myra that you're about to see me again.

You know what that makes me think? That makes me think that maybe some little part of you does love me just a tiny bit. And I think that scares you.

I realize I'm being intense again. My mother always tells me I'm too intense. Lots of people tell me that. Everybody tells me that. They just don't tell me how to stop. Or why. It's the way I am. I don't tell them not to be the way they are.

So, this is me. And if you didn't want anything to do with it, you wouldn't have purposely kept my worry stone.

That's the truth, Richard. I hope you find it inspiring.

Love,

Vida

PS: I love that you're rubbing my worry stone. That's a good thing. Please keep doing that.

From: Richard Bailey
To: Vida Angstrom

Dear Vida,

I told Myra you'd be coming by sometime soon to pick up something important that you left here.

I asked her if she wanted to meet you.

She doesn't.

Please don't take this personally. It's not that she has anything against you. But she was the mother of that heart. She formed it in her womb, and meant it for her daughter. Not that she begrudges it to you in any way. Just that it would be very painful for her to see you and know you had something in your body that she grew herself, from her own blood and cells and DNA, to create Lorrie.

It's more than she can take on right now.

I could tell she was curious to meet you, and that part of her wants to. She's like me in that respect. But she can't bring herself to do it. In that respect, she is not like me. She takes better care of her own interests.

Did I say she was practical? I'm beginning to think she's more cautious than practical.

But really, to be honest, she was right when she said that meeting you could turn out to be stressful and complicated. Sorry if that doesn't feel good to hear, but it's the truth.

I also think that she believes it could open up a whole can of worms for her, too. And she is definitely less fond of canned worms than I am. Not to suggest I'm overly fond of them either. But I seem to find myself among them all the same.

So how about we meet at some neutral location, like that coffee house where I met Abigail when she wanted to talk?

Just so you know, Myra will know I'm doing that. There will be nothing short of the truth. I think you've spoiled me for anything short of the truth. I think there will be no going home again.

Love,

Richard

Matricide

I sat at that same table with her. The table I'd shared with Abigail, some time earlier. How much time earlier, I wasn't sure. I guess about . . . I have no idea. Seemed like years ago, but probably a couple of months. I'm no good with time any more. But I probably said that already.

Vida's feet reached the railings of her tall chair.

The worry stone sat on the table, looking weighty and important – at least to me – next to my cup of black coffee. I had not yet slid the worry stone over to her side of the table. And she had not yet reached for it. I don't know what that was about. I don't know much of anything. I guess I used to think I did, but it's funny how entirely wrong you can be about a thing like that.

'How did you get here?' I asked. 'Did Abigail drive you? Or did you take a cab?'

I had more or less decided, without checking, that Vida had never learned to drive.

'Neither,' she said. 'I took the bus. Well. I took three buses.' A silence, while I wondered why I thought that would pass for conversation. 'I brought you some things I wanted you to see,' she said.

She slid them across the table to me. Papers. Print-outs from the Internet. I could tell because she'd printed the navigation bars and the ads as well as the text. There appeared to be three or four separate articles, a few pages each, carefully stapled at their corners.

'I forgot to bring my glasses,' I said, turning the top one around and glancing at it. 'So I can't read it.'

'Oh,' she said.

But that was not entirely true. The headline was large enough to read with uncorrected vision. Just not the text.

Only Vida always tells the truth.

It read, ORGAN TRANSPLANTS AND CELLULAR MEMORY.

'I'll take them home and read them,' I said.

'No, you won't. You'll take them home, but you won't read them.'

I bristled, of course. Because she couldn't possibly know what I would or would not do. And because she was right. I almost said, 'How did you know that?' I stopped myself in time.

'Why would you say a thing like that?' I asked instead.

'Because you said it in the exact same voice as when you said you'd come visit me again in the hospital.'

This time I was the one who could only manage, 'Oh.'

'It's like this,' she said. 'I understand how you don't believe me yet. Because you're not in this body, and you don't know what I know. But I'm trying to spell it out for you. I'm trying to tell you that . . . when you walked into that hospital room . . . I don't know how to explain it. I thought it might help if you read the articles. I asked you if you believed in love at first sight, but I'm not sure that's what it was, really. It was just the only thing I knew to say about it. But it's not exactly like I started loving you the moment I saw you. More like I'd already been doing it for a long time.'

At a loss for what else to say, I said, 'OK. I'll read them.'

It didn't change her trajectory.

'I guess I thought it was love at first sight because I've heard of that. And how did I know it wasn't that? Because I don't know how that would feel. I don't really know much about love in general. No experience. So I just figured that must be what it was. I was guessing.'

A little snorting laugh escaped me, followed by the sting of immediate regret. I apologized in a mumbly voice.

'What's funny?'

'The idea that you've never been in love before. I thought you always told the truth.'

'I do always tell the truth. Why would you think that isn't the truth?'

'Because Abigail told me,' I said. As if from a distance, I heard my voice harden and come up in volume. I wondered why there was emotion behind the words, and what kind of emotion it might be. 'Abigail told me the truth. She told me that every couple of months you meet a guy and decide it's love at first sight.'

In the silence that followed I thought, There. I did it. I punctured that weak balloon of fiction. It was messy and painful, but it needed to be done. I thought all this with my eyes trained down to the worry stone, which I had begun to absent-mindedly finger.

When I looked up, Vida's face was white. Shockingly white. Drained of all color. I found it hard to look away.

'Oh my God,' she said.

'Look, I'm sorry. But it's better to get the truth out on the table.'

'Why would she lie?' she asked, her mouth remaining open long after the words had fallen out.

It struck me hard in my unusually vulnerable gut that she was probably not faking it. At least, my gut said she was not. It said you just can't fake that level of shock.

Maybe Vida really did always tell the truth. Maybe Abigail was a liar.

'Where was I supposed to have met all these guys? I was too sick to even go out of the house. Why did you even believe that, Richard? How could you believe that? It doesn't even make sense.'

I opened my mouth but no words came out.

She was right, of course. I should have at least doubted Abigail's version of events. I guess, in the absence of first-hand experience, I still had a sort of 'default' image of Vida living a normal life before I met her.

Why *hadn't* I at least considered the possibility that the picture Abigail had painted wasn't even possible? I guess when a tiny pink-cheeked pixie like Abigail opens her mouth to speak, I somehow expect truth to spew forth.

I thought I had plenty of time to answer. I glanced down at the stone again, and when I looked up, Vida was off her chair and halfway to the door.

'Vida!' I called out, and everyone in the coffee house turned around. As if everybody's name was Vida. I hadn't meant to shout. 'Where are you going?'

'I'm sorry,' she said. 'I hope you'll excuse me. I have to go kill my mother.'

The door made a whooshing sound as it closed behind her.

I sat nursing a deep disappointment. I'd allowed

myself just so much time to indulge my strange and ambivalent experience with Vida's company, and it stung to have it prematurely yanked away.

I turned my attention to the printouts, planning to gather and neatly stack them to take home.

That's when I realized that our worry stone was still firmly gripped in my right hand.

I waited until Myra had gone to bed in my bedroom. I'd given her my bed for the duration of her visit. And, let me tell you, it took everything I had not to call it 'Lorrie's and my bed'. There was only one bed in the house. So I was sleeping on the couch.

I took out my glasses, and the stack of printouts I'd brought home from the coffee house. They had been hiding in a scandalously old stack of unreturned student papers.

Vida is right. I'm a liar and a coward.

But I'm not a complete coward, I guess. Because I began to read them.

The first, the one whose headline I had already read, turned out to be a surprisingly scholarly article from some type of medical website. I tried to divine what type, based on the link text in the navigation bar, but it didn't help. In any case, very little was anecdotal. It outlined a new theory that suggests that the mind-body connection is so complex that memories are stored not solely in the brain, but in virtually every cell of the body. A prominent psycho-neuroimmunologist suggested that every living cell of a living system has the capacity to remember, creating pathways that extend to the skin and to internal organs . . .

I stopped reading briefly to attempt a breath. Something akin to a hiccup seemed to have emptied my lungs.

'Richard?' Myra said. And I jumped the proverbial mile. She couldn't have missed seeing it, either. She stood in the bedroom doorway, her shoulder against the jamb. 'I'm sorry, did I startle you?'

I shook my head in place of words, because if I'd tried to speak she would have learned more about my reaction. I couldn't breathe. I couldn't calm my heart. And I had no idea why her sudden presence should have jolted me so deeply.

'I thought I might start for home tomorrow,' she said. 'If you think you'll be all right here by yourself.'

'I think I will,' I said, trying to disguise my breathlessness. 'I think you should be allowed to get back to your life.'

She tilted her head at me oddly. I wasn't sure how many observations she was making at the same time. 'Are you all right, Richard?'

'Yes. Fine. Silly, I guess, but it did startle me. I don't know why. Just a voice when you don't expect one. You know.'

She regarded me for a while longer, while I wondered

if she would change her mind about my ability to cope without her.

'Well, goodnight,' she said.

'Goodnight, Myra. Thank you for coming. It meant a lot.'

When she'd closed the bedroom door again, I slid the printouts back into their hiding place amongst the student papers.

I stood in my own driveway, watching Myra drive away. Waving in that phony way we're taught to do when we're barely old enough to toddle. With one hand. Rubbing the worry stone hidden in my pocket with the other. Waiting to feel that pull of loss I'd felt when I'd watched Vida retreat down the same street. But Myra's leaving pulled nothing out of my gut and strung it painfully down the asphalt.

Then I went inside and closed the door. My plan was to finish reading Vida's printouts. I think I used to have a better track record with plans, but maybe I'm remembering wrong.

Not even a full sixty seconds later I heard the knock.

Of course I assumed it was Myra. The timing dictated that it would be. She'd forgotten something. A belonging she'd suddenly realized she'd left sitting on my bathroom sink. Something she'd meant to say. Though, looking back, she could have phoned in any final thoughts, I suppose.

Speaking of looking back, the knock itself told me it was not Myra. The very essence of what it conveyed was all wrong. Not a Myra knock at all. This knock was panicky, insistent. But I shuttled that instinctive information aside.

I threw the door wide and found myself looking over the head of the diminutive Abigail. My face fell, and I knew she saw it.

She did not look pleased.

'Where is she?' she demanded.

'I don't have her.'

'I don't believe you.'

'Well, believe what you want. But I don't.'

'I'm coming in to look.'

She barged past me and headed straight for my bedroom. I caught her by the back of her shirt. She was wearing a pink long-sleeved tee-shirt, and I watched the material stretch as she pulled forward on her Vida-finding crusade. As if nothing could stop her. But in time she snapped back again and stood, still facing the bedroom, still stretching her shirt by pulling, looking oddly like a marionette at the end of my string.

'Actually . . . you're not,' I said. 'Not unless I invite you to. This is my house, Abigail. In purely human terms, it's quite rude to barge in here and inspect it as if it belongs to you. In more of a law-enforcement sense, it's a type of illegal entry.'

She stopped pulling. 'So you *are* hiding her,' she said.

I sighed.

'OK. Look. Abigail. I will escort you to every room of my house so you can see for yourself that your daughter is not here. I just wanted to make the point that you ask someone's permission before you inspect his house.'

I let go of the tee-shirt.

'I'm sorry,' she said. Still facing away. 'I'm very worried about my daughter. May I see with my own eyes that she's not here? Because I really don't know where else she would go.'

'Well, it's a small house,' I said. 'So this won't take long.'

I took her into the bedroom, the bathroom, the kitchen. Even the garage.

She seemed to deflate further in every successive room. In the garage, I think she more or less gave up the ghost of her crusade. And with it, her abundance of energy.

'How long has she been gone?' I asked, belatedly feeling sorry for Abigail.

'Since yesterday.'

Still we just stood there, staring at my car. As if expecting it to do something. I noticed with some shame that it hadn't been washed in months. But I felt unmotivated to do anything about that.

'What about her friend Esther?'

I watched her eyebrows raise slightly. Almost stealthily. As if she would have preferred to hide that reaction from me.

'She talks to you quite a bit, then, does she?'

I sighed again. I had taken to doing that a lot. Especially around Abigail. I didn't answer. I felt sharply aware of the lie she had told me, and more sure than ever that she was the liar, not Vida. It was something I could almost feel in receptors on my skin. Not the lies, exactly, but the desperation to control the uncontrollable. Which is both the motive and the opportunity for manipulating the truth.

I don't like to give information to liars. I guess I'm not unique in that.

'I tried Esther's,' she said. 'She was very rude to me.'

'Similar to the way I was rude when you barged through my door?'

She looked briefly over (and of course up) at my face, then quickly away again.

'If you see her, or hear from her, please call me immediately.'

'Only if that's OK with Vida.'

I felt a tangled mass of her energy return. My God. I'd had no idea of the fireball hiding underneath the skin of this tiny, seemingly mild-mannered woman.

'You're conspiring to keep her away from me?'

'She's a grown woman.'

'Ha!' A snort pushed the word out into my garage.

Aimed it at the window of my filthy car. 'That shows how little you know about Vida! Turning Vida out into this world is like turning a puppy loose on the freeway.'

'Maybe so,' I said, thinking it Abigail's fault that Vida wasn't better prepared. 'But, legally, she's over eighteen and can do what she wants.'

'That's exactly what Esther said. And what Vida's doctor said, too.' She reported these opinions in a tone that made it clear she felt she'd been repeatedly given bad advice. There was a kind of spitting in her reportage.

I wanted to say, 'Oh. *That* kind of rude. The kind where people tell you the truth.' I wanted to quote my friend Fred who used to say, 'If three men call you a jackass, buy a saddle.' I didn't say either of those things. What I said, at least from Abigail's point of view, was likely a great deal worse.

'I think you need to accept the idea that if you lie about your daughter . . . make her out to be some kind of tramp . . . especially to someone she cares a great deal about . . . it's going to infuriate her and drive her away.'

No immediate response. I stood nearly shoulder to shoulder with her for a beat or two, trying to read her energy by feel. But she'd managed to draw some kind of curtain around her reaction, and I felt only blankness coming through.

Then she turned on her heel and stomped off.

I didn't follow. Just noticed the puckering of the stretched-out back of her tee-shirt as she stormed away. Just stood there in my own garage, listening for the slam of the front door. When I heard it, I pressed the button to power open my garage door, then went inside the house to fetch my keys. I pulled the car out into the driveway and set up with a bucket and hose to give it a good wash.

While I worked, it dawned on me, as if for the first time.

Vida was gone. I had no idea where she was, if she was OK, or if she was ever coming back.

And she had taken the heart with her.

VIDA

So Much to Learn

This morning I cleaned out my bank account.

Believe me, it wasn't much. But it was all I had. And then, suddenly, after all those years of saving it up, I had it all in my hand. All $576.22 of it.

It mostly amounts to birthday money I've been given over the years. I think I had this idea that I'd save it up and spend it all in one place. Not waste it. But do something kind of . . . lavish with it. And it would be fabulous. Of course, I was picturing this truly impressive wad of cash.

I think I forgot to allow for inflation.

I stood out in the street and hailed a cab. While I was waiting, I breathed. I mean, even more so than usual. More deliberately than normal. It was morning, and I could already feel the summer in the air. And I could smell the bay. I wasn't in the part of San Francisco that's the most wonderful part. Not my favorite part, that great downtown part of the city where you can just look down steep hills and see the bay stretched out in front of you.

But with a little luck I was about to be.

A cab stopped, and the driver got out and put my suitcase in the trunk, and while he was doing that I got in.

The guy was about fifty, and had black hair with a big round patch of bald scalp in the back, facing me. His name was Lawrence. I know that because it said it on his license, which was up on the dashboard where I could see it. I guess it has to be.

'Where to, miss?' he asked me while he started to drive.

I told him I wanted to go to a hotel.

He wanted to know which one.

I said I wanted it to be one that was close to the bay, so I could look right out my window and see water. I've never looked right out my window and seen water before. I told him that.

By now he was pulled over to the curb again, but I wasn't sure why.

'You don't know what hotel you want to go to?'

'I was hoping you might be able to recommend one.'

'Depends on how much you want to spend, I guess. Right down on the water, you're probably looking at three to four hundred a night.'

'Dollars?'

Yeah, I know. That was an extra stupid thing to say. But that whole moment caught me off-guard.

'Unless you went on Expedia, or something like that online, and got one of those nice deals on rooms. But it's summer. So I don't think they're exactly giving 'em away.'

There was a partition between us, like Plexiglass, and he didn't turn around when he talked. It felt weird to be talking to a bald spot through a barrier.

'I don't suppose they give a discount for cash.'

'Is that a joke?'

'Not really.'

'I don't even think they take cash.'

'How can anybody not take cash?'

'You're not from around here, are you? Where're you from?'

'I grew up here.'

'Where've you been?'

'I was always sick.'

'Oh. Sorry. Didn't mean to get personal. I thought you just landed here from some foreign country or something, except you don't have an accent. Didn't mean to pry. In the old days if you checked into a hotel with cash, they'd make you pay up front. So you couldn't skip out on the bill. These days, they got phones you can use to make long-distance calls . . . well, I guess they could lock the phone. But also they got a minibar, and even if they don't give you the key to the minibar they have all these snacks sitting out, and you can eat in the restaurant or order room service and it goes right on the bill. I guess there's some kind of arrangement they can make if you only have cash. But it'll be weird. I bet you'll end up feeling like some kind of second-class citizen. You know the meter's running, right? You OK with that?'

'Yeah, I guess,' I said.

I already owed him more than eight dollars. And we hadn't gone much of anywhere yet. But I was getting an education, so I figured it was worth it.

'How 'bout I take you to a store where you can buy a pre-paid credit card? You just give 'em your cash. There's a fee, I'm sure, but then they give you a card that looks just like a Mastercard or a Visa but it has a limit. The limit is just whatever you paid for.'

'That would be good.'

So he took me there. Which felt like we were making better progress. Because, so long as the meter was running, we might as well go someplace.

While I was inside getting a card with $500 of my life savings, turns out Lawrence was looking on Expedia. When I got back to the cab, he had a thin little laptop computer on the seat beside him, and he was clicking around online. I couldn't figure out what he was hooked up to. Must have been a Wifi zone. I have no idea how much of the city is a Wifi zone, because I never took my computer out of the house. Even taking myself out of the house is pretty new.

'What do you think of this?' he asked me.

He held the computer up so I could see it through the partition.

He'd found one room in one nice hotel near the water, and it was going for only $115 a night on Expedia.

'You want it?'

'Absolutely.'

'Read me your card number. I won't memorize it or anything.'

'No. I know you won't.'

I don't know why or how I knew that, but I did. He was a stranger. The fact that I would even say what I said must've sounded like another one of those things. You know. Those things that made me sound like I'd just arrived in the country. If not on the planet. I wasn't stupid. I know you can't just automatically trust any cab driver. I just trusted Lawrence. My gut just said I could.

After we were done making the reservation, I owed Lawrence about sixty dollars so far for the cab ride. But since he saved me a couple hundred dollars a night for the hotel, I didn't feel like I was getting a bad deal.

'At least we know where we're going now,' he said when he pulled back out into traffic. 'That's gotta be some kind of progress.'

'I'm worried,' I said. A few blocks later.

'About what?'

'I only have a little over sixty-seven dollars left in cash. And I don't think that'll be enough to pay you.'

He smiled at me in the rear-view mirror. 'Lucky thing I take credit cards. That way you'll have money left over for a tip.'

'A tip?'

'You don't know about tips? Wow. You really did just fall off the turnip truck, didn't ya?'

'I don't know what that means.'

'Doesn't matter. Look, you're on your way to a hotel. So you need to know this stuff. Anybody helps you with that bag, you gotta give 'em at least two or three dollars. If not five. If you order room service the tip is already added, but if you really wanta make 'em happy, write down a couple dollars more. It's not required. They can't make you tip 'em. But you want good service. Right? So this way they'll like you. And they'll treat you real good.'

By now we were at the hotel, and a door man was opening the cab door for me, but I had to stay inside while Lawrence was running my credit card. So the door man got my suitcase out of the trunk instead.

'What about cab drivers?' I asked.

'What about 'em?'

'How much do you tip cab drivers?'

Yeah, I know. Sounds too trusting. All he had to do was say fifty per cent. But I knew he wouldn't.

'Ten per cent's a good rule of thumb. Some give more. Up to you.'

Ten per cent would have been seven dollars and some change. Closer to eight, really. So I gave him ten.

Then I thought better of it.

'Wait. Lawrence.'

'Larry,' he said. 'What?'

'Give me back that ten, OK?'

He looked over his shoulder at me. For pretty much the first time. He looked disappointed. Actually, he looked like I'd just stabbed him or something. But he handed back the ten. Stuck it through the little window in the Plexiglass like it hurt him to even hold it.

'Thanks,' I said, and gave him a twenty instead. 'I decided the education was worth something, too. Boy. There's so much to know. I had no idea how much there was to know.'

I remembered something my father said once. To his friend Moe from work, when he was over at our house playing cards. He said, 'Moe, buddy, you don't know what you don't know.' It's a statement that makes a lot of sense in a weird sort of way.

But, back to what I was saying to Larry. 'So thanks.'

I watched his eyes get soft.

'You don't have to pay me for that, and you don't have to thank me, either. The meter was running the whole time.'

'I know. Can I pay you and thank you anyway?'

He reached his hand through the partition. I shook it.

'That's very generous, miss. You got anybody looking after you? You seem a little lost.'

'Yes and no. I'll be OK.'

'I got a daughter about your age. But you seem like maybe you need a little extra looking after.'

By this time the door man was back, and waiting to help me out.

'He's got it covered,' I told Larry, pointing to the door man.

'I wish you the best, miss.'

Like last words or something. Like I was about to jump off a cliff. But I felt like I was fine.

I'm Fine

I'm not sure what everybody was so worried about.

I stayed for three days, and it was really nice. I could see the bay right out my window. I could pick up the phone and order food and somebody would bring it up. I could watch TV without my mom yelling at me to turn down the volume.

But that's not why it was nice. Here's why it was nice.

Because it was the world.

I was not at home. I was out in the world. This was life. And I was in it. I was doing everything totally by myself. I was not relying on anyone. I was not attached to anyone. No supervision. No assistance.

Nobody even knew where I was, except Larry, and he didn't know *who* I was, so that doesn't count.

It was such an amazing feeling.

If it hadn't been for the enormous sea of brown

plastic prescription bottles on the nightstand, I would've sworn I was just a normal person, free.

But then, after three days, I figured I should leave. While I still had plenty of money left for a cab ride home. Or a cab ride somewhere, anyway. I guess my plans were not what you'd call firmly nailed down.

Also, another reason why it started feeling like maybe time to go: even though it was beautiful and comfortable, and even though it was the world, it was also a little bit boring.

No, wait. Maybe boring isn't the right word. What's the word I'm wanting here?

Lonely. That's it.

It was a little bit lonely.

Being Uncharacteristically Sneaky

Is sneaking around anything like lying?

I don't think so. Anyway, I sure hope not. I hate to think I'm spoiling my (almost) perfect record on that.

Still. I waited until it was dark to go up the stairs to Esther's. I also wore a knit scarf over my head. In the middle of summer. Right. Like nobody's going to wonder about that. And I kept to the side of the stairs that's hardest to see from our window.

It sounds terrible, I know. But I just needed more time to be on my own, and to think about things. And if my mom had seen me, she would have marched up the stairs and dragged me out, or refused to leave, and then the whole world would have been about making things right with her, which I will in time, but which I just didn't have the energy for right at that moment.

I hope that makes sense.

I rang Esther's doorbell, because I know you can only hear the doorbell from inside Esther's house. A knock you can more or less hear everywhere.

After a second I heard her call out, 'Who is it?'

But I couldn't exactly yell back, 'It's me, Vida!' Could I, now? So I just rang the bell again and waited.

She had to know I'd gone missing. My mom had to have told her. I mean, where would my mom look for me first thing? Richard's. And Esther's. So I figured she'd get the idea in a minute. Figure out who it was. Or at least who it might be.

A minute later I heard Esther's special sound. The sound she makes when she sits down in her chair, or gets up out of it. That sort of groaning elderly-lady complaint.

'Who's there?' she asked again, this time from right on the other side of the door.

I put my face right up near the crack of the door and said, 'Vida'. Kind of quiet but forceful. Like I could will my voice to go forward, nice and strong into her house, but not leak over, or make any turns, or go anywhere else.

Nothing happened. So I figured she didn't hear me. Being in her nineties, Esther doesn't have the very best hearing of anybody in the world.

After a minute I heard the sliding chain go on, and then the door opened about three inches, and I saw her beautiful face.

Well. *I* think it's beautiful, anyway. Especially right then, when I needed it most.

'Oh,' she said. 'Vida.'

And I said, 'Shhhh.'

The door closed again, I heard the chain slide, and then she opened wide and I slipped in.

We stood there in her bare living room, looking at each other.

'So,' she said. 'The prodigal daughter returneth.'

'OK,' I said. 'I have no idea what that means.'

'It's biblical.'

'Which would explain why I have no idea what it means.'

'It's not important. Where were you? Your mother is frantic.'

I told Esther all about how I went to a hotel, and how I got there and why and all. I told her I knew my mom would check here first thing. (Here and also Richard's, which is nice, because then he would know I was gone. But let me not get off track.) Anyway, I explained how I didn't come to her house right away because I was waiting for my mom to ask her where I was, and for her to say she didn't know. I wanted her to be telling the truth.

'Besides,' I told her. 'I'd never stayed in a hotel before. I wanted to see what all the fuss was about.'

She asked me if I enjoyed it.

I said it was very nice.

'Why did you leave, then? Not that I mind having you here. I just wondered.'

'That was all the money I had.'

'Oh,' she said.

She doesn't get all excited and nervous like my mother, and talk and talk and talk even though nothing more needs saying. If something doesn't need saying, Esther doesn't mess with it. And I guess it would be pretty hard to make her nervous. After everything she's lived through already.

'So, she asked you where I was,' I said. 'Right?'

'More times than I could count.'

'Think she's done asking?'

'I can only hope.'

'Can I sleep on your couch for a few days?'

'Of course. But let's try to be sure your mother doesn't know. I would never hear the end of it. You'll tell her where you are in time, though, right? Because, even though I understand your hesitance, it must be terrible for her.'

I got an attack of the guilts. And of course I promised.

I asked her why my mother would do something so horrible as to lie about me like that to Richard.

'There's only one reason I can think of that makes any sense at all,' she said. 'You are everything in the world to your mother. And she wants to be everything in the world to you, too.'

'Wow,' I said.

'Wow in what regard?'

'I guess I'm just really surprised I didn't think of that myself.'

I think that might have been when it dawned on me that I'm going to have to give this life thing a try.

There's a reason why I thought that. Sounds sort of weird and out of place, the way I just said it, but it made sense at the time. I just don't have the energy to write any more about it tonight.

More About That

So, here's the deal behind what Esther said, and why it made me want to give the whole life thing a try:

Esther knew why my mom lied.

And I didn't. Until Esther told me.

Even though it was about *my* mother. Even though I was right there while all this was happening. Esther wasn't even there, but I ask her one sentence about it, and she tells me what's what, just like that. Like pulling a key out of her pocket and fitting it into a lock. A lock *I* should've had a key to, because, after all, it's my lock.

There's only one explanation for that. Life experience.

It was so obvious that Esther knew stuff and I didn't. So it must be because she's lived. And so far I've only rested and waited for a heart.

I decided it's time to learn some of this stuff on my

own. That it's high time I jumped the nest. I mean, even more than I already have.

So I told her. I told her I was going out into the world.

It was first thing in the morning. Barely light. I was lying on the couch, not sleeping. And even though I hadn't even heard her and didn't know she'd gotten up, at least not that I was consciously aware of, I saw her moving around in the kitchen in the nearly-dark, making a cup of tea.

So I said, 'Esther. I'm going out into the world.'

She said, 'I had no doubt that you would. Sooner or later. Would you care for a cup of tea?'

'That would be very nice,' I said.

Survival

'How will you survive?' Esther asked.

Not right then. Later in the day. When I'd made it clear that I meant sooner. That I was going out into the world sooner. Not so much later.

'How will I not survive?'

'There are many ways not to survive. You could starve. How will you eat? Where will you stay?'

'I don't know,' I said. 'But it seems to me that most people who don't have much money don't starve. Mostly they figure something out.'

'Just so you know it's possible that you could die out there.'

'I guess,' I said. 'But I've been dying all my life. So that's nothing new.'

'You and I are so much alike,' she said. 'For a long time we thought we would die anytime, and then we found out we had much more time than we thought. So I think maybe it is our duty to protect that time wisely.'

I thought that over for a while. I was eating my half of a turkey sandwich she had made for us to split.

'I would think it would be our duty not to waste it,' I said.

Esther sighed. She looked sad, which made me feel guilty. I'm not sure I've ever seen Esther sad before. Wait, no. That's not right. Esther is always sad. But always the same amount. So far as I know there's never been a time when she was any sadder than any other time.

'In a way I hope that's not the case,' she said. 'Because, if so, I have made a terrible mistake. All these years mostly just trying to stay safe. But I'm sorry to say you might be right. I hate to think so, but maybe.'

Then we just chewed and looked out the window. The window was open, like it usually was, and there was nothing on the windowsill for the birds, but the birds were there anyway. Like the situation could change at any minute, without warning. Like all they had to do was wait it out.

For a while we didn't talk.

Then Esther said, 'Are you sure you're not doing it to see if the heart man will come looking for you?'

'Oh, yes, of course,' I said. 'Definitely that, too.'

When

Later, when the sun was almost down, and I was sitting watching it out the window, Esther said, 'Exactly when do you plan to do this thing?'

'I'm not sure,' I said. Because, frankly, it's one of those things that sounds better in the very moment it bursts out of your mouth. 'Definitely not today.'

'Well, of course not today,' she said. 'Today is more or less over.'

'Probably not tomorrow, either.'

'I see,' she said.

And I could tell she did see. In fact, she probably saw way too much.

Manzanar

'I've been thinking about what you said,' Esther told me at breakfast.

She had served me tea with milk and sugar, and I was sipping it. Wondering if, out in the world, somebody hands you tea with milk and sugar in the morning.

Probably not.

'Which thing?'

One of the shoulders of her housedress was falling down, and I could see her bra strap, which was held in place by a little pink safety pin.

The flesh around her neck and shoulders was all soft-looking and 'ample'. That's what my mother always says about Esther. She's an ample woman. I think it's a polite way to say fat. I think when you have watched every friend and relative you ever had starve to death, or nearly to death, while nearly starving to death yourself, ample starts to seem like the way to go.

'About our extra life, and how it's our duty not to waste it.'

'Oh. I'm sorry if I made you feel bad. I didn't mean to make you feel bad.'

'Well, not so very bad,' she said. 'If it was too late, then I would feel very bad. But I'm not dead yet. So it's not too late. It's late. But it's not completely so late that nothing can be done.'

'So . . . what are you going to do, Esther?'

'I would like to go somewhere.'

'Can I come with you?'

'I was hoping you would. I need that you would. I am too old a woman to be traveling alone.'

'Where do you want to go?'

'Not every place, like you. You are young enough for every place. I'm thinking I had better stick to only one.'

'Do you know which one yet?'

She absent-mindedly pulled up the shoulder of her droopy dress.

'Yes,' she said. More than firmly. Regally. As if she'd been thinking about it for a long time. A lot longer than just since last night. 'Yes, I have always known where I should like to go if I were ever to decide to go somewhere. I would like to go to Manzanar.' A silence. Then two pieces of toast popped up from the toaster, and she gave one to me and kept one for herself. I watched her slather on a great deal of butter, then wipe the knife carefully on her napkin before dipping it in the jam. 'Do you know what it is, this Manzanar?'

'I think so,' I said. Looking at the toast and thinking I didn't feel very hungry. Not that my lack of hunger was exactly breaking news. 'I think I saw a movie about it once. Isn't it that place where we sent all the American Japanese people during the World War?'

'That is correct,' she said.

'It's an interment camp.'

'Let us hope not,' she said. 'To inter someone is to bury them.'

'Oh. I always get that wrong. So what's the word, then?'

'An internment camp.'

'Oh,' I said. 'Funny how that one letter changes everything.'

'Not so much,' she said. 'It doesn't change all that much. I'm sure plenty were buried there. Besides, that's the wrong word, too. It was really not an internment camp. That's just the way you say something when you want it to sound better than it really is. It was really a concentration camp.'

I stared at my toast a bit longer. I was more sure than ever that I didn't want to eat it. But I bit the edge of it to appear cooperative.

'But they didn't kill people there.'

'Not as far as we know, no. I didn't say it was a death camp. I said it was a concentration camp. When you round up a people and make them live all on top of one another you are concentrating them.'

'Yes,' I said. 'I guess that's true. Are you sure that's where you want to go?'

'Oh, yes,' she said. 'Very sure.'

'I was just thinking that if you were only going to go just the one place, then you would want it to be some-place really wonderful.'

'Are there still innocent Japanese people being held prisoner here in this camp?'

I think she knew there weren't. She said it like she knew. Like she just wanted to hear me say it out loud.

'No. They let all those poor people out a long time ago.'

'Then it will be wonderful,' she said.

Just one thing, though. Just one little problem

Esther doesn't drive and neither do I. So it's going to be a bit of a challenge. Figuring out how to get us both to Manzanar.

Victor

'I was thinking I would call Victor,' Esther said. 'And see if he would drive us on our trip.'

'Victor who drives you to your doctor's appointments?'

'Yes, but I think he won't.'

'Why won't he?'

'Because I can't really afford to pay him what a trip like that is worth. It will take six or seven hours each way. We will have to stay over one night. The money I pay him per hour, I could not afford to pay him that much. But I can ask.'

I got a little sulky, then. And stayed sulky most of the day. But I didn't say why.

But I'm going to write down why, now, because I think that's what this book is for: if Victor said yes, then Esther wouldn't need me to go. She would have Victor.

I hate being left out.

Though you would think I'd be used to it by now.

More About Victor

'Victor will take us,' Esther told me later that day.

'Us?' I said.

'You don't want to go?'

'I do want to. But you don't need me to. You have Victor. So you're not traveling alone.'

I think she caught on that I was feeling a little sulky. I don't hide stuff like that very well. I think it's part of that whole never-lying thing.

'First of all,' she said, 'you are always invited if you want to go. Second of all, I think I need you to go. I think you are the reason Victor will do it.'

'How could I be the reason?'

'You tell *me*,' Esther said. 'I only know that at first he didn't think he could. He was worried that his car would break down on such a long trip. And he didn't want to take that much time away from his band.'

'Victor has a band?' I asked. Knowing I was only help-ing us get off track. But then, that's me. Isn't it?

'Apparently so. But then I mentioned that you would be coming along, and then right away he said he would trade cars with his mother and charge me only for the gas.'

'Hmm,' I said.

I've only met Victor once or twice, on the stairs. On his way up to get Esther for the doctor's, or whatever. He seemed kind of odd to me. I didn't pay very much attention.

'Well. Then I guess I have to go.'

It was all I could do not to smile a little. Because I really did want to go.

Esther Mentioning My Mother

Right around the time I said goodnight and told her I was going to bed (to couch, actually, as I think I've made it clear that Esther doesn't have a second bed), Esther said, 'I wrote a note to mail to your mother.'

'Why would you do that, Esther?'

'Because she is your mother. It's a very sacred trust, that motherhood. Not that I know for myself, because I have no children. But I had a mother. So to that extent I know. No matter how she handled that trust she was given, she still needs to know you are OK. So I told her you are OK. I told her I had heard from you. Which is true. I heard from you. Correct?'

'Where did you say I was?'

'I told her you had sent me a postcard from Independence, California. I thought that was very close to the truth. Because you will be in Independence, California so soon.'

'Oh,' I said. Or if not 'Oh', then something very much like it.

'We will leave the day after tomorrow,' she said.

'Why not tomorrow?'

'I thought it would be better to go on Wednesday because your mother will not be home. I know you don't want to run into her on the stairs. And I don't wish that she would know you have been staying here. Good God, I would never hear the end of it. So, Wednesday morning. That's the day she goes to her missing-child support group.'

A silence, while I counted the number of ways in which that last sentence was strange, surprising and pretty much all wrong.

'My mother goes to a missing-child support group?'

'So she says.'

'Shouldn't that pretty much be for mothers whose missing children are . . . you know . . . children?'

'One would think, yes,' Esther said.

'Do you think she lies and tells them I'm younger than I am? Or do you think she gets some kind of special exception because I've had to live like a child all these years?'

'I'm sure I wouldn't know,' Esther said.

I'm sure I wouldn't know. That's what she said. It sounds like the kind of thing a person says when they're feeling a bit peeved. And I think she was. But not with me, I don't think. I was sensing that second-guessing my mother was not her favorite hobby.

I don't like it much myself, but for me it's been more of a career.

'What if she goes running out to Independence to find me?'

'If I mail it on the day we leave, then by the time she gets the note in the mail we will be on our way back.'

'Oh. OK.'

'It seemed the only humane thing to do. To tell her you are OK.'

I guess I wondered for a minute if I was being in-humane to my mother. Probably, huh? But it made my head hurt to think about it. So after a while I stopped.

Even More About Victor

Victor has a dog. He's part German shepherd and part collie. Not Border collie like everybody has these days, but the real old-fashioned Lassie kind of collie. You can tell by the shape of his face, which is very narrow and long. But he looks something like a German shepherd, too.

His name is Jax.

Victor forgot to tell Esther that Jax was coming along.

I guess he figured it went without saying. If you're going away overnight, you have to take your dog. You can't just leave him home alone all that time. I guess he thought, Why would anybody mind?

Now from Esther's point of view: people who have been in concentration camps tend to have issues with dogs. Maybe if they were Yorkies or chihuahuas, that might not be so bad. But a German shepherd can trigger issues.

We were actually standing in front of Victor's car before we got the news – in a purely visual way, that is – that Esther was going to have to share the trip with Jax. I mean, there he was, in the back seat. So it was pretty obvious.

As if I might have been foolish enough to think things couldn't get much worse, Victor held the back door of his car (well, OK, his mother's car) open for Esther. You know. Thinking she was going to get in the back. With Jax.

I guess when Victor drives Esther around, she sits in the back. And Jax sits at home.

I can't quite describe the look on Esther's face. Victor missed it, because by then he was loading our overnight bags into the trunk.

Esther hissed at me to quick get in the back, and I did. Jax kissed my ear.

Then Victor came back around from the trunk and said, 'Oh, no, I was going to have Vida sit up front with me.'

'Then I hope the dog will fit in the trunk,' Esther said.

Everybody just looked at everybody else for a long time. Even Jax was checking out all the faces. I think he caught a whiff of the unrest. Dogs are good at that.

I always wanted a dog, but my mom thought I would

get some kind of deadly germ from one. Which is stupid, because other people are like this hotbed of diseases, but there's very little a person can get from a dog. One of my doctors even told her that, but she got it in her head that it would be dangerous, and I couldn't knock it loose again.

I think I know what happened to my mother. I think she opened up this mechanism for keeping me OK, and just couldn't figure out how to shut it off. Like when you open a computer program, but then it hangs up and stops responding, and you can't get out of it again.

It's very hard on the user. But in this case I'm not sure if that's her or me.

Both, I guess.

But she is still my mother. Esther was right about that. So I've made up my mind I will send her a nice postcard from Independence. That way at least she won't have to feel bad, thinking I sent a postcard to Esther but not to her.

And I definitely want to send a postcard to Richard, too, because I think about him all the time and I want him to know.

Wow. I really got a long way off the track there, didn't I?

Long story short. Esther sat up front. And Victor was not happy about it. I guess he was really looking forward to chatting with me the whole way. He tried to, anyway. At first. But I had to keep asking him to repeat what he said, because of the road noise and all. So after a while he just gave up and brooded.

Every time I looked up I could see him looking at me in the rear-view mirror. I could see the back of his long black hair, which seemed kind of stringy and limp, and maybe even too black to be real. I was looking at it, thinking he must dye it black to look more punk. He was definitely the Goth type. I figured that out by his nose and eyebrow rings and his very heavy black lace-up boots, and the fact that he wore a black trench coat even in extra-hot weather. Making black the hair color of choice, I'm sure. But then I'd catch his eyes in the mirror, and they were black, too, or at least dark enough brown to pass, so then I decided maybe that was his natural color.

He was so tall that his head literally pressed up against the headliner and lifted it up higher, which looked pretty uncomfortable. I wondered if his own car was better for a tall person. Probably so.

Esther kept looking over her shoulder to convince herself that Jax was still lying down, and not just about to touch her or sniff her or something. She'd made me swear I would keep him away from her, and I'd made a solemn vow, but I guess that wasn't enough to make her feel safe.

It was shaping up to be a pretty interesting trip.

About Real Mountains

Moving cars put me to sleep. Always have, since I was a little kid. And I guess in that one way, I never outgrew being a little kid. Actually, according to my mother there are other ways, but most of them involve how I sleep. I sleep like a kid, I guess, which maybe is why she feels so free to treat me like one. But that doesn't really seem fair to me, because I'm only asleep one-third of the time, and besides, she mostly treats me like a kid when I'm awake. I mean, so far as I know.

Then again, if she treated me like a kid when I was asleep, I wouldn't know.

I think I'm getting off track again.

What I'm trying to say is, I fell asleep.

When I woke up, Jax was sleeping with his head in my lap, and I was sleeping all bent over sideways, with my head on his back. I straightened up and stretched, and I had a dog hair in my eye, and I really think I tweaked some muscles in my side, because they were acting up and sore for pretty much the whole trip, but I think I'd better be careful not to get too far off track again.

When I looked out the window, I saw the mountains.

I knew that Manzanar was really close to the mountains, and that those mountains are called the Eastern Sierra Nevadas. What I didn't know is that they would have snow on top of them in the summer. I didn't think anything would have snow in the summer.

I also didn't know how beautiful they would be, and how they would be unlike any other mountains I had ever seen.

We have mountains in the Bay Area. At least, I always thought we did. Now I think they're just hills. The ones I know have grass and brush on them; they're not sheer gray rock reaching up for ever with folds and seams full of snow. It was like looking at the Swiss Alps or something. Although I guess it goes without saying that I never saw the Swiss Alps. But this is kind of the way I imagined them, or maybe I saw a picture of them in a book or on the Internet. Or maybe I imagined them and saw a picture of them, both.

I sucked in my breath, and I guess it was so loud you could hear it in the front seat, because Victor looked at me in the mirror. I could see his black eyes and the little earring in his pierced eyebrow, and some fresh red marks and old scars from his having bad skin. His eyes looked like they were wanting something, hoping real hard, and I wondered what he thought he was going to get from me.

'They're beautiful, aren't they?' he said, in his deep voice.

And then Esther, who I guess did not hear me suck in my breath and had not known I was awake, whipped her head around to make sure that Jax wasn't awake, too. He was, actually, but his head was still down on my lap. I was petting it.

'Yeah,' I said. I'm not at my most articulate right after I just woke up.

'Did Esther tell you I hiked Mount Whitney?'

And I said, 'Excuse me? What did you say?' Because, you know, the road noise and all.

'Did Esther tell you I hiked Mount Whitney?' Louder this time.

Esther never told me anything about Victor. Why would she? I didn't even know him. He was just a guy I saw on the stairs if Esther had a doctor's appointment. But I didn't say that. It would have been mean.

'No, I didn't know. Is that near here?'

'Oh, yeah,' he said. Yelling to be heard, and kind of directing the words over his skinny right shoulder. 'Really near where we're going. The Portal Road is, like, ten miles from Manzanar.'

Esther winced and put one hand over her left ear because he'd been yelling in it.

Esther is usually pretty patient with me, but not always, and she is definitely not patient with everybody. Believe me.

I said, 'I'm sorry?'

Thing is, I'd heard him. I just wanted not to talk. I wanted to look at the amazing real mountains in peace, and not be part of Esther getting her left ear yelled into. So, even though I didn't actually say, 'I didn't hear you,' I said something that definitely gave the impression that I didn't. Which is further from the truth than I usually let myself get.

'Never mind,' he said. 'I'll tell you later.'

So I just looked at the mountains and petted Jax, and thought about how that was the second time I'd said something that maybe wasn't one hundred per cent true, and how both times were recently. Both since I got the heart. It made me wonder if always telling the truth was a thing only for people who are about to die. And who know it.

That would explain why it's not such a common thing.

Manzanar Again

This time I don't have to only write about *talking* about going to Manzanar. I get to write about actually being there.

The first thing I want to write is that it was hot. Very hot. The second thing is that even though I think there were lots of buildings at one time, they are now almost all torn down.

There was a wooden guard tower, though, which was sort of creepy.

We tried to get Esther into the interpretive center (which is what they call it), but she didn't seem interested. Victor and I went inside, and I thought it was sad, but worth seeing.

'There's a movie,' Victor said when we came out.

'I don't need to see a movie,' she said. 'A movie I can

see at home. Victor, take us on the driving tour. Please. I wish to see the cemetery.'

So we started driving down these dirt roads, with signs that mark what buildings used to be where, before they tore them all down. It looked . . . what's the word I'm searching for here? Desolate. Like one of those patches of land the government gives to the Indians for a reservation, because they don't want it for anything else. Nobody would.

'I'm not sure where the cemetery is,' Victor said, pointing at the map in Esther's lap.

'Well, it isn't hard to know,' she said. 'Don't you see that memorial?'

We all looked, even Jax, and there was the top of a white stone memorial. I think you call the shape an obelisk. It was huge. I'm not sure how tall it was, but maybe twice as high as a person. I'm guessing. It had some Japanese alphabet symbols on it. I don't read Japanese, in case that doesn't go without saying.

We drove to that, and we all got out to look.

There were a few graves around it. Just a few. And a fence most of the way around that was made out of sticks in a criss-cross pattern. At the open part, where you can go in, there was a big rock right in the middle of the dirt in the entryway, and it was all covered with change. Coins, I mean. Money. I put about fifty-two cents on it, but I'm not sure why.

We walked in the dirt, in the sun, up closer, to see what was all over and around the memorial. Turned out to be things people had left, like rocks and coins and lots and lots of different-colored origami cranes.

Esther was being really quiet, standing in front of the few little graves.

I stood there beside her, kind of worrying about how hard she was breathing, and listening to Jax panting real loud on the other side of me, and watching those surreal waves of heat that rise up in your line of sight when it's, like, a hundred degrees.

I said to Esther, 'Did you know it was almost all torn down?'

'Oh, yes,' she said. 'Always when a camp is not needed they tear it to the ground. Because no one can deal with the memories. Because all the excuses are gone, and then nothing is left but the shame, and then it must go.'

'Oh,' I said. Then I listened to the panting some more. From both sides of me. 'But you still wanted to see it?'

'Not exactly,' she said. 'I wanted to feel it.'

Before I could ask her what that meant she turned her head and looked past me to Victor and Jax. 'Get some water for that dog,' she said. 'He has a fur coat. It's inhumane.'

And Victor hurried off without saying a word.

I asked Esther, 'Was it hot at Buchenwald?'

'Maybe it was,' she said. 'But that's not what I

remember. What I remember is the cold. I can never forget the cold. When you have almost no food, almost no fat on your bones, the winter cold is unbearable. And unforgettable. Maybe there was summer heat and I have forgotten. I have forgotten a lot about Buchenwald. As much as I can.'

'Maybe we should find some shade,' I said, because I was starting to worry about Esther.

'In a minute. Right now I need to feel what's here. Even though it's in the sun.'

I just waited for a really long time without saying anything. Because, you know. If she was feeling something, I didn't want to interrupt.

I watched her take out a lacy white cloth handkerchief and wipe the sweat off her forehead and neck.

Finally I asked, 'What are you trying to feel, Esther?'

'I have always believed,' she said, 'ever since I was a young girl, that the spirits of the people who were entrapped in a place like this get to go free. But the spirits of their jailers return, and stay. And are chained here. Don't get me wrong. I'm not saying God is vengeful and does this terrible thing to them. Only that guilt is very powerful, and must be served.'

'Wow,' I said.

Just then Victor and Jax got back.

Victor brought Esther a folding chair. And he brought us each a bottle of cold water. Where he got a chair, I don't know. It looked too big to be from his trunk. I figure he must have told the ranger or whoever was at the visitor center . . . I mean, interpretive center . . . that he was worried about Esther. He tried to set it up for her, but she pointed to the only shade there was, a little patch cast by the obelisk.

'Maybe over there. I have felt here long enough, I think, and the sun is too hot.'

She actually looked like she was about to pass out.

Victor tried to take her by the arm to lead her over there, but she wouldn't walk that close to Jax. So I took hold of Jax's leash and walked behind them. I was feeling a little woozy myself. While Victor was setting up the chair in the shade, Esther looked at my face.

'You don't look good,' she said. 'Victor, you should have brought a chair for Vida. She had a heart transplant, you know. She's no stronger for this trip than I am, even at her young age.'

But then she sat down in the only chair. So I guess she meant he should have brought another.

He ran off again to get another chair, and Jax pulled hard and jumped and whined to go with him, so I let go of the leash and he ran and caught up to Victor.

I squatted in the shade next to Esther's chair.

'So . . . what do you feel?' I asked.

'Nothing.'

'Really?'

'Really. Nothing. This place is in absolute peace. Isn't that interesting? A place like this. Where people were imprisoned just for their ancestry. People who were born in this country just like you, people who had done nothing, rounded up as if they were cattle. And now all is at peace. You know what this means, don't you?'

I thought a minute, but I wasn't sure I did.

'Not really.'

'I think it means that the slates are wiped clean after we die. That we get to leave our guilts and our sins behind with this old piece of real estate,' she said, indicating the body she currently sweated in. 'And if they can leave their guilt, surely we can leave our wounds. Wouldn't you think so?'

'That's a nice idea,' I said.

'I have never in my entire life been so happy to be wrong,' she said.

The Mountain Victor Climbed

It was late. Victor and I were out sitting by the pool.

The motel where Esther got rooms for us (two – one for Victor because he's a boy, and one for her and me, and Jax had to sleep in the car) is in Lone Pine, and it has a pool. I didn't bring a suit, and neither did he. But it was nice out there, because everybody else was asleep, and it was super quiet and kind of cool compared to earlier that day, and the moon was a few days before full, and you could see the mountains. Almost as well as if it had been light. Well, not the same as during daylight. But you could really see them.

Victor was telling me all about hiking Mount Whitney.

He showed me which one it was, too. There's a special way you can tell which one is Mount Whitney, because on the left it has these spires, and then it's sort of like a spire itself, only wider, sitting just to the right of them.

The weird thing is, it doesn't look like the highest.

But Victor told me it's not just the highest in the Sierra Nevadas, it's the highest in the whole United States, unless you count Alaska and Hawaii, and then it's not.

I asked why it didn't look like the highest. He said it's because it's a lot farther back than the others that look higher.

He talked a lot about the hike. And about how it felt to be on top of Mount Whitney, looking down. He told me it took ten hours to get up there, and he didn't get to the top until nearly four in the afternoon, which is dangerous, because a lot of times there's lightning in the afternoon, and it was a cloudy, sort of stormy day. He said it took him another seven hours to get down, and then he had to walk most of the way down in the dark.

'Didn't you keep tripping?' I asked. 'Or get lost?'

'I had a little headlamp.'

'What kind of a lamp is that?'

'It's like a flashlight, but you wear it on your head.'

'Oh.'

We were quiet for a while in those nice cool lounge chairs, and I could still see which one was Mount Whitney.

'Do you like to hike?' he asked.

'Oh, yeah,' I said. 'I love it.' And then I just sat there

trying to figure a few things out. Because I have never once gone hiking in my whole entire life. 'Actually,' I said, 'I don't know. Because, you know. With my heart and all. I never got to go.'

'But you just said you loved it.'

'I know. That was weird, huh? I guess I meant I always thought I would love it. You know. If I ever got to go.'

'Tomorrow,' he said. 'We'll get up super early. And we'll drive up to Whitney Portal. And I'll show you the trail.'

'Victor. Don't be stupid. I can't climb Mount Whitney.'

'Well, I know *that*. But you can walk up the trail. Maybe a mile. Maybe half a mile. Maybe ten feet. I don't know. But at least you can say you were on the Mount Whitney Trail. Even the drive up there is really cool. The road goes up to over eight thousand feet.'

'You said you need a special permit and it's hard to get.'

See? I was paying attention.

'Not from the trailhead to Lone Pine Lake. Anybody can do that as a day hike. Beyond the lake you need a permit. But we can do the first part of the trail, and Jax can go as far as the lake, too. I really want you to see it. It's amazing.'

'Maybe,' I said. 'What about Esther?'

'She looked like she was feeling really crappy. I think she'll sleep in. We could leave her a note and say we'll be back by nine. We could leave before the sun comes up.'

'I don't even have good shoes,' I said, pointing to my sandals.

'We don't have to go very far.'

I felt like I was running out of excuses. But I still didn't want to go. So I had to ask myself why. Why didn't I want to go up there and see Whitney Portal and walk on a tiny bit of the trail?

The answer was pretty simple.

'I think I'm scared,' I said.

'Of what?'

'I don't know. It's just all new, and I've never done anything like that before, and it's just scary, that's all.'

He didn't answer. I guess because he didn't have the kind of answer that would get me to go.

We sat there for a while and looked at the mountains, and the way the moonlight made the snow glow white, like it glowed in the dark all by itself. Like snow was its own light source. I could hear Jax whimpering from the car because he wanted to be with us, but dogs are not allowed in the pool area.

'Why didn't you get him water?' I asked.

'I did.'

'I mean, until Esther told you to. It just seems weird. You love him, and Esther hates him, but you didn't go get him water until she told you to.'

'I thought maybe I wasn't supposed to leave,' he said.

'I thought maybe she was going to pass out from the heat, and I felt like I couldn't leave if she didn't say I could. She can be really . . . intimidating. You know?'

'No,' I said. 'I don't know.'

'You don't think she's intimidating?'

'Not at all. She's just my friend.'

'Wow. That's weird.'

'What?'

'Being afraid of Whitney Portal, but not being afraid of Esther. I just can't picture that at all.'

More sitting quietly, and then I said, 'I'm going to go away soon.'

'Where are you going?'

'I don't know. But I'm going.'

'Do you know where you want to go?'

'There's a place,' I said. 'I can almost see it in my head. But I don't know exactly where it is.'

'But it's a real place?'

'I think so.'

'How will you find it?'

'I don't know.'

'Don't take this the wrong way,' he said, 'but isn't that a lot scarier than driving up the Whitney Portal Road?'

I thought about that for a while, and then I said, 'Yeah, I guess I see your point about that.'

'So you'll go?' He sounded all happy and excited.

'Is there a place up there to buy postcards?'

'Yeah! There is. There's a really cool little general store.'

'OK,' I said. 'I'll go.'

I'm going to need to get a whole lot braver, and I'm thinking that's one of those things that you just need to keep working on. You know. Like if you wanted to play the piano. Like practice.

Esther Snores

So when she's quiet, I have to figure she's awake.

So I was just lying here writing in my book about Victor and Mount Whitney, and then I got that she was awake, and then she talked to me.

'So, I'm thinking you are less nervous and scared,' she said.

And it was weird, because just for a second I thought she knew everything about tomorrow morning. Already. Which would have been a little spooky.

'Why do you say that?'

'Because you used to rub the worry stone all day long, and now you don't.'

Sometimes I hate being someone who always has to tell the truth.

'It's at Richard's,' I said.

'Richard?'

'The heart man.'

'Oh. Yes.'

'I dropped it by mistake when I was at his house. And he's keeping it safe until I can get back to get it.'

'Oh. I see.'

'It was just an accident. It doesn't mean I love it any less than ever.'

'I know that. I understand.'

'Esther? Are you really OK with finding out that all the slates get cleaned after we die? Or are you partly mad because that guard doesn't still have to be suffering?'

'I am mostly happy to know I will not need to be bumping into him again.'

'Oh. OK. Good.'

'You are almost a third of the way through that book,' she said. 'This is good.'

'There's been a lot going on to write about. Oh. By the way. Really early in the morning Victor is going to take me up to Whitney Portal. Maybe I'll hike just a little tiny bit of the trail.'

'Are you sure that's a good idea? You just had a heart transplant.'

'Well, not *just*. It was months ago. I mean, I had my eight weeks of follow-ups. And everything is fine. And anyway, I'm not going to go very far on it.'

I did not mention that, although it's true that for eight weeks you have to do follow-ups twice a week, after that you still have do them, just farther apart. And I had already missed one.

See? There I go again.

'Be careful. Because it's very high altitude. Not much air up there. Be very careful.'

Poor Esther. She's spent so many years being careful that she doesn't know how to stop now. Like my mother.

Somebody should put a warning label on everything in life that's about fear. Being afraid to die, being afraid your daughter will die, being afraid of getting hurt in love. It should all have a warning label to let people know it can be habit-forming.

Once you decide to put all your energy into being scared of something, you might wake up one day and find out you have no idea how to stop. It happens to people. More often than anybody seems willing to admit.

The Portal

The road was very winding and tight, and it looked most of the time like Victor was about to drive right over the edge. Which is why I closed my eyes.

'Isn't it beautiful from up here?' he asked.

And I said, 'I don't know. I have my eyes closed.'

'Why?'

'Because it's a scary road.'

'I'm not going to drive off it, if that's what you mean. I'm being careful. You need to look. You're missing a really nice view.'

I opened my eyes and we were about two-thirds of the way up to the top of the road.

I looked down. It made me dizzy, but it was pretty, too. Like just a little wedge of high desert below us, because the mountains on both sides covered up the view of the rest, and a lake that was almost all dry, and the little town of Lone Pine, which was not so little compared to Independence, but it was little.

The sun wasn't even up yet, but it was just barely light.

We came around another curve, and I turned my head even farther to look and Jax kissed my nose.

We had to park in the overflow extra trailhead parking. There weren't too many people around, and I couldn't figure out who owned all those cars. Usually when you see that many cars parked you see a few people to go with them.

'Where are all the people to go with these cars?' I asked while he was locking up his mom's car.

'They're on the mountain.'

'They went up in the dark?'

'Some of them. Some people start at midnight or one in the morning to get up there before noon. Some camp on the trail and do it in more than one day. This is the most popular time of year for Mount Whitney. Because there's so much snow on it the rest of the time.'

I looked around at all the gray, granitey-looking mountains on each side of us, and the little seams of snow in them. I could hear a waterfall somewhere but I couldn't see it.

I felt weird being up here in just sandals.

We walked kind of slow to the trailhead, which was pretty steep uphill, and already I was getting really out of breath. It was scary. Like all the air got sucked out of my lungs, no matter how hard I tried to breathe in. Like it used to be.

I stopped and leaned my hands on my knees, and bent forward and tried to catch my breath.

When I looked up, there was a group of three hikers walking by very close to us. Two guys and one woman. They had those huge packs that look really solid and go up higher than your head, and they had rolled-up stuff – maybe sleeping bags or pads – strapped to the packs. And they had poles, those kind that are like ski poles but they're for hiking. And they were wearing shorts, and very big solid boots, and incredibly thick socks with thinner socks underneath. You could see their underneath-socks sticking out at the top.

I looked at the packs, and I looked at the woman's legs. They had these muscles in the back that were really nicely visible. They were all ropey and fit-looking. And I got this attack of something, but I swear I don't know what it was. It just hit me. But I'm still not sure exactly what it was. Just that it hit me.

It's like I really missed having legs with ropey calf muscles, and a big tall pack on my back. Which doesn't make a whole lot of sense, because I never did. But that's what it was, even though it was impossible that it could have been that. I'm sorry, it just was anyway.

I know how it feels to miss something. And I missed ropey calf muscles and big backpacks. It made a spot inside me ache. I mean, really ache. A big, ugly ache.

And then all of a sudden that missing made me miss Richard. Not that I didn't usually. Not that I didn't in general. But suddenly, and much more. In fact, it hit me so hard that I said it out loud.

I straightened all the way up and said, 'Oh my God, I just miss Richard so much.'

I didn't mention backpacks and ropey calf muscles. Just Richard.

It was just light enough that I could see the look on Victor's face. It wasn't good.

'I didn't know you had a boyfriend,' he said.

'Well. I don't know that he's my boyfriend. But I sure miss him.'

'You feeling OK to walk some more?'

'Yeah. OK.'

I thought we'd talk about Richard some more, but I guess Victor didn't want to. I took a bunch more steps uphill, and right away my lungs emptied out again. I wondered if Richard missed me, and if he was scared for me.

'Don't let me forget the postcards,' I said. It was hard to even breathe enough to say it. I mean, to say it well enough that he could understand.

'OK.' Long pause.

I was starting to think I couldn't walk any more.

Then he said, 'Is the postcard for Richard?'

'One is. And one is for my mom.'

'Oh.'

'I don't think I can walk any farther.'

'But that's the trailhead right up there. Here. Take Jax's leash. He'll pull you.'

I took the leash and it did help a little bit. At first. But it also made me walk faster than I wanted to.

But we got to the trailhead.

I sat down on a bench and tried to catch my breath.

'I can't do this,' I said. 'I don't have strong muscles like you do. And like those people that went by us. You need to practice to be in shape. I've never been in shape, not once in my whole life. And I can't breathe. And I can't do this.'

'We'll just sit a while,' he said.

The sun was almost up, and it was pretty there at the trailhead, even though I had to watch guys with big calf muscles go by. At least seven of them. I mean, at least seven guys. Which would be fourteen calves. At least. But I guess I sort of lost count.

'Maybe I'll just go get some postcards,' I said.

'You see that shelter?'

I looked up. The trail went up a few switchbacks to sort of a . . . well, I don't think I would call it a shelter. I'm not sure what it was. Just sort of a big framework of wood that you walk through. But it was made of slats, so it wouldn't shelter you from much. I'm not sure what it was supposed to be for.

'Let's just try going up there,' he said.

'Yeah. I guess.'

I swear, I must have made the worst showing of anybody who ever set their feet on the Mount Whitney Trail. Because this shelter thingy was like about as far from the trailhead as your car is when you park in a parking lot to go to the store. I mean, if you can't get a close space. And I barely made it, even with Jax pulling me.

Maybe it was the lack of air, or the fact that it was pretty steep uphill. Maybe it's because I was letting myself get scared. Oh, yeah, and the recent heart-transplant thing might factor in there somewhere. That and the fact that I really never got a lot of exercise pretty much anytime in my whole life.

When we got inside the thing, there were all these signs with pictures and information about all the horrible stuff that could happen to you when you hike up to Mount Whitney. I couldn't figure out how anybody could walk by signs like that and not be afraid.

Except . . .

Except I remembered something. Only I'm pretty sure it was something that never happened to me. I mean, it didn't. I know it didn't. It couldn't have. But I know how it feels to remember something, and I remembered this.

I remembered a sign with a drawing on it of a man

staggering from exhaustion. He had one hand up to his head, like he was in pain. And under that were the words: 'Warning: Do not attempt to hike to the river and back in one day.' Or maybe a slightly longer version of the same message. And then under that it had some more stuff on it in other languages.

And I walked by it. And I wasn't afraid. Well, maybe a little. But I didn't stop. Maybe partly because I wasn't coming back that same day.

Except none of that ever happened to me.

But I still remembered it. I could actually see a picture of the sign in my head.

'Let's go back now,' I said. 'I just want to get some postcards and go back.'

I was feeling a little weirded-out and confused.

On the way back down, I said, 'Have you ever missed something that never happened to you?'

'Well, sure,' Victor said. 'I think everybody sits around and thinks about stuff they didn't get to do.'

I don't think that was what I meant. But I didn't want to try to explain it. It made me tired even thinking about trying to explain it.

'Have you ever *remembered* anything that never happened to you?'

'Uh. No. That would be impossible. Wouldn't it?'

'Yeah,' I said. 'I guess that would be impossible.'

*   *   *

While we were driving back down the terrifying Portal Road, I took a pen out of the glove compartment and wrote on Richard's postcard.

I wrote, 'Dear Richard, I miss you so much. I hope you miss me even a little bit. I was on the Mount Whitney Trail today, but don't worry about the heart, because I didn't go very far. Did Lorrie like to hike?'

I swear I didn't know I was going to write that last sentence until I did.

Then I wrote, 'Well, I guess you can't answer. But I'll be back. Sometime. Love, Vida.'

Maybe he was off looking for me. Wouldn't that be the coolest thing?

Then I tried to do the one to my mother, but I couldn't think what to write, so I had to save it for later.

About Germany

When I got back to the motel, it was still only about eight o'clock in the morning. Esther was snoring.

I lay down on the bed real quietly, but she seemed to figure out I was there, even in her sleep, because she stopped snoring and then she talked to me.

She said, 'It's early yet. Did you go up the mountain?'

'Yes, but I didn't walk very far.'

'Just as well,' she said.

'I don't think so,' I said. 'I think it would have been better if I'd walked farther. I could have. I could have just stopped and sat down on a rock and rested as long as I needed to, and then I could have gone farther. I just got scared. And I have to stop doing that.'

'What do you have to stop doing?'

'Getting scared.'

'I wish you all the best of luck with that,' she said. 'I'm not sure fear is a part of life that can be stopped at will.'

'Oh. Well, then, maybe I'll just have to start getting scared but not letting it stop me.'

'You're a better woman than I am if you can.'

I think neither one of us really knew what to say after that, so we just lay there, each on our own little beds, and stayed quiet for a while.

Then Esther said, 'You know where I really wanted to go, don't you?'

And I said, 'No. You said it was Manzanar.'

'Well. That's where I wanted to go that was possible. But you know where I really wanted to go, right?'

I thought about it for a while. But I definitely didn't.

'Not a clue,' I said.

'Really? I thought you would guess right away.'

'Sorry. You're going to have to tell me.'

'I wanted to go back to Buchenwald. But I knew I didn't have the money to go all the way back to Germany, plus I'm too old now for such a long trip. I should have done it while I had the chance. I see that now.'

I was surprised, so it took me a while to say anything.

Finally what I said was, 'Why would you want to go back there?' I was thinking, with all the time it took me to talk, I should have come up with something better than just that.

'Two reasons. One, for the same reason I came to Manzanar. To feel it. To see who is still hanging around. But now I know the answer to that. Because what is true at Manzanar will be true at Buchenwald. Not that they are the same thing. But they are different degrees of the same thing. And I don't think that the degree of a wrong will change anything so basic as whether or not it can be wiped clean. The second reason is to tell it something. I wanted to look Buchenwald in the eye – figuratively speaking of course, because Buchenwald has no eyes – and tell it, "I won and you lost."'

'Does it still have the buildings and all?'

'Not many, no. It is much like Manzanar in that respect. All the barracks were blown up or burned to the ground. There is still the fence, and the gate, and the guard towers. A few buildings, I think, but I'm not sure which ones. But the ground is sacred because so many died there. So many spirits, or so I thought. So much energy of what came to pass. So people still go to visit. To work out their own feelings about such a thing, I suppose. But I have missed my chance now. I will never go.'

'You might live long enough to go.'

'No,' she said. 'I won't.'

I didn't want to argue with her about a thing like that. What did I know about it, anyway? But it made me sad.

'Maybe *I'll* go,' I said.

'Well, if you do,' she said, 'give it that message from me. Tell it, "Esther Schimberg won and you lost". I would have preferred to tell it myself. But that will be better than nothing.'

The Ride Home

Esther wasn't feeling too good. I had to help her get dressed, which was kind of weird and embarrassing. Not that I minded. I mean, it's just life. It just is. But I think she might have minded some.

And then when she was decent I had to go get Victor, and he had to help her out to the car.

I think we might have had a plan to go see more of Manzanar in the morning before we left. We had talked about that, anyway. But it was so obviously out of the question that no one even brought it up again. We just headed for home, where she could rest.

We gave her the whole back seat, and Jax rode up front between Victor and me, which was a tight squeeze.

She fell back asleep almost right away.

I asked Victor if we could stop at a mailbox on our

way through Independence. So I could mail my post-card, but I didn't volunteer that part. I just wanted to mail the one. To Richard. I still hadn't thought what I was going to say to my mother.

'Why, so you can send a postcard to that Richard guy?'

'Right.'

I knew he didn't like it, but what was I supposed to do about it? I can't be in charge of what he likes, and my life just is what it is, no matter what he feels about it. I can't stop loving Richard just to make Victor feel better.

He stopped at a mailbox in front of the post office, but he didn't say a word. I had to get out and walk around. For one awful minute I got it in my head that he might drive off without me. Esther was already asleep and wouldn't be able to tell him to stop.

All my medications were in my overnight bag in the trunk, and I have to take them every day. For the rest of my life. I could literally have died if he drove off with them. Depending on how long it took me to get home, I guess.

But he didn't do that, of course. It was just my brain playing tricks on me.

We drove north for about an hour, and the moun-tains were on our left now, so to look at them I had to look past Victor's face. He kept looking back over at me, like maybe I was looking at him and not the mountains.

And, I mean, he did that so many times that I started to wonder why he wasn't getting it yet.

Finally I gave up and just closed my eyes and saw the mountains in my head instead.

Then something weird happened. Something very weird.

Jax sort of whimpered once, and then he jumped into the back seat with Esther. And he lay down with his head on her lap.

'Holy crap!' Victor said, and started looking for a place to pull over. But there wasn't anywhere. 'Oh, God, if she wakes up she's going to have a fit. She's going to kill me. Jax!' He kind of hissed it. Like, trying to sound really mad, and strong, so the dog would obey him, but without making too much noise. The dog looked up at him. His eyes looked guilty. But he didn't come. 'Jax!' A little louder this time. He sounded really panicky. I wondered what it would feel like to be so scared of Esther. 'Jax, goddamn it! Get up here!'

That last time was too loud. He woke up Esther.

She stirred a bit. Her eyes flickered and she looked down.

She picked up her hand and patted Jax three times on the head. Nice firm, thumpy pats. Then she went back to sleep.

Victor and I looked at each other. For as long as we could before he had to look back at the road. You know. Watch where he was driving.

'What do I do?' he asked. 'Should I stop? Should I try to get him back up here?'

'I don't know. I guess not. I guess it's OK the way it is.'

I could just feel how nervous he was, though. I started to write that he was nervous the whole ride home. But I don't really know that. Because moving cars put me to sleep. Like I said before. So after a while I was asleep. And I really don't know how Victor felt after that. But if I had to guess, I would guess that he was nervous.

Next thing I knew, Victor was shaking me by the shoulder. Still all panicky. Still or again, I'm not really sure. He wasn't in the driver seat any more. The passenger door was open, and he was on the sidewalk by my shoulder, trying to get me to wake up.

I opened my eyes and we were in front of our building. We were home.

I was wondering why we didn't have a plan for getting back in without my mother noticing.

'What?' I said. 'Yeah, we're home. I get it.'

'We got a problem,' he said.

'Yeah? What kind of problem?'

'The kind where I'm pretty sure Esther's dead.'

On the Stairs

We sat on the stairs outside where Esther and I used to live. And where I used to live with my mother. And where my mother still did. Waiting.

I cried. A lot.

Victor didn't cry. I guess I shouldn't have expected him to. He wasn't really Esther's friend. He was just her driver.

Jax was still in the back of the car with Esther. He wouldn't leave her.

We were waiting for somebody to show up, but I'm not sure who. Victor made the calls. Not me.

I was busy crying.

After a few minutes my mother came out and stood in front of me with her mouth open. It was like she wanted to say so many things at once that they jammed up and got stuck, and then she couldn't say anything at all.

'Hi, Mom,' I said. I think I was hugging my own knees by then.

She didn't seem to notice that I was crying.

When she finally got unstuck, she shrieked at me. She shrieked, 'Vida, where on earth have you been?'

I didn't really feel like fighting or anything. Because, you know, Esther just died. And I wasn't feeling so great.

So I just said, 'I went to Manzanar with Esther.'

'You were with Esther?' The shrieking was getting louder. I was wishing she'd get stuck again. 'She swore you weren't!'

'Well, at the time she swore that, it was true.'

'I am going to give that woman a piece of my mind,' she said.

It made me tired. It reminded me how incredibly tiring it is to be around my mother. I almost didn't have enough energy to answer.

But I understood how she felt and all. I'd left her pretty much completely out of the loop, which I guess is a very bad place for a mother to be left. I should have known that. Well, I guess part of me did. It must have been hard for her to suddenly find out that Esther was in the loop all that time, when she wasn't.

I should've done better.

Interesting how when I'm talking about my mother I

use the word 'should' a lot. Interesting to me anyway. I just can't help noticing that lately.

'No,' I said. 'I don't think you can give Esther a piece of your mind.'

'I'd like to see you stop me. I'd like you to tell me what's going to stop me.'

I looked over at Victor. I couldn't be the one to say it. And I told him so with my eyes. Now, at the moment I did that, I really didn't know Victor well enough to know if I could tell him something with my eyes. Some people you can do that with. Some you can't. But he seemed to pick it up just fine.

Score one for Victor.

'Esther passed away,' he said. 'She's down there in my mother's car. You can tell her anything you want, but I don't think it's going to make much difference.'

My mother gave him the evil eye, one eyebrow raised. She looked over her shoulder. Down the stairs, toward the car.

Then she went down there and looked for herself.

Jax growled at her. Like he was protecting Esther. It was so sweet.

My mother came bounding back up the stairs. 'Well, don't just sit there!' she said. 'Call somebody! Do something!'

'I already did,' Victor said. 'I called the police, and they called the medical examiner. We're just waiting for them to show up.'

I thought it was weird that he seemed completely unintimidated by my mother. How could anyone find Esther intimidating but not my mother? It's weird how we're all scared of such different things.

She was still staring him down.

'Who are you?' she said.

I said, 'That's pretty rude,' but she didn't pay any attention.

'I'm Esther's driver,' he said. Without much emotion.

I could tell that my mother definitely got it that she was getting nowhere with Victor. She turned her wrath back to me.

'You missed an EMB.'

'Yeah. I know. But it's going really well. You know that. You know what Dr Vasquez said.'

'What did he say?' Victor asked. Like he'd been very interested in my health, but hadn't been able to bring himself to ask until now.

'She. Dr Vasquez is a she. And she said I'm showing less of a tendency toward rejection than any patient she ever treated. I haven't had one single rejection episode. Not one. Which is so far above the curve I can't even tell you. And you were right there when she said it, Mother. So I don't see what you're so worried about.'

'That doesn't mean you have a right to miss an EMB.'

'Mother. I just turned twenty. I have a right to do

anything I want. Including go someplace else. Some-place that isn't home.'

'You had a birthday?' Victor asked. 'When?'

'While we were on our trip.'

'You should have told me. We could have cel-ebrated.'

'We had a nice trip. I mean, until Esther died it was nice. So, that's a celebration. Sort of.'

'You should have told me. Why didn't you tell me?'

'I don't know. There was a lot going on.'

Speaking of which, my mother was getting even madder, if such a thing is possible, because we were talking about something that had nothing to do with this important thing that was all she could think about, and that she wasn't done talking about yet.

'Vida! Pay attention! Are you going to stay and have the EMB?'

'Yes. I will. I promise. Now, please, Mom. Please. My best friend just died. And I don't want to talk about this right now. I'll come in and talk to you soon. I just can't talk right now.'

'I was worried out of my mind,' she said.

And Victor kind of stood up – but only figuratively speaking, because actually his tall body was still sitting there on the stairs – and said something really brave.

He said, 'You obviously didn't hear what Vida said. She said her best friend just died and she doesn't want to talk right now.'

Amazingly, my mother backed off two steps' worth.

For a long time she just stared. Her eyes were kind of narrower than usual.

Then she said, to me, 'I'm going to go back in now, but I'll expect you in soon.'

'Well, I don't know how long this will take. Because I never turned a dead person over to the medical examiner before. But when I'm done, I'll come in.'

She turned to leave.

'Mom,' I said, and she turned back around. 'Here. I have a postcard for you.' I dug it out of my overnight bag and handed it to her.

She turned it over in her hands twice.

'There's nothing written on it.'

'I couldn't think what to say.'

'Oh. Well. Thanks, I guess.'

Then she went back inside.

I sat watching the empty spot where she had just been. Kind of amazed and grateful for the silence.

'So that was my mother,' I said.

'Yeah. Got it.'

'You were really good. You didn't let her back you down at all.'

'I'm sick of being intimidated,' he said. 'I've had it with that.'

'Good. Good for you.'

'What's an EMB?'

'Oh. Endomyocardial biopsy. Yeah, before you say it,

I do realize that doesn't answer the question. It's this really yucky test where they go in through a vein, like my jugular. They're monitoring for allograft rejection. Oh, my God, listen to me. Talk like a human being, right? It kind of warns them if my immune system is trying to kill the heart. Which I'm pretty sure it isn't. But they still like to run a lot of tests. You can't just tell them you're pretty sure it isn't. They want answers they can take to the bank.'

We were quiet for a little while longer.

Then I said, 'I really am going to go away now. Well, not right now. I'll go see the doctor, like my mother wants. Make sure everything is good with the heart. But then I'm going. I can't stay here without Esther. She was the only thing keeping me here. It would break my heart to be here when she's not. I just don't know how I would cope.'

'Wow, you were really close to her, huh? I could go away with you. Let me go with you.'

'Why?'

'Why? Why would you want to go off all alone? It'll be safer this way. And not so lonely. And you don't even have a car. I have a car.'

'Which car, though? Your car? Or your mom's?'

'Oh. Well. I can't exactly run off in my mom's car, now can I? She'll need it.'

'Yeah, but you told Esther your car might not even get to Manzanar without breaking down.'

He chewed on his lip for a minute.

'Well, which would you rather have when you want to go away? A car that might break down, or no car at all?'

'That's a good point,' I said. Then I thought about it a while longer. 'But what about your band?'

'Screw the band. Who cares? They suck. They can get a new bass player. They're never going to amount to anything anyway. I'd rather go with you.'

And, you know, really, it *was* pretty terrifying thinking of running off all by myself. I'd walk away from the front door and then . . . what? What would I bring with me, and would I have to carry it all? How could I carry it all? Where would I go to lie down when I got tired? At least you can sleep in a car. Even if it breaks down, you can sleep in it.

'Maybe,' I said. 'Only . . . just friends, right?'

He squirmed a little. But then he said, 'Yeah, OK. If that's the only way it can be. Just friends, then.'

'OK. I guess that would be good. If you're really sure you want to go with me. Leave me with your phone number. When I find out how soon I can get this lovely EMB experience done, I'll give you a call.'

'We need to go through her place,' he said. 'See if there's somebody to contact.'

'Esther doesn't have any family. They're all dead.'

'Oh. Well, what do you think she would want for a funeral?'

'I have no idea,' I said, and right away started to cry again.

So Victor waited on the stairs for the police and the medical examiner, and I went through Esther's stuff. It didn't take long. She wasn't what you might call a pack rat, like I guess I've mentioned before. She lived like a person on a camping trip in a solid wood tent in the city. Only what she needed to survive.

I found some bank statements in a file. The most recent one showed she had $148 in a checking account. And I found a certificate for a pre-paid cremation.

Cremation.

Doesn't that seem like a weird choice for somebody with Esther's background? Cremation.

But that's what she wanted.

I took it back outside to show to Victor and whoever was about to show up.

When I Went Back In

Of course, sooner or later I had to go in and talk to my mom.

I hit what I hoped was a happy medium. Not so much sooner that I couldn't bear it, but not so much later that she exploded or anything.

'OK, I'm back,' I said. 'Sorry.'

She had calmed down quite a bit by then. Not that she was any less mad. She was just mad in a way that made a lot less noise.

'Just out of curiosity,' she said, 'which part are you sorry about?'

So I said, 'Well, I guess the part where I didn't handle leaving very well, and also the part where you were worried out of your mind. Which I guess isn't really two parts, exactly. I guess it's really more like one part. One thing pretty much being the result of the other and all.'

I was making it a point not to look at her eyes. Because she was using them to punish me. Maybe I deserved some punishment, but I was still a little raw and sort of in shock about the whole Esther thing.

Didn't she know that Esther was really important to me? She should have.

Then again, I should have known that being told where I was going and when I'd be back were really important to her.

There I go with the 'shoulds' again.

But really, I guess you can't go around knowing nothing about other people and expecting them to know everything about you. It's common enough. And it's easy enough. But it isn't really fair.

'Why didn't you tell me where you were going?'

'Because if I had, you'd have run right out there and dragged me home by the ear.'

'You need to be home taking care of yourself.'

'So you admit that's what you would have done.'

'I would've done what needed doing.'

'So that's why I didn't tell you.'

I braved a quick look at her eyes. They were busy wrestling with something, which I guess had made them lose that intense focus on making me feel bad. Just to be safe, I didn't look for long.

'I'll make you a deal,' I said. 'I'll tell you my decisions if you'll respect them.'

'Only if they're decisions worthy of respect.'

CATHERINE RYAN HYDE

'You don't get to be the judge of them. I'm twenty, Mom.'

Then nobody said anything for a long time. So I went to my room to lie down.

On my bedside table I found this huge bouquet of dead flowers, with a teddy bear sitting next to them. I opened the card. It was from my dad. He said he was sending a teddy bear with the flowers because 'nobody should have to be a grown-up at a time like this.'

Then I felt bad because I went off and became a grown-up without ever hugging the teddy bear, and because the flowers were dead by the time I saw them.

I curled up on the bed with the little brown bear, and, sure enough, I found a part of me that still didn't want to have to be grown-up yet. It made me cry again.

After a while my mom stuck her head in and said, 'We didn't really settle anything.'

'That's true,' I said. 'We really didn't.'

But at least I could say I'd tried.

On Calling Richard

I called Richard three times in the three days before I left. I was hoping I could go get my worry stone back. To have with me on the road. And of course seeing him would have been nice.

Actually, seeing him would have been wonderful.

But he was never home. All I got was the machine.

I think the third time I might have called just to listen to the outgoing message again.

It was Lorrie's voice. He still hadn't changed it. It gave me goose bumps and tingles to listen to her voice. Like she was some long-lost love of mine or something.

Not that I really know how it would feel to have one of those.

I wondered if he was out somewhere looking for me.

I left messages every time, and I thought maybe he would call me back before Victor and I hit the road. I was sure hoping he would.

He never did.

RICHARD

White Crows

I stood in a fairly long line in front of the microphone, waiting to ask Dr Matsuko a question. The mic had been set up at the front of the center aisle just seconds after she announced that the lecture portion of her talk was about to yield to Q&A.

My face burned, I felt a little dizzy, and I couldn't stop clenching and unclenching my left hand. I had my right hand in my pocket, rubbing the worry stone. More or less as usual.

I missed most of the early questions due to my stage fright, and my inability to stop obsessing over whether or not I had felt this kind of fear before, standing up in front of classes all those years. I knew in the back of my mind I had felt some kind of fear in that professional forum, but could no longer recreate what kind it was.

I'm not sure whether or not I felt any of what I felt until after I lost Lorrie.

I also couldn't help noticing that everyone in line ahead of me and behind me seemed to be college age. Students. The audience for this lecture appeared to be comprised of about eight-five or ninety per cent students. Based on my knowledge of university doings, I had to guess that some professor or other had offered extra credit for attending this lecture. I had made a point of sitting next to an older couple, because it made me feel like a fish out of water to be surrounded entirely by students.

I was just reminding myself to breathe when the young woman in front of me peeled away, and I found myself staring directly into the microphone. And the face of Dr Matsuko.

She was a bit younger than I had thought, from this close angle. Not that she had looked older from my seat. More that I hadn't been able to see her well, and had just assumed she was older. She was still a good bit older than me. Maybe late forties, I guessed. She was not what you might call pretty, but she was pleasant to look at. She appeared to be mostly, but perhaps not one hundred per cent, Asian. Very American-Asian. She spoke with not a trace of an accent, so I assumed she'd been born here.

Meanwhile I wasn't asking a question, which was problematic. I could feel the audience shift slightly in its collective seat.

'Dr Matsuko,' I blurted out suddenly, startling myself with the sudden amplification of my voice. I'd held my face too close to the microphone. I backed off an inch or two. 'I noticed that in your book you made just a handful of references to cellular memory as it relates to transplant recipients. And that all such references were citations from other researchers. You never gave us your own opinion of the phenomenon of transplant recipients who seem to experience the memories of their donors. Would you be willing to do that now?'

To my surprise, she smiled broadly. And rather . . . humanly. As if genuinely amused and unguarded. As if she were a person and a woman as well as just a scientist and a researcher. Imagine that.

'Well, well,' she said, still smiling. 'I've been waiting for this moment. Sooner or later someone was going to pin me down on that in public.'

'Sorry,' I said, once again too closely into the microphone.

'Don't be,' she said. 'I should have taken a bolder stance in my book. If I had it to write over again, I would. So here's your answer: I'm a scientist. So I wanted to disbelieve it. I leaned hard toward disbelief. Which is my job, I think. If I'm not a skeptic, I can't very well ask you to take me seriously when I say I believe something. Are you familiar with the theory of the white crow?'

I shook my head. 'I'm sorry,' I said. At proper mic distance. 'I'm not.'

Some of the stage lights had been trained on the audience, and I was aware of sweat dripping down my forehead. If I'd had a handkerchief, I wouldn't have hesitated to wipe it away, even while under scrutiny. But I didn't.

'It's courtesy of the psychologist William James. He wrote, essentially, that if your goal is to upset the law that all crows are black, it's enough to prove one single crow to be white. And I think it goes without saying that the transplant field has more than its share of white crows. Of course, the doctors pass it off as a response to the massive drug cocktails that are a part of the recipient's life. But they can't explain away something like the little girl who helped catch and convict her donor's murderer by repeatedly dreaming the exact details of the crime. And there are others, but . . . just for the sake of conversation let's call her our white crow. So then if another recipient comes to me and says his taste in food or music has changed, and then only later he asks about his donor, and sure enough, he has changed to the donor's tastes . . . could this be a hoax or a coincidence? Yes. I suppose it could be. But I can't tell this person, "No, that's impossible. All crows are black." Because we've already established that there's at least one white one. And there are so many reports of this . . . and I can only imagine how many more there would be if someone could lift the stigma and the disbelief these people face . . . I guess what I'm saying is that after a certain number of fairly credible reports, it becomes unscientific to believe too strongly in coincidence. Because the statistical likelihood of that many co-incidences is simply unscientific. So, long answer to a perfectly simple question . . . I guess I'm stretching it out because I'm still not entirely comfortable with this . . . the answer is yes. I do, myself, believe that it's possible for a transplant recipient to experience distinct donor memories as a result of cellular memory. At least for the first few months.'

I stood, stunned by her last sentence.

She gently indicated with her body language that she was done. She shifted her gaze up the aisle to the person behind me and pointed slightly. As if to say, 'Next.'

But I didn't move. I couldn't move.

A moment later the young man behind me reached around me and pulled the mic off the stand and back to his lips.

'Dr Matsuko . . .' he said.

And I peeled away back to my seat.

I had read as many as seven books on the subject of cellular memory. I had read Dr Matsuko's book twice. Nowhere in any of them had anyone suggested that donor memories in a transplant recipient could be a temporary phenomenon.

If Dr Matsuko was right, I had only just so much time to share this bizarre bond with Vida. And I had no idea where she was.

*   *   *

I expected Dr Matsuko to exit from the stage when it was over. Duck behind a curtain and disappear. I was wrong.

I stood in front of my seat, my thighs leaned on the seat-back in front of me, and watched her gather her notes and tuck them into a soft-sided, natural-colored leather briefcase. I watched a student, a young man, approach her, and wait for her to finish gathering. I waited for her to brush him off. Act busy, and brush by him and out of the auditorium.

She didn't. She stopped and talked to him.

I'd been sitting close to the back wall, a testament to my inability to appear front and center in my own life, so by the time I made my way through the crowd to the podium, there were at least a dozen people waiting to talk to her. A dozen twenty-year-old students and me.

I stood, looking away. I wanted to pretend to be looking at something else, but what? I settled for scanning the room as if trying to locate a lost companion. Why, I'm not sure. Maybe for the same reason that people who are dining alone will attempt to fix their attention on some imaginary interest or concern.

It took a good ten minutes before I realized that this was going to take a long time. I rubbed the worry stone hidden in my pocket and waited.

I glanced at my watch. It was nearly nine. For some

irrational reason I had thought I'd drive home after the lecture. Pure insanity, as it was nearly an eight-hour drive. I'm not sure what I was thinking, other than having been away from home for a day and a half already. Which was perhaps a thousand times longer than I'd been out in the world since Lorrie's funeral.

I gave up locating my imaginary companion, and instead just half-leaned, half-sat on a table on the stage, my arms crossed, looking down and pretending to be lost in thought. Distantly hearing the chatter of the doctor and whoever remained of the students, but not really focusing on words.

I have no idea how much time elapsed.

I know only that at some point my charade of deep thought turned over on me, and I became lost in genuine thought, almost without noticing. Crazy though it sounds, even to me, I was weighing the possibility of contacting a valid psychic – if indeed such a thing exists – regarding Vida's whereabouts.

It took me a moment to register the silence.

Then I heard Dr Matsuko's voice slice through it. She said, 'Are you the recipient?'

I looked up. Surprised. I glanced around to see if she could be addressing someone besides me. But everyone else had finished engaging the doctor and wandered away.

'No. I'm not. I'm the donor.'

She stood before me, briefcase dangling from both

hands in front of her. Smiling in a way that felt surprisingly familiar. I don't mean to suggest that there was anything familiar about her to me. There wasn't. More that she was treating me with a familiar air. Not like the total stranger I so obviously was.

She raised one eyebrow. 'Living donor? Kidney? Partial liver?'

'Oh. No. I guess I don't mean I was the donor. I mean, I donated my wife's organs. After her death.'

'Recent?'

'Yes.'

'I'm sorry.'

'Thank you. So am I.'

'Don't tell me. Let me guess. You're confused because I suggested it might be temporary. I could see the way it hit you.'

'I haven't read that in anybody else's research.'

'Well, they're not sure. And, actually, neither am I. There's not much hard evidence to go on. It gets down to that wacky, unpredictable world of quantum mechanics as it relates to the increasingly holographic view of human anatomy. And just between you and me . . .'

It took me a second to realize she was pausing so I could supply my name.

'Richard.'

'Between you and me, Richard, if anybody tells you he or she fully understands the subject on anything

other than a gut, instinctive level . . . hell, even that
. . . he's either a liar, or his brain needs to be studied.
Except, look what I just did. I passed it off as relating
to his brain. Which is the old-school science. The old
way is to believe all knowledge and understanding
comes from the brain. Even after all my research into
how every cell in the human body carries the memory
and experience of the whole. But those old habits die
hard. For so many years we thought our brain was
the determinant. That the heart could only beat if
the brain told it to. But we know for a fact that the
heart will beat valiantly for a time after disconnection
from its brain. Literal disconnection. In fact, the new
school is that, if anything, it's the heart that runs the
show. You know. Puts the "us" in us. Please don't repeat
what I said to an actual MD. Not to say they're old
school, though God knows some of them are. More
like it's not even the same school. Medicine doesn't
think the heart runs the show. Just the oddballs like
me.'

She stopped and looked at my face. I think it had
turned white. I thought I could feel the blood draining
out of it.

'Oh,' she said. 'Right. Sorry. You donated your wife's
heart. Didn't you?'

'Yes.'

'I should think before I talk.'

'Maybe I wouldn't have. If I had known all this.

You know. That it was still alive and still . . . her. You know?'

'But your only other option was to let it die and then bury it in the ground, or throw it in the cremation furnace. Does that really sound like a more appealing option?'

'When you put it like that, I guess not.'

'Look, Richard. I like talking to you. But I'm absolutely famished—'

'Right. I understand. Absolutely. Thanks for your time.'

I turned and began to walk off the stage, not wanting her to see that I was stung by her abruptness.

'Richard.'

I stopped, but did not turn. I still wanted to hide my reaction.

'Yes?'

'You're jumping ahead and ending up in all the wrong places. I wasn't brushing you off. I was about to ask you if you've eaten.'

I turned back, and looked into her face. It seemed open. Impassive, yet somehow invested. Curious.

'Actually, no. I haven't. Not since breakfast.'

'Do you have a car here?'

'Yes. I do.'

'Good. Because I don't.'

'This is very generous of you.'

'No, it's very generous of *you*. You just volunteered to pick up the check.'

My mouth smiled without warning. Without permission. It felt out of place, as if I had suddenly begun speaking a foreign language.

'My pleasure,' I said. 'The least I can do.'

Connie, Or Else

'Tell me about your wife,' she said, tearing into a fresh, hard-crusted roll and then buttering it with a molded pat of butter which had not been properly softened.

'What about her?'

'Whatever you want.'

'Do you really want to know about her?'

'I want to know about *you*. And she's obviously the biggest part of you there is to know about right now. And I know from experience that people who've lost loved ones are comforted by sharing about them. And we do have time . . .'

I sat without speaking for a moment, and she held the basket of rolls in my direction. I could well have reached for them myself. I got the impression that she was encouraging me to eat. I knew I should. My blood sugar must have been regrettably low.

I took one, but then just set it on its little plate and forgot all about it again.

I wanted to ask *why* she wanted to know about me. But it was too loaded a question. It suggested, hinted at, a subtext I was pretty sure did not exist. I was convinced I would only make a fool of myself, and perhaps embarrass her as well, if I asked.

'I don't know what I should tell you about her.'

'Tell me how you met.'

'OK,' I said, gathering up the story inside me. I sat back and smiled slightly. She was right. It was a comforting memory.

'She was a big hiking enthusiast,' I said. 'And so was I. And so one early October I was camping up at the North Rim Grand Canyon, and then I hiked down to the river and spent one night at the bottom. And that was where I first saw her. At Phantom Ranch. I never even talked to her. Not then. I just saw her there. I was camping at Bright Angel, right nearby, but I had reserved meals at the ranch. And I guess maybe she was in a women's dorm. I didn't really know, but I was guessing, because she seemed to be alone. Anyway, I saw her in the dining room at dinner, and I noticed her, but it wasn't a big deal. I just noticed. And then at the first breakfast – the five thirty breakfast – I came in and there she was again, but she was at a table with all other women and there were no empty seats near her. I guess it's easy to gravitate toward the people in your dorm.

Maybe you don't really know them, but there's some familiarity.

'So then after breakfast we took off hiking. I was headed back to the North Rim, and so was she. Which is interesting, because probably more than nine people out of ten hike from and to the South Rim. I found out later that she was hiking rim-to-rim. South Rim to North Rim, and then she was going to take a shuttle bus back, but I ended up driving her back.

'But I'm getting ahead of myself.

'Anyway, I had this insane, chauvinistic notion that I'd slow up my pace so that we'd keep passing each other every time one of us took a rest break. Which turned out to be really funny. Because I nearly killed myself trying to keep up with her.'

Dr Matsuko laughed, and in nearly that same instant the waiter arrived.

'Well, now,' he said, 'are we ready to order or do we need a little more time?'

I'm not fond of those who use the editorial (or royal?) 'we', but maybe if I were to be completely honest with myself, I might have had a chip on my shoulder because I'd been lost in my story, and happy there, and did not like being bumped back into my current reality.

I said, 'Dr Matsuko, are you ready to order?'

'Connie,' she said. 'And I'm going to be incredibly sinful tonight and eat red meat. The New York strip steak. With salad. Whatever you serve as your house dressing will be fine so long as it's not made with soy oil.'

'Yes, ma'am,' the waiter said. 'How would you like your steak done?'

'I know it's very gauche, but I would like it as close to well done as I can get it without making your chef cry.'

I smiled and so did the waiter.

Then he turned his attention to me, and I realized I'd done no homework whatsoever pursuant to ordering dinner.

To get out of it, I said, 'I'll have the same. Medium rare.'

'Soup or salad?'

'What's the soup?'

'Cream of mushroom and leek, or clam chowder.'

'Clam chowder.'

He whisked away our menus and blessedly retreated.

'Now let's see,' I said. 'Where was I, Dr Matsuko?'

'First of all,' she said, 'if you call me Dr Matsuko one more time I swear on my honor as a scientist that I will shamelessly bitch-slap you in front of this entire restaurant full of people, as loudly and flamboyantly as possible. It's either Connie or suffer the consequences, and don't say I didn't warn you. Secondly, you were struggling to keep up with the pace of your future wife, you chauvinistic, overconfident male hiker, you.'

'Right,' I said, shaking off the fact that it was hard to

know how to react to her effusive, joking candor. 'I was just getting up to Cottonwood. Which is a campground part-way up to the rim. Supposed to be sort of a half-way point, but it's really closer to the river. I had fallen behind by then, but when I got up there she was there, and it was clear she was going to set up camp. And my plan had been to hike to the North Rim all in one day. But I changed my plan.'

'Ah. And that's where you talked to her.'

'Oh. Yeah. Sure. That would be a much better story. The real story is very embarrassing. We were there most of the afternoon and all evening – along with dozens of other people of course – and I smiled and said hi to her once at a water spigot, and she said hi back, but I never actually got up the courage to talk to her.

'When I got up in the morning, it was just barely light, but she had already broken camp and gone. I practically ran up the trail, but I never saw her. She had a head start, and she was fast. So, that was it. I'd blown my chance. I was absolutely morose.

'I got up top, and I was just going to go back to my campsite, but then I suddenly got it in my head that an iced drink would be nice. Even though it was pretty cool out. You know, North Rim. Eight-thousand-plus feet in October. But still, I was heated up from the hiking. So I walked over to the lodge. Well, limped over to the lodge. And they have this thing called the sun porch. Have you ever been to the North Rim Lodge?'

She shrugged and shook her head. 'I've never even been to the Grand Canyon.'

'Oh, you should. You must. Anyway, the sun porch. Part of it is inside, but with big windows. And then there's this big open outdoor stone patio. It's right at the edge of the canyon. And I mean that literally. Right at the edge. So you can sit out there, near a low stone wall, and drink your cold drink, and stare out into that beautiful red-rock abyss . . . So, anyway, I got myself a lemonade and limped out there, and—'

'And don't tell me. Let me guess. There was your future wife.'

'No. She was not there. And I sort of had it in my head that she might be. But she wasn't. Not yet. There were only two seats left, and they were together. Literally. Like a chair for two. So I took one side. And about two minutes later I heard this woman's voice asking if the seat next to me was taken. And I looked up . . .'

'Please tell me you at least got up the nerve to tell her the seat was not taken.'

'I did. Indeed. I said it wasn't. And she sat down and then she asked, "Aren't you that guy I kept seeing on the trail . . . ?"'

'And the rest is history,' she said. 'Her recipient is very lucky. To get a hiker's heart.'

I didn't answer.

'Sorry,' she said. 'Too much reality too fast. I pulled

you up out of your happy place so fast you got the bends. It's written all over your face.'

'Not your fault.'

'I do have a bad habit of dumping the truth on people like ice water from a very large bucket. Ask anyone.'

But I wasn't sure who I was supposed to ask. And I had no idea what to say any more to Dr Matsuko. Connie.

She caught my stress and talked right through it.

'What's that thing in your hand? If you don't mind my asking. That thing you keep fiddling with.'

I opened my left hand, exposed the worry stone, and looked at it blankly, as though surprised to see it there.

'Oh. That's a worry stone.'

'Ah.'

'It's not mine, actually. It belongs to . . . the recipient.'

'Ah,' she said. 'I'm sure there's a story behind that.'

'There is,' I said.

But I didn't tell it.

Unintended Consequences

'So, let me explain why I said what I said. The thing that made your face turn green.' She sawed a long slice through her decidedly crispy New York steak. Looked up at my confused face. 'About the first few months.'

'Oh. Right,' I said. 'That.'

'Here's what we know. And what we don't know. We know that cells die. That's a given. So, after a good long length of time . . . seven years is an acceptable rule of thumb . . . there won't be one living cell in the heart that was alive at the time of donation. Now, does that mean those cells, aggregate that heart, will now bear no relation to your wife's heart and be purely a product of its new host? No. It does not. The cells will still be the daughter cells of the donor heart. Cardiac stem cells may never die. And they're the seed for new cells, but the new cells will be raised by the new host.

And a cell is not an island. It's constantly influenced by conditions external to it, which is to say, conditions in the new host body. Everything from what he eats . . .' She paused. 'He?'

'She.'

'Right. She. No wonder it's so complicated for you. Everything from what she eats, to what she worries about, to her opinions about herself. Stress. Environmental factors. Cells are constantly being bombarded by nourishment – or lack of same – information, energy, including what we call "non-local" energy: biochemical influence, hormones, drugs. The more time goes on, the more the transplanted organ becomes some combination of its original owner and its new owner. But what combination? How much of each? And when? That's the part we don't know. There hasn't been a lot of pure scientific research on this. Most of what we know about it is entirely anecdotal. All I can tell you for sure is that your wife's heart is most purely your wife's heart closest to the actual date of transplantation. Everything else is still a mystery at this point.'

'So the memories will get lost, is that what you're saying?'

'Well, no. How can they, really? Once you remember that you remember something, you don't forget it again. And then the memory rightly belongs to the new host, and is stored in every cell of the new host's body, and then there's just no telling what's what. This is where our current science just falls flat on its face, I'm afraid. This is where a scientist with any humility at all will need to admit that God or nature or what-have-you has created something quite beyond our understanding in the human being. And even if we did understand it, this is something outside nature. God did not create a donor heart sewn into a new body. That's our handiwork. And privy to all sorts of unintended consequences, I'm sure.'

'Yes,' I said. 'I'm sure you're right.'

'I'm not speaking against organ donation.'

'Never thought you were.'

'It's a modern miracle. Saves thousands of lives. I'm just saying that when modern scientific miracles meet natural miracles, some very interesting outcomes occur. And the only thing we can predict with any certainty is that they will be completely unpredictable. So, why is it such a problem for you to think that the effect might fade in time?'

I looked up from my plate for the first time in a long time.

'Because . . . when she was here . . . I treated her like she was faking, or crazy, or acting foolish, or otherwise just plain wrong. And now I don't know where she is.'

'Hmm. That would be a problem. Yes.'

*   *   *

Connie spent most of the rest of the meal explaining all the different ways in which sugar degrades human cells. So when the waiter arrived with a tray of sample desserts, and a line about whether or not he could tempt us, we both burst out laughing.

'Just a check,' I said, masking my disappointment as best I could. I had watched that tray of desserts make its way over to a nearby table earlier in the meal, and could practically taste the chocolate cheesecake.

Connie looked up at me, hands clasped on the table in front of her, in a kind of summing-up mode. A close to the hugely unexpected evening. I found myself knocked off-guard and off-center by her frank visual assessment of me.

'I have a couple of articles I drew on for the book that seem relevant. You might find them interesting. I'll send them to you if you like. Have you got a card?'

'Oh. Do I? Let me see. I mean, of course I have cards, in general, but did I bring one? I usually keep two in my wallet. Unless I gave them out. It's been so long since I've been in a normal flow with things like that. You know, even to check.'

While I babbled, I dug my wallet out of my back pants pocket and admonished myself with an inner litany of, 'Shut up, Richard,' and, 'You're talking too much again.'

I opened the wallet and found two of my cards.

I handed one across the table to Connie.

She put on her reading glasses – they'd been hanging on a chain around her neck – and examined my card for a bizarre length of time. Longer than it should have taken her to read every word and number on it twice.

'You live in San Jose?'

'Yes.'

'I just assumed you lived here in LA.'

'No, thank you.'

She laughed.

'So where are you staying?'

'At the Doubletree, just a few blocks from the university.'

I did not mention that I had checked out, and had not planned to stay another night. I was hoping they still had a room available. If not, I supposed some hotel would.

'Oh. Good. That's just about three or four blocks from my hotel, I think. Maybe I can trouble you for a ride back. Save me calling a cab. I didn't get a rental car because I hate to drive in strange cities. And what city could be stranger than LA? I ask you.'

I smiled slightly, and found myself wondering if she ever berated herself for talking too much. Then her expression changed subtly. Became less light-hearted.

'You didn't drive down just for this, did you?'

I felt uncomfortable, as if caught in a lie or a sin.

'I did, actually. Yes.'

'You know, there are other researchers whose body of work is more relevant to transplantation.'

'They weren't speaking anywhere in the west, though. And you were.'

On the drive back to the hotel, Connie asked, 'What does your recipient remember?'

'Just me. I think. She just remembers me. She swears the minute I walked into her hospital room she knew me. And loved me.'

'Common,' she said. 'If the heart is going to remember anything, we have to assume a dear loved one will be high on the list.'

I drove in silence for a few blocks. I was amazed by how tired I was. I found myself working hard to be sure I didn't slip, while still driving, into a mode too akin to sleep.

Connie's voice startled me. 'Do you love her?'

'Who?' A stupid question, I suppose, but she might have meant Lorrie.

'Your recipient.'

I was stunned, and completely thrown by the question. I had no idea why she would ask such a thing.

'No. I don't love Vida. How could I? She's just a kid.'

'Oh,' she said, her tone changing. 'She's a kid. That's very different. Wait . . . how could she be a kid? How would the size be a match for transplantation?'

'No. Not a kid kid. She's something like nineteen. Or maybe she's twenty by now.'

'Ah. That kind of kid.'

I tried hard to read her tone, but came up empty.

'She's . . . really, she's a kid. She's anorexic and completely scattered, and she's lived outside the world for almost her whole life, and . . . well, believe me, if you met her, you'd see what I mean. She's just a kid.'

'So what you love is something more like the heart that beats in her chest.'

'Yes. Something more like that.'

'I could tell you loved something very strongly here. It comes through.'

We pulled up in front of her hotel. Not a moment too soon.

She turned and took me in, assessed me as she had at the end of dinner, and I felt no less alarmed. Perhaps more so, in light of the strange turn the conversation had taken.

'Well,' she said. 'It's been very nice meeting you, Richard Bailey.'

She thrust her right hand forward, and I shook it.

'I really appreciate your time, Dr— Connie.'

'Close one,' she said.

Then she opened my car door and stepped out into the dark street.

I winced and jumped as she slammed the door behind her, and I watched as she made her way to the hotel doorway. I watched in that sort of gentlemanly way. Waiting to be sure she got in all right. Despite the fact that a door man appeared, ready to play that exact same role.

Or maybe I was just too stunned to drive away immediately.

Or maybe I was waiting to see if she would look back.

She didn't look back.

What Doesn't Upset Us

I thought I would fall asleep the moment my head hit the pillow.

I was fortunate enough to get a room in the hotel where I'd stayed the night before. Why that one was better than any other, I don't know. Only that I drove to it first thing, and hated to think of driving any farther.

I could not have been more wrong about the sleeping.

I lay awake for hours in the glow of the overly aggressive lighted clock radio, exhausted to the point of pain, but nowhere near sleep.

At about three thirty in the morning I got up, dressed, and wandered down to the hotel business center to check my email.

Truth be told, I had checked it quite often, obsessively in fact, up until leaving for LA. Hoping for some word from Vida. And I had thought of it many times since leaving home. And I couldn't sit on that urge any longer.

With my room key, I let myself into the dim and deserted business center off the lobby. There I sat in front of one of the two computers, racking my brain for my webmail password. I don't use webmail often. I got it on the third try. I tried first Lorrie's birthday. Then our wedding anniversary. The day I met her – which was the same month and day as our wedding anniversary, but two years earlier – proved to be the charm.

There was no email from Vida. I found, instead, about thirty pieces of spam and three messages from Myra.

I'll paraphrase.

To sum it up, she had emailed me shortly after I'd pulled out of my driveway for this trip, to inquire about my welfare. When I hadn't responded, as it was my habit to respond within half a day at most, she'd gotten downright panicky. In the last message, she asked me to please call her as soon as possible, and said that if she didn't hear from me by tomorrow, she would have no choice but to begin the long drive down.

I looked at my watch again. Silly, as I knew it was well after three. I certainly couldn't call her now.

I trudged back upstairs, prepared to lie awake for the rest of the night and then some.

I lay down on my hotel bed, still dressed, and closed my eyes.

When I opened them again, it was after noon.

In my hurry to check out of the hotel, at which check-out time was the standard twelve noon, I forgot about calling Myra.

I remembered just as I got on the freeway.

I had not thought to bring an earpiece with me for my cell phone, and my car was a slightly older model and did not have Bluetooth or any type of hands-free feature. And handheld cellular use while driving had been declared illegal in California. But this was import-ant. And I knew I had to call.

She picked up on the first ring.

'Richard,' she said. 'My God. You're all right.'

I wondered what had been going on in her head, but didn't want to ask.

'You won't believe this,' I said. 'But I managed to get myself up and out of the house. I've gone on a little trip. Sorry if I scared you. I never really thought about that. It just never occurred to me that it would.'

'That's wonderful,' she said. 'A trip. You must be getting your head up some.'

'Some,' I said, thinking it to be fractionally the truth. Some doesn't have to be much.

'Where are you?'

'Just driving out of LA.'

'Oh. But you hate LA.'

'Yes, but there was an event here I wanted to attend.'

'Concert?'

'No. Not a concert.' I didn't want to say. But I knew, in that instinctive, non-verbal way we all have, that she could tell I didn't want to say. And that the more I didn't want to say, the more she wanted to know. 'A lecture.'

'On . . .'

'Cellular memory.'

A long silence.

I dropped the phone into my lap as a highway patrol car, which I'd spotted in my left-hand mirror, drew level and then passed me. When I was sure he'd gone, I picked it up again.

'I'm sorry, Myra. If you said something just then, I missed it.'

'I hadn't said anything.'

'Oh. OK. Good.'

The final word of my response could have been taken a couple of different ways. In fact, I wasn't even sure which way I'd intended it.

'I'll feel a lot better when you get through this phase, Richard. I think it will bring you nothing but pain. But I guess I've made that clear already.'

'Yes,' I said. 'You have. I wish you could have heard

this lecture. This researcher, Connie Matsuko, she's really old-school science. Or anyway, she was. She was as skeptical as you about all of this. But it's won her over to a great degree.'

'Richard—'

I did not let her have her say. I was feeling emboldened. I was not going to be pushed or cowed.

'She brought up that case of the little girl who helped catch and convict her donor's murderer. The girl remembered every minute detail of the crime in dreams.'

I was contemplating pulling off the freeway to discuss this, but traffic had slowed to a crawl going over the Hollywood Hills, so I sat, stopping and barely starting in heavy traffic, near the Skirball Center and the Getty Museum.

'Maybe the little girl was psychic,' Myra said.

'Now that's interesting. Why would you believe in ESP and not cellular memory? Aren't they just about the same degree off to the left?'

But in the silence that followed, I knew why. She believed that which it did not deeply upset her to believe. Like all of us, I guess.

'It's just that ESP is so well proven. Some people are psychic. We know that. Why, just yesterday or the day before there was an article in the Portland paper about a psychic who consulted with the local police and helped them solve three cold cases. Now, if the police believe in her, who am I to question? Besides, she was right. We've always known, as long as I've been alive at least, that humans are only using a small percentage of the potential of our brains. So I guess this must be one of the parts most of us don't use. That's not so hard to understand.'

Ah, yes. The brain. The determinant of everything. I pictured Connie laughing. Quite literally saw it, vividly, in my head.

'Look, Myra. The connection is breaking up, and I'm not supposed to be talking without hands-free. So I'm going to let you go now. I'm sorry I scared you. I'm fine. Really.'

'Thanks for calling, Richard,' she said. Hesitantly. Making it clear, by her tone, that there was much more she wanted to say.

'Goodbye, Myra,' I said, and clicked off the phone before she had a chance to say more.

I arrived home well after eight.

I checked my email immediately. But, other than spam, there was nothing new.

Then I opened my web browser, and did a search for *The Oregonian*, the Portland newspaper. Once on their site, I searched the word 'psychic' along with the phrase 'cold cases'.

It came up immediately. The article Myra had referred to. The woman's name was Isabelle Duncan, and she had received this 'gift' (she made it clear later in the article that she did not consider it a gift and, in fact, did not want it) fairly late in life, after dying during a surgery and being brought back by the doctors two and a half minutes later. She approached the police after reading a human-interest story about a cold murder case, written on the tenth anniversary of the victim's death. She didn't particularly care to mix in, but she knew who did it, and when, and why, and where the murder weapon was hidden, and felt it her civic and human duty to say. The Portland police were skeptical, of course, but they followed the lead to an easy arrest and conviction. Every one of her details checked out. The police were so impressed that they convinced her to reluctantly take on two other cold cases, which were quickly solved.

I read the article twice.

I found the link to the reporter's email address, and sent him the following painfully simple inquiry:

Is there any way that one can get in touch with this Isabelle Duncan? Thank you.

Richard Bailey

Then I went to bed.

I noticed that the message light was flashing on the answering machine, but I was sure I would only discover that Myra had left panicky messages. Or, failing that, I was sure it would prove to be something I wouldn't want to deal with, and which would only keep me awake. So I let that go for the time being.

Postcard from Independence

It was after eleven the following morning when I put on my bathrobe and wandered out to collect my three days' worth of mail.

I carried it all in, weeded out the junk and catalogues, and dropped them in the recycle bin.

There was a notice from the phone company that might well have been final, and a second notice on the gas bill. With a deep sigh, I knew I would need to pull myself together to pay bills. Which meant I would have to confront and absorb the truth about my rapidly dwindling bank balance. I supposed I could always take another credit card advance.

I briefly put them aside.

Under them was a postcard. A photo of a snowy Mount Whitney. I turned it over. My heart literally missed a beat to see that it was from Vida.

I read it three times. Held it in my hands. As if it could tell me something.

Then I remembered my phone messages, and played them.

Two panicky messages from Myra. Three calm ones from Vida. She was home, and hoping to get her worry stone back.

I picked up the phone, and called her house. Abigail picked up on the first ring.

'Vida?' Not even hello. Just, 'Vida?'

'No. It's not, Abigail. It's me. Richard Bailey. I was hoping to talk to Vida. I was returning her call. Calls. But, from your greeting, I'm guessing she isn't there.'

'She's gone again. She was home three days, and now she's gone again. Do you have any idea where she is? Tell me the truth.'

'If I did, Abigail, don't you think I would have called there instead of here?'

'Oh.'

'I know she was recently in the Eastern Sierras. She sent me a postcard of Mount Whitney. Postmarked Independence.'

'Yes. That's on record. That's pretty well established. Did yours have any writing on it?'

'Of course it did. What would be the point of a post-card with no writing on it?'

'I've been wondering that myself lately. If she turns up, I'll let you know.'

'Thank you.'

But six long days went by. And nobody let me know anything.

Six days later, at ten minutes to nine in the evening, the phone jangled me out of sleep.

I grabbed it up, hoping it would be Vida, or, failing that, Abigail, with news.

'Richard?' A woman's voice.

'Yes, this is Richard.'

'I'm sorry. Did I wake you?'

I'm loath to admit how early I go to bed these days. It's humiliating. 'Well, I cannot tell a lie,' I said. 'I fell asleep in front of the TV.' Obviously, I could tell a lie. Obviously I was lying when I said I couldn't lie. I had gone to bed. Purposely.

I still had no idea who I was lying to.

'Well, I'm sorry I woke you,' she said.

A long silence, which I hoped would speak for itself. I felt an aversion to having to ask.

'This is Connie.'

'Oh. Right. Connie,' I said, waking up fast. 'I didn't recognize your voice. Interesting you should call. I've been wishing I had your phone number. Because I got a postcard from Vida. And I was wrong when I told you that she only remembers me. Apparently she also remembers that Lorrie was a hiker. She asked me if Lorrie was a hiker.'

'But you can't answer her. Right? Because she's gone.'

'Right. She's gone.' A long silence. Long. Horrifically, painfully long. 'But I didn't mean to talk over your reason for calling.'

'Oh, no, please do,' she said. '*Please* talk over my reason for calling.'

More silence. The uneasy feeling in the pit of my stomach callously announced that this was no surprise, and I should not even bother to pretend otherwise. And that it had warned me. What it said, more or less, was, 'You knew this all along.'

Connie jumped into the gap.

'OK. I'm a total idiot. That's just a given. I have a good grasp of certain scientific details, but it doesn't mean I necessarily handle the rest of my life like a science. I'm just like everybody else. I called to make a confession.'

'OK.' My lips felt numb as I said it.

'Those articles I told you about . . . I don't need to send them to you. They're right out on the Internet. I could have linked you to them, very easily. I could have written two or three links on a cocktail napkin right then and there. I just didn't want to completely drop out of touch with you.'

'Oh.'

'Look, don't even say anything, OK? Because I know. I know it all. I know you just lost your wife. Please don't point out that you just lost your wife, because I know. And please don't pass judgment on the fact that I would even find myself drawn to a man who just lost his wife, because I have two best girlfriends and a therapist to do that job for you. And I also know you're a good ten years younger . . . I know all of it, so just don't say anything.'

I waited. Having been told not to say anything.

'Oh. Right. You can say *something*,' she said.

'Can? Or may?'

'OK, you may. Can you?'

'Not really. No.'

'Look. All I'm saying is, maybe we can not drop completely out of touch. I'll be up in San Francisco in October. Maybe we could just get together and have coffee or something. Maybe go for a hike!'

'Sure. That would be fine.'

'You sound totally lost and confused.'

'I am.'

'I'm sorry.'

'Don't be. I was before I met you.'

'So . . . where did she send you a postcard from?'

My brain raced to keep up with her sudden change of tack. Nearly tripped over itself and went flying.

'Oh. Vida? From Independence. California.'

'Seriously? Independence?'

'Something special about Independence?'

'There is to me. It's about eleven feet from Manzanar.'

I knew what that was. Manzanar. I just couldn't access what I knew. Not on short notice, anyway.

She raced on.

'The Japanese-American internment camp. My grand-father died there during the war.'

'That's horrible. I didn't know people died there.'

'Lots of people died there. Take that many people and hold them for years, some of them are going to die.'

'Oh. I see. You don't mean they killed him.'

'Open to interpretation. He had a heart attack. He was a big stress monster, you know? And then all the added pressure of being interned against his will, and especially not being able to save his wife and son from that same fate. His barrack-mates tried to get him some medical help, but nobody got to him for hours. My father was six, and he stood there and watched his father die in his mother's arms. I'm not going to make a big, sweeping statement about the state of healthcare at Manzanar. Because I wasn't there, thank God. I wasn't born yet. But it sure let *my* family down.'

'I'm really sorry. That's unforgivable.'

'Yeah. Well. Here's the problem with unforgivable. The more I research the bodymind, the more I get that the only workable path to workable health is to forgive the unforgivable in spite of its unforgivability. Otherwise we just destroy our own cells with the byproducts of all that hate. We don't hurt Manzanar any. Just us. You don't suppose Vida was there because of the camp, do you? No, that doesn't make any sense. She's not Asian, is she?'

'No.'

'Couldn't be, then. Got to be coincidence. I just couldn't think of any other reason why someone would go to Independence.'

'The postcard had a picture of Mount Whitney.'

'Yeah. That makes more sense for a white girl. Not sure what I was thinking there, for a minute.'

Another deadly silence, during which I was grateful for the diversion, yet at the same time realized it had played out and abandoned us.

'So . . . I'll give you my phone number,' she said. 'Do you have anything to write with? And on? Handy?'

I looked around blankly. The lights were off but it was summer, and not even entirely dark at nine o'clock.

'Not really.'

'I'll email it to you.'

'OK.'

'Go back to sleep now. I'm sorry.'

It took me a while to think what to say in return. And, besides, before I could, my train of thought was broken by a dial tone.

From: Isabelle Duncan
To: Richard Bailey

Dear Richard Bailey,

Sorry it's taken so long to reply, but the newspaper forwarded me a number of requests like yours, and it's been quite overwhelming, and it's taking me some time to get through them. Most are missing children. And I won't do missing children. I just can't. It would tear me apart. You didn't specify. If this is not about a missing child, I'll help if I can.

Isabelle Duncan

From: Richard Bailey
To: Isabelle Duncan

Dear Isabelle Duncan,

The missing person is not a child. She's nineteen years old. And I don't think she's come to any harm. So I don't think it would tear you apart. Thank you for your offer of help. It means more than I can say. How do I proceed?

Many thanks,

Richard Bailey

From: Isabelle Duncan
To: Richard Bailey

Richard,

If you could bring something that belongs to her, or even just something that she touched, that would help. If you can make it tomorrow at about 1 p.m., let me know, and I will give you my address.

Isabelle

Tired

It was raining on and off in Portland. In fact, it rained on and off all the way from the northern California border. But that hardly qualifies as a surprise. When is it not raining in Portland?

When she opened the door, Isabelle Duncan looked as though she hadn't slept in days. If not weeks. She looked to be fifty-something, with hip-length hair of pure white. The circles under her eyes looked nearly black in comparison to the rest of her pale and pasty skin.

Her house smelled distinctly of the three large, aged dogs that circled my legs, wagging feebly.

'You look tired,' I said.

'So do you.'

'Oh. Yeah. I guess I must. It's a long drive.'

'Come in,' she said. 'Come in.'

I had to walk slowly and carefully so as not to trip over the dogs, who seemed intent on reading fascinating smells on my pant legs.

'Where did you drive from?' she asked, indicating her worn couch.

I sat, and she sat very close to me. More or less in what I like to think of as my personal space. The one I've been guarding so cautiously lately. I owed her a debt of gratitude, so I let it go by. But it kept me on edge.

'The Bay Area,' I said. 'California,' I added. Because there are bays in Oregon, too.

To say I'd driven from the Bay Area was only very loosely true. I said it because San Jose was even farther, and I wanted to make the drive seem less insane.

'You don't live in Portland?'

'No.'

One of the dogs settled heavily on to the carpet with a deep grunt.

'How did you even read that article?'

'My mother-in-law lives here. She told me about it, and then I read it online.'

She clucked her tongue.

'Word does travel,' she said, making it clear that it would do far less traveling if she had her say. 'You couldn't have driven up just today.'

'No. I left late yesterday, after I got your last email.

It's more than a ten-hour drive.' A couple hours more, actually.

'This must be important to you. Where did you sleep?'

'In my car at a scenic overlook. Overlooking Lake Shasta. I'm sure I could have gotten a ticket for it if anybody had noticed. But nobody did.'

'That explains why you look tired.' She did not explain her own exhaustion, and I didn't consider it my business to ask. 'Well. Not to be rude, but let's get started. I have a couple coming at two. Missing child. Yeah, I know. I broke my own rule. Shouldn't have taken it on, and I know I'll regret it. Already do. But I agreed, and there's no getting out of it now. What did you bring?'

I gently placed the worry stone in her hand.

She didn't close her eyes, or become trance-like. Nothing stereotypical. She just held it. Curiously. As if it were talking and she were listening with some detached interest.

'This belongs to a lot of people,' she said. 'At least three.'

'It's Vida's. Really.'

'But it has three distinct energies. One is yours.'

'Yes.'

'So I'll put yours aside for now. You said she was nineteen?'

'That's right.'

'Good. Then she's not the one who's dead.'

'Dead? Somebody's dead?'

'The person who first put her energy into this stone is dead. Yes.'

'I don't think Esther is dead,' I said. 'She's old . . .'

'She's dead.'

'Really? How long?'

'That's not the type of thing I could really say for sure. It doesn't feel like ancient history, though. I'd say it's recent.'

'That's awful. I wonder if Vida knows.'

'She does. She's very sad about it.'

'Oh. Wow. I had no idea. That must be awful for Vida. She was close to Esther, I think.'

'Yes. She was. Very close. But she's OK. She's strong, this Vida. Stronger than she looks. Stronger than anybody gives her credit for. But it's hit her very hard. I'm not entirely sure, but it feels like this might even be her first deep loss. So she feels it very strongly. But she's OK.'

'So . . . do you know where she is?'

'Wheres are also very hard. I do get that she's been moving. Traveling. And it feels like there's someone with her. A young man is how it feels.'

I could barely speak. I had no idea how to express my shock. I stumbled over my first words, and she waited patiently. Tiredly.

'She's with a guy?'

'I'm not positive, but it feels that way.'

'How could she have a boyfriend? That doesn't make sense.' Had she really gotten over loving me, just like that? Was Connie right about the first few months? 'She was so clear that . . . that she thought she loved me.'

'I didn't say he was her boyfriend. The sense I get is that he *wants* to be her boyfriend. But it doesn't feel like he is. And she doesn't *think* she loves you. She loves you. With all her heart. That's the one thing so far I can tell you with complete confidence. That's coming through loud and clear.'

I held still for a long time while nothing more was said on that score. If I was thinking, or feeling, it was nothing I could identify. Maybe I was feeling so many things simultaneously that no one reaction could rise to be recognized.

One of the ancient dogs, a mastiff type, stuck his head into my lap and I stroked his ears absent-mindedly.

'This is very confusing,' she said. 'This is the most confusing reading I've ever done. Even putting aside you and the dead woman, there are two completely different energies here, but I don't think it's two different people. I don't understand this at all.'

'Maybe the worry stone has been in too many hands. Here. Try this.'

I pulled the postcard from Independence out of my pocket and handed it to her. I waited while she communed with it in her way.

'Still two distinctly different stories. Like, for

example, I'm getting that she met you many years ago. And you said she's nineteen. Which means that you were romantically and sexually involved with her when she was . . .'

'No, of course it isn't like that.'

'Better not be, or you're out of here on your ass. And then I'm also getting that she's just known you for a few months. It's very strange. And I'm definitely getting that she has something that belongs to you. No. Not to you. It belongs to your wife. Wait. I thought *she* was your wife. No, she couldn't be. Your wife passed away, didn't she? But this Vida has something that used to belong to your wife. But you still feel like it belongs to you. But it doesn't. It's Vida's now. And you have to let it go.'

She looked directly into my eyes. I froze.

'It's something very personal,' she said. 'So I can understand that it's hard. But you have to. It belongs to Vida now. You have to let it go.'

I felt my own heart groan under an actual physical strain in my chest. As though someone had run it through with a weapon of some sort. So I guess Connie was right about at least one thing. We don't receive all information through our brains.

'What does she have of your late wife's?' Isabelle asked. 'Maybe that will help me make sense of this jumble.'

'Her heart.'

She received the news more impassively than I expected. It seemed so monumental to me as I said it.

'Literally? She received it in a transplant?'

'Yes.'

'Well, that explains a lot. That explains why she's known you for many years, and also for just a few months. It also explains why you're having so much trouble letting it go.'

I had thought – assumed, really – that this session would be all about Vida and her whereabouts and nothing about me and my own shortcomings. But I didn't say so.

'So . . . she's moving,' I said instead. 'Do you know where she's going?'

'No.'

'Oh. Too bad.'

'*She* doesn't know. If she decided, then I might know, or I might not. Hard to say. Things like how she feels are easier than things like where she is and where she's going. She's looking for something. But she doesn't quite know what it is or where to find it. So I can't tell you what she doesn't know.'

'Do you get *anything* that could help me with where she is now?'

Isabelle breathed for a long time. I watched her, thinking how far I had driven to get here. It was nobody's fault but my own, though.

'It's hot. I can definitely feel the heat. Has to be the

desert. She's looking for *you*,' she said. Suddenly. Firmly. As if that were the solid answer I had come here to un-earth.

'How could she be? She knows where I am.'

'Yes. She knows where you are. But she feels there's another place to look for you. And maybe for part of herself at the same time. I wish I could be clearer, but like I say, I can only be as clear as she is. And a lot of this hasn't quite revealed itself to her yet. But one thing I can say for sure: what she's looking for has a lot to do with you.'

And, through the emotional backlash of that rather general information, I had to pull myself together one more time and go after something solid. Something that would actually help.

'Can you tell me *anything* about where she's going? I mean, you said it was hard to be specific about where she was. But then you told me it was hot, like the desert. Can you give me *any* detail like that about this place she's trying to find?'

She closed her eyes and sighed.

'Vast,' she said.

'Vast?'

'Right. Someplace huge and beautiful.'

'So, someplace really big.'

'The word vast keeps coming up. Vast and beautiful.'

I swallowed several times, wondering if we were done.

'Leave me with your phone number,' she said. 'If I get more, I'll call you.'

'Thank you. Have you got a pen?'

I pulled my wallet out of my back pants pocket and drew out my one remaining card. It had only my home number printed on it, and I wanted to write my cell phone number on the back of it as well. It would be a long ride home, and I was on the fence about seeing Myra before leaving, and I wanted to hear news as soon as possible. I mean, on the off-chance that there might be any.

She lumbered heavily to her feet, and all three dogs rose to follow her into the kitchen. She emerged holding a pencil with a bright purple eraser glued to the top end.

'Thanks,' I said, and wrote my cell number on the back of the card. 'I really appreciate your taking the time to do this. I get the sense that it takes a toll on you.'

She eased herself back on to the couch again.

'You have no idea,' she said. 'But this one was easy. Not like the next one. The next one will be hell. I already know their child is dead. I wish there was some way out of this next one. But I committed to it, and now there's no way out.'

'I'm sorry.'

'As am I. As will they be.'

I had no idea what to say, and found myself anxious to leave.

'I guess I should have asked in advance . . .' I tailed off, hoping she would finish the sentence for me. Spare me from having to ask. But she showed no evidence of knowing where I was going. '. . . what you charge for this.'

She seemed genuinely taken aback. 'Charge?'

'You don't . . .'

'I don't do this for money.'

'Oh. I'm sorry. I just assumed . . .'

'I do it because it needs doing, and not many people can.'

'I'm sorry. I just . . . how do you make a living, then? Not that it's any of my business.'

'I work at the phone company. This is my day off.'

I was speechless. And quite tired of my repeated forays into speechless, a territory so recently unfamiliar to me. Once upon a time words were my strong suit. A specialty.

'I'm getting a big thermometer,' she said. 'But I don't guess that helps you much.'

I stared at her blankly. I thought she meant she was planning to purchase a large thermometer. Had I been right, it could easily have qualified for non sequitur of the century.

'I'm sorry?'

'Where she is. There seems to be a big thermometer. But I'm not really sure what that is or how it gets you closer to where you need to be.'

'Oh. Well, then. I really owe you a debt of gratitude,' I said, not positive if that was entirely true or not. The whole thing still hadn't put me any closer to where I so desperately needed to go.

'You're welcome. Best thing you can do to thank me, not to be rude, but I could use a good rest before this next couple shows up.'

'Of course,' I said. 'Thank you again.'

'I'll call you if I get more information.'

'Thank you.'

Isabelle and her ancient dogs walked me to the door.

It had begun to rain again. Quite hard this time.

I was just breaking into a run in the sheeting rain in her driveway when I heard her call my name.

'Mr Bailey.'

I stopped, and turned. Against my better judgment I just stood there, with no hat or coat, getting drenched.

She stood in her open doorway, one hand on the door. The dogs stood beside her, watching me with measured enthusiasm. Still wagging amiably.

'Yes?' I said, hoping to hurry this up.

'Not to pry, but what's the connection with this other woman? Not the woman we've been discussing. Someone else. The recent one. What is that?'

I stood watching her a moment, having long since given up staying dry.

'I don't know what that is,' I said at last.

'Interesting.'

'I don't even know if it's interesting.'

'We never really know what's interesting, do we? Seems like part of the human condition, how we always guess wrong about that. Even me sometimes.'

'Really? Even you? That seems surprising.'

'Yes, I guess it would seem surprising, from the outside. It's easier to see for somebody else than it is to see for yourself. I can't explain it any better than that.'

I stood, getting soaked, for another brief moment. Wondering if we were done. Questioning myself about whether I'm too polite for my own good.

'OK,' I said. 'Thanks.'

Then I trotted to my car and jumped in.

There I sat, soaked to the skin, shivering slightly, and one hundred per cent unsure of my next move.

The World's Tallest Thermometer

'Oh, my goodness,' Myra said. 'You're soaked. Come in, Richard. Come in and get dry.'

She briefly left me standing in her foyer, dripping on to the mat, while she rummaged around in the master bedroom and came back with an oversized soft towel, and a dark blue man's bathrobe that I could only imagine belonged to her late husband. Unless she was seeing somebody these days.

Either way it made me uncomfortable to take it. But I did.

I closed myself into the bathroom off the hall, peeled out of my wet clothes, dried off, and put on the robe, carefully transferring my car keys, wallet, and Vida's worry stone into its big terrycloth pockets.

Meanwhile Myra put on a pot of coffee, and when I came out of the bathroom, she took my wet clothes from me and loaded them into her dryer.

During all of this, she did not ask.

But when we sat on the couch together, looking at the pewter coffee pot and cups and cream and sugar servers, sitting on their pewter tray, she asked.

'So at some point,' she said, 'I'm trusting you'll tell me.'

I believe that qualifies as asking.

When I had called earlier to ask if I could come by and see her, I had pointedly avoided answering the obvious question, which of course is why I would be in Portland without having mentioned anything about the plan in advance.

'Very short-notice trip,' I said.

She poured two cups of coffee, because all I was doing was *staring* at coffee.

'You had the whole long drive up and a cell phone, though.'

'Yes. I did. Look, Myra. This brings me to what I came by here to say. I mean, I guess I mostly came by here because I can't imagine being in town and not seeing you. But I did have something on my mind. Which is this. It should be obvious by now that the reason I'm not telling you why I came up here is because it's one of those things you wouldn't approve of. And I'm wondering . . . maybe this is too much to ask . . . but I'm wondering if maybe you could just let me go off in these directions that seem ill-advised to you. Even if it's a mistake. Even if you're right about that. But maybe you could just . . .' I wasn't sure if I could say this last bit. But I felt I had to try. '. . . love me anyway.'

To my surprise, she put down her coffee cup and threw her arms around me.

I don't believe we had ever embraced before. Myra was not the huggy type, and I was never the type to push in that regard.

'Oh, Richard,' she said. 'I always love you. No matter what. I always will.'

'You will?' I sounded five years old to myself. Seven, tops.

'Of course I will. I never realized you could think otherwise.' Her voice projected bizarrely close to my ear. I could even feel the breath of her words as she spoke them. It made me feel vulnerable and small. 'Oh, Richard. You mean so much to me. You're the only person in the world who loved my daughter as much as I did. And that includes her own father and her two sisters. I don't know if I could have survived these last few months without you. I think I would have gone insane. I just don't want to see you get hurt. That's all.'

Amazingly, she was still holding on.

'Sometimes people have to get hurt, though. Sometimes they just do.'

'I always feel like I want to give them the benefit of my experience.'

'That never seems to work, though. At least, not for me. Have you had any success with it?'

'Very little,' she said. 'Now that you bring it up.'

I had just tucked into bed in Lorrie's old room, which had long since been converted to a generic and rather feminine-looking guest room. High canopy bed, dust ruffles, pillow shams. Matching window treatments. I was under the covers in just my boxer shorts, which Myra had so nicely dried for me.

I heard a soft rapping at the door.

'Come in, Myra,' I said, pulling the covers up over my bare upper body.

But the head that peered through the half-open door did not belong to Myra. It belonged instead to Lorrie's sister Rebecca.

'Richard! Mom said you were here. Are you sleeping?'

'No. Not at all. I just crawled into bed. Come in.'

She did. And sat on the edge of the bed and gave me a big hug, which felt awkwardly intimate. Not sexually intimate. Just awkwardly close.

She was Lorrie's oldest sister, which made her a year or two older than me, and enough of a ringer for Lorrie to make my heart flip over twice. Figuratively speaking. But I swear it felt like it was flipping around in there.

'I haven't seen you since the funeral,' she said. 'Are you OK?'

'Depends on the standard of measure, I guess. I walk and talk on a daily basis. I didn't know you were here visiting. Myra didn't tell me.'

'Visiting? I live here.'

'Since when?'

'Since the bottom dropped out of the real-estate market. Don't get me started. It's totally humiliating. And very temporary. I hope.'

'Probably a good time for Myra to have one of her daughters at home.'

'Yeah, I thought of that. She acts like everything is under control. But I know her too well. So, listen . . . don't take this the wrong way, but what did you say to Mom to make her feel guilty? She has her guilty face on.'

I pulled the covers a little more snugly to my chest.

'I didn't mean to make her feel bad.'

'Don't take it on. I just wondered.'

'I just sort of . . . asked her to let me make my own mistakes.'

Rebecca burst out laughing. It was a deeply familiar sound. Not only did she laugh like Lorrie, but she flipped her hair back the same way, and the expression she formed with her mouth made my teeth ache in a sudden acute attack of missing what I'd lost.

'Why are you looking at me like that?' she asked.

'Just for a minute you looked so much like her.'

'Oh, Richard. Honey.'

She slid closer to me on the bed. Touched my face. I saw her face move in close, and just for a moment I thought she was going to kiss me on the mouth. But the kiss landed warmly on my cheek.

'Poor Richard,' she said, and rose to go. 'By the way. I wish I had a nickel for every time I told Mom I needed to learn things for myself. Good luck with that. But she needs to keep hearing it anyway. I'll leave you to get some sleep,' she said. 'Goodnight.'

Then she was gone.

I sat up a while longer, wondering over an odd dichotomy. The more I found myself surrounded by people, the lonelier I felt.

I arrived home about eight o'clock the following evening to find Abigail sitting on my doorstep.

My heart fell.

My threshold for human contact had worn painfully thin. I felt like a car that had been running its lights too long on battery alone. I felt fresh out of charge, and as though I needed to plug in for days before I could have one more conversation with one more human being.

But there she was.

I wondered how long she had been sitting there. Waiting to talk to me.

I pulled my car into the garage, then came out through the front, hitting the button to close the automatic door behind me. I stepped up to my own front porch, and she looked up at me.

Right away I noticed a difference in her energy. She looked like Abigail, but felt like someone else entirely. The fire had gone out.

'How long have you been sitting here, Abigail?'

'I'm not sure,' she said faintly. 'I'm not wearing a watch.'

'I've been gone for days.'

'I haven't been here for days. Maybe an hour or two. Or three.'

'Would you like to come in?'

'Yes, please.'

I let us both in with my key, and she sat on my couch, slumped over herself and looking about half her normal size; which made her look the size of a child. I offered her coffee or fruit juice or wine, but she shook her head.

I found myself leaning against my writing desk, facing her, because I wasn't sure I wanted to get too close to this new energy, or lack of same. I didn't have much margin for error in that department.

'I've been wondering how everything went so horribly wrong,' she said.

'That actually sounds like a worthwhile use of time.'

She looked up at me suddenly. Examined my face, as if trying to assure herself I wasn't being sarcastic.

'That means a lot to me,' she said.

'What does?' I had no idea what I had done.

'Just the fact that you would give me credit for doing something right. I feel like nobody gives me credit any more. I feel like I've become the villain, and I don't know how to make it stop.'

I sighed deeply. And knew I had to risk sitting closer. I joined her on the couch.

'People used to give me credit for being a good mom,' she said. 'No, a great mom. And now all of a sudden they're treating me like a terrible mom.'

I sighed again. 'Well,' I said. 'I guess it's strange that I would be dispensing advice on motherhood to you. You obviously know more about it than I do. Only . . . have you ever noticed how easy it is to solve somebody else's problems? I'm wondering if maybe I can make an observation here, based on the fact that I'm looking at the forest from a reasonable distance and perspective, whereas your view is blocked by all those damned trees.'

I pictured myself standing in the rain in Isabelle's driveway while she said, 'It's easier to see for somebody else than it is to see for yourself.' I wanted to weave that into my point somehow, but I knew it wouldn't make much sense out of context, and I was hardly prepared to supply the full context of my meeting with Isabelle now. Or, really, anytime. To anyone.

'Go ahead,' she said, still gazing at my hunter-green rug. 'I'm listening.'

'It seems to me there are two phases of motherhood. The one where you have to nurture and protect your kids, and the one where you have to let them go be their own person. You know. Let them be grown-ups. I think some people are really good at one but not the other. I'm sure it takes practice.'

'It just all happened so fast,' she said. 'I was taking care of her, all her life, and I got along fine with that, and all I wanted was for her to live, and I thought if she got a heart everything would be perfect; and then she got a heart and then it didn't turn out the way I thought.'

'Things rarely do,' I said. As sympathetically as possible.

'I didn't get to ease into it gradually, the way most mothers do. Do you have any idea how hard that is? To build your whole life around somebody, and then you just turn around and they're gone? Just like that? No warning?'

I didn't even answer. I knew it would hit her soon enough. So I just waited.

I saw it on her face, when she got it. I could see her face fall.

'Oh, that's right,' she said. 'You do.'

I expected her to cry. She didn't. She didn't seem to have access to enough energy. She just continued to stare at the carpet.

Then she jumped, as if she'd just remembered

something important. She fished around in her purse for a long moment – there must have been a lot to fish around in – and pulled out a postcard. She waved it around as if it were live, incapable of holding still in her hand. On one pass, I thought I recognized a photo of Mount Whitney.

'Tell me what you make of a thing like this. How do you give somebody a blank postcard of someplace you've been? What kind of message is that supposed to send?'

She was poking it in my direction, so I took it, and looked at it, but I'm not sure why. If Abigail said it was blank, who was I to question? But I was curious about it all the same, and wanted to hold it, the way Isabelle had held the one Vida sent me. As if it carried its own well-guarded secrets, and I could coax a few of them out of hiding.

I looked at the photo, and noted that it was not identical to the photo on mine. But it was still Mount Whitney.

I turned it over to see if it had a postmark. It didn't. But that wasn't the most surprising thing about the back of it. The surprise was this: it wasn't blank.

I just stared for a moment, wondering what this said about Abigail. Was she delusional? Had she really imagined the string of men she'd lied about, reducing the false information to something other than a conscious lie? Or had she lied again, about this, to make a point about her abuse at the hands of her daughter? In which case, wouldn't handing me the card seem an odd choice?

I took the opportunity to read it.

'Dear Mom,' it said. 'I'm sorry I'm not the same daughter I used to be, even though you need me to be, and I'm also sorry I keep expecting you to suddenly be a whole different mom, even though I guess you can't be. I have to go find something, but when I come back, which I will, we'll see who we can be to each other now.'

And she signed it, 'All my love, Vida.'

Meanwhile Abigail had been going on and on about . . . well, I have no idea what, actually. I hadn't caught so much as a word.

I looked up at her, and she stopped talking abruptly when she saw the look on my face.

'What?' she asked. A little defensive.

'It's not blank.'

'What do you mean it's not blank?'

'I mean it's not blank. It has writing on it. From Vida.'

She snatched it out of my hands.

I watched her read for a moment, and then she melted into tears.

'Oh, my God,' she said. And then she just cried for a while longer.

I wanted to ask how she could make a mistake like

that, but all the phrasings I tried out in my head felt insensitive.

'She must have slipped it out of my purse before she left again.'

Ah. Finally, something that made sense. And it was a relief, too. I wanted the woman sitting on my couch to be something at least resembling a reliable narrator.

'Be patient with her, Abigail. Everything is changing suddenly in her life, too.'

'How am I supposed to be something different to her?'

'Oh. I don't know. I wish I did. It's a whole big process, this letting-go thing. I'm not exactly the expert guru you need in that department. I think I've barely scratched the surface myself.'

'I don't think I know how. I only know how to protect her. It was all she ever needed. She never needed any letting go before. So I don't think I know how.'

'Maybe you need some help.'

'What kind of help?'

'Professional variety.'

Silence. Then, 'That makes me feel . . .'

I waited.

'That makes me feel like I'm supposed to be defective or something. Like you think I'm crazy.'

'Maybe just look at it more like your world has gone crazy. All around you. And you just need some help adjusting to it all.'

We sat that way for a long time. Literally minutes. How many minutes, I couldn't say. Three or four maybe.

'I'll think about it,' she said, and stood to go.

I almost let her. But then I caught up to her, turned her around, and gave her a long hug. She allowed it for a surprising length of time. Melted into me and let herself be completely held.

'Thank you,' she said.

'Anytime,' I said.

She let herself out. I watched her walk halfway down the driveway before I remembered what I wanted to ask.

'Abigail,' I called, and she stopped and turned. 'Did Esther die?'

She nodded sadly, sobbed once in a hiccupy sort of way, then walked away without further comment.

I checked phone messages before bed, but there was nothing. I checked my email, but found only spam. Not even an email from Connie with her phone number, as promised.

I didn't have the energy to wonder why. I just needed sleep. I needed fuel. I needed life force. I needed repair.

Actually, I think I needed my life back the way it was before. But that was off the table, so I settled for a night's sleep.

*   *   *

I hurried out to get my mail in the morning, suddenly and oddly sure I would have a postcard from Vida.

I was right.

What did that mean, I wondered? I had never before known something in advance like that. Not that I was aware of, anyway.

The front of the postcard said, 'Greetings from Baker, California, home of the world's largest thermometer.' And of course it had a picture of the thermometer in question. It was a towering spire of many storeys which had been photographed showing a readout of 100 degrees.

I turned it over, feeling oddly empty. But I did note that my heart was beating harder and faster than normal.

'Dear Richard,' I read. 'Car trouble for days and it's very hot here. Hope to get back on the road soon. The car has no air conditioning but at least you can roll down the windows and drive fast. When it's running, that is. I'm looking for something but I don't know what it is. But when I figure it out, you'll be the first to know. Well. The second, actually. I'll know first. Love, Vida.'

VIDA

The World's Tallest Thermometer

Eddie asked me, 'What's that little book you keep writing in? Is it a diary?'

So then I took about twenty minutes to tell him all about Esther and the blank book she gave me, and the worry stone, and how she died (which made me cry again), and a bunch of other stuff he didn't exactly ask about.

But I really needed something to do.

Eddie is the mechanic who is fixing Victor's car. Only not right then, he wasn't. Right then, when he asked about my book, he was fixing somebody else's car. A nice blue BMW that belongs to some other poor fool who was just trying to get through the desert in one piece.

He can't work on Victor's car yet because he had to special-order a water pump and it hasn't even shown up.

It's taking a long time. Longer than anybody thought it would.

And besides, even when the water pump shows up, he still needs to put paying customers first.

I like Eddie. He's my friend.

He's older than us. Forty or fifty. And he's Indian. I don't mean like an Indian from India, I mean like an American Indian. Or I guess I should say Native American. It's probably more respectful and more right. After all, how long can you hold on to a name just because Columbus was an idiot out looking for spices who didn't even get that he ran into something that wasn't nearly India?

But I should be careful not to get too far off track.

Anyhow, Eddie has a long ponytail that goes way down his back, and he keeps it tied in three places. He ties it with leather thongs. It's tied close to his head, but the bottom of it is tied tight, too, and it's also tied in the middle. So it's thin. And black. And he has a great big stomach.

He's also very nice.

He knows we don't have much money, so he's been sending Victor out on errands in his truck. Picking up parts and stuff. He's been letting him work it off. And he let us put up Victor's tent behind his gas station. But I can't be out there until at least four in the afternoon, because that's when the gas station gets in-between the sun and the tent, so there's some shade. Otherwise you could die out there. Literally. I'm not just being dramatic.

He also lets us take ice out of his ice-machine anytime we want, which may have saved my life, and definitely saved Jax's life. About once an hour I hose Jax down with the hose at the side of the station, and then I feed him ice and hold some ice on his paw pads, and then he perks up a little, like a sad, droopy plant when somebody waters it.

Jax will be happier than anybody when we get back on the road. And Victor and I both want it pretty bad ourselves.

Victor isn't here now because he's off working, running errands in Eddie's truck.

If I wanted, I could be in the little tiny snack shop that's part of Eddie's gas station, and which is air conditioned. (Because if it wasn't, people wouldn't stay in there long enough to buy anything.) But right now I don't want to be in there because the bad cashier is on duty. And besides, there's no place to sit. I have to sit on the floor, and the customers look at me funny.

The good cashier likes dogs, and she lets Jax lie on the floor behind her counter, where nobody even sees him except her. That way he gets to be where it's cool. The bad cashier hates dogs (and actually, people, too, now that I think about it), and says she will report her own place of work to the health department if she sees that dog inside.

I asked Eddie once why he has her working here, and he said he would get somebody with a better disposition if he could, but it's not likely that anyone will be looking for a job here in the summer.

I almost offered to do the job myself. At least it's in the air conditioning. But we'll be moving on soon.

I'm getting off track again.

So I was sitting in the shop area with Eddie, in a service bay, talking to him. My back up against the wall. Jax was lying on the concrete beside me, freshly wetted down and sleeping flat out on his side in a little shallow puddle, with his tongue hanging out on to the floor. It isn't air conditioned in the shop, because the service bays are all open in the front. But at least in here we're in the shade. And there are two big fans blowing, which is better than nothing.

So back to where I started.

I told him all about Esther and the book. And he listened, and nodded. He was leaning over the engine of this BMW. He had the hood off, and he had these vinyl drapes (printed with STP motor-oil company logos) over both sides of the fenders so he could set his tools down without scratching anything.

He said, 'Victor told me you had a heart transplant. I wasn't sure if he was lying or telling the truth.'

'Why would he lie?'

'I don't know,' Eddie said. 'I don't know why anybody would lie, but I know some people do. Don't get me wrong. He seems like a good guy. But I don't know him very well. I just never knew anybody who had a heart transplant before. It's so rare.'

'It's not that rare.'

'I thought it was really rare.'

'Not any more. Thousands of people have them every year. I'm pretty sure it's something like between two and three thousand just right here in the US. Unless I'm remembering wrong. But I don't think I'm remembering wrong, though. It's a lot.'

I pulled down the collar of my tee-shirt a little, to show him the top of the scar. He winced, like it was his chest getting cut down the middle.

'Ouch,' he said. 'How far down does that go?'

I pointed to the spot where it ended at the bottom, and he winced again.

'That must have been quite an ordeal.'

'Yeah. But better than dying. But I guess I really shouldn't say, though, because I've never died. But it sure seemed like a better idea than dying at the time.'

'Oh, you've died,' Eddie said. Going back to his BMW. 'We've all died. Numerous times. You just don't remember.'

'Maybe so, yeah. That could be. I'm going to go see how hot it is.'

'114,' Eddie said.

'Can you see the giant thermometer from here?'

'Nope.'

'Do you have a little one in here?'

'Nope.'

'Then how do you know?'

'I just know. I've lived here all my life, and I just know. Bet I'm not off by more than one degree. You don't believe me, go look.'

I got up and walked out of the shop. Jax stirred, and got up, and came with me to the open doors of the shop, dripping all the way, but then he stopped before I got out into the sun. He wouldn't walk out into the sun. He stopped and waited for me.

I walked out across the baking tarmac until I could see the giant thermometer. I could see and feel these waves of heat, shimmering all around me. Baking me. I knew I'd have to hurry up and get back in the shade before I got too crispy and well done.

The world's tallest thermometer is sort of what Baker is known for. Seems like a strange thing to be known for, but I guess every place has to have something. It's 134 feet tall. A foot for every degree it should ever have to be able to read. Because in something like 1913, it was 134 degrees at Death Valley. At the bottom, it says, 'Baker, CA, gateway to Death Valley.' And then it has a lighted sign for every ten degrees, with lines in-between.

It was 114.

The Water Pump

Maybe this is weird. No, definitely this is weird. But anyway, here goes.

I started thinking that a water pump is to a car what a heart is to a body. And then I started feeling like maybe there would never be a pump. Like we were in the hospital waiting for a pump, and maybe it would just never show up.

God knows, it hadn't been showing up so far.

And then Victor's poor car would never live and breathe and drive down a road and see the world again. And we would still be alive, of course, but pretty well stuck. Pretty stranded.

But then, the next day after I told Eddie about Esther and the book, there was Victor, standing in the heat waves outside the doorway of the service bays, freshly back from a parts run. And he was smiling really wide, just standing there with the sun beating down on his head, until Eddie said, 'Hey, gringo, get out of the noonday sun.' Like I say, Eddie is Native American. Not Spanish. But he calls people gringo if they don't know enough to get out of the sun, which he thinks is pretty funny.

By the way, I was wrong when I said Victor wears his Goth black trench coat even when it's really hot. Not when it's 114, he doesn't. He just wears a tee-shirt. He's getting one of those truck-driver tans from his upper arms down to his hands, and on his neck, but I better not get off track again.

Victor came in the shop, still smiling, and Jax got up and wagged like crazy.

And Victor said, 'Guess what just came in today?'

We knew it was the water pump. He didn't even have to say it. Victor and Jax and I did the water-pump dance together for a minute, but then it got too hot for dancing, so we stopped.

Victor went out to unload all the parts and bring them in.

I sat back down with my back against the wall, and Jax lay down beside me with a big sigh – I call it his heat sigh – and Eddie went back to his BMW.

'I'm going to miss you when we move on, Eddie.' I said that. Even though I knew it would be another day or two before he put the water pump in. Or longer. A day or two meant figuring no more paying customers would break down near Baker.

'You'll have to come back through sometime and say hi.'

'Maybe in the winter.'

And he laughed.

'Gringos,' he said.

On Finding the Someplace

Eddie worked all next morning to finish the BMW so he could start on Victor's water pump. He sent Victor out on one last set of errands, which worked out pretty well, because they both figured that would be just about enough work to pay off the job. I think he was giving us a little break, but he wasn't giving it away or anything. He was being fair to everybody, I think, himself included.

I spent the morning in the air conditioning with the good cashier, Ellie, with Jax hiding behind the counter. But then I had to get him out the side door and into the service bay fast when she saw the bad cashier, whose name was Crystal, coming down the road for her shift.

The heat hit me like walking into a blast furnace. Not that I ever have, but I've read about them. But it was worth it. Because Eddie was already working on Victor's big old American car. It made me really happy. I think it might have been the first time I really believed, for real, deep down in my heart – well, somebody's heart, anyway – that we were going to get out of the desert and go someplace cooler.

'How long do you think it'll take?'

'Oh, it's not a very big job, now that I can finally get to it.'

I sat down on the concrete with my back up against the wall, as close to one of the fans as possible, and Jax paced back and forth and whimpered, which was his way of complaining because we couldn't sit inside. After a while he gave up and flopped.

'Who are you going to have run your errands when we're gone?'

'I guess it'll have to be like the old days. If something needs doing, I have my three trusty employees. Me, myself and I.'

'I think you should make Crystal do it. That way she wouldn't need to be around real people. She'd just be in the truck.'

'There's real people at the auto-parts store. And I can't afford to piss 'em off.'

'What about your snack-shop customers?'

'She's actually pretty civil with them. She saves the mean mouth for us, I think. I never asked where you two kids are going.'

'Don't know yet,' I said.

'Just traveling for the sake of traveling?'

'Not exactly. It's like there's someplace calling me. Like I half-remember it. But I'm not quite sure what it is. Or where it is. I know some things about it, though. Like I know a lot of people go to it. It's busy. It's not like some out-of-the-way place in the middle of nowhere. And I know it's one of those places where, when you first see it, you make a noise out loud. Like you say, 'Ooooh', when you didn't even mean to. Or you suck in your breath so loud the person standing next to you can hear it. And I know it's red. I mean, not bright red, but like the way red-rock places are red.'

Eddie whistled softly. 'You got your work cut out for you there, kiddo. In the southwest US of A, that does not exactly what you might call narrow things down much.'

'Where would you start looking if you were me?'

'Maybe the Zion and Bryce Canyon area. Sedona's like that. Grand Canyon, of course. Glen Canyon. Maybe Escalante and Capitol Reef. Or Arches or Canyon-lands.'

I sighed, thinking that was a lot of places, and they were probably all hot.

'I guess we'll have to try them all, then.'

I saw Eddie look up, so I looked up, too. Somebody was driving up to his shop. It was a couple, not too old, maybe late twenties, in one of those really old American pickup trucks that's been cherried out to look real nice.

A classic. But it didn't sound as good as it looked. It was sputtering and coughing, and there was something like either smoke or steam coming out from under the hood.

'Pull her in here,' Eddie yelled, and motioned for him to take the empty bay, but the engine died, and then it wouldn't go any farther than that.

Shit, I thought. Even though I usually don't swear, not even on the inside. We're not getting out of here after all.

The guy stepped out and walked around the back of the truck and started yelling and cussing and stomping over something he saw there. I was thinking it was too hot to be so mad, but he seemed to manage. He was wearing one of those wife-beater tees to show off his arm muscles, and tight jeans with a big oval belt-buckle about the size of a flat lemon.

Eddie walked out into the sun and around the back of the truck, and looked at the something with him, and then they pushed the truck inside. I heard just enough to know that the reason the guy was so upset was because water was coming out of his tailpipe. I guess that's not a good thing.

'You limped it too far to get it here,' Eddie said. 'Huh?'

'I could've walked, I think, but she didn't think she could. Or she said she couldn't anyway.'

He pointed to the back of his girlfriend, or wife, or

whatever, who was disappearing into the cool snack shop, shaking her head. Her perfect hair never even moved. She had this look like she was done with this whole mess and wanted no more to do with it.

I guess I shouldn't make assumptions that she was his girlfriend or wife. I mean, Victor isn't my boyfriend or husband, just because we're on the road together. But I still think I was right, because they were ignoring each other with that quiet sort of fighting that friends mostly don't do.

'It wasn't even that far, but it was so hot. I think she just wouldn't. And now I bet I blew a head gasket.'

'Just hope that's all you did, son. Hope you didn't warp the heads. Or even crack your block.'

'Oh, shit, man. Don't wish all that on me.'

'I don't wish any of this on you. I hope it's the easiest thing possible. I got more work than I know what to do with. Don't have to make my whole living just on you. It's gonna be a big job one way or the other. Even if the heads are just warped, I have to send 'em off to the machine shop in Barstow. We're probably looking at a few days minimum.'

See? I was right, I thought. We're never getting out of here.

'How soon can you look at it?'

'Maybe near to the end of the day. Maybe morning. Depending on when I can get done with this water pump for this nice young lady.'

I caught Eddie's eye. Like asking him what he was doing. What he was saying. But he just looked away again. I looked up to see Victor drive up in Eddie's truck.

'Oh, look,' Eddie said. 'You're in luck. Here comes my assistant. If you like, I'll have him drive the two of you to a nearby motel where you can cool down some and get a hold of your nerves. And I could call you. Keep you posted.'

'That would be good,' the guy said. 'Yeah. That would be nice.'

'Hey, Victor,' Eddie called as Victor got out of the truck. 'Don't even unload those parts yet. I got another little job for you to do.'

Victor came into the shade of the shop and Eddie pulled him aside and slipped him some money. I wasn't close enough to see how much it was.

But I heard Eddie say, 'Take these people somewhere they can get a room, and then let me know where they land.'

Victor looked at the money and said, 'What's this for?'

And Eddie said, 'Well, your repair is all paid. So I'm paying you to do this extra job for me.' Victor tried to argue, but Eddie said, 'Don't argue with me. The longer you stand here arguing the hotter these two are gonna get, and they're hot enough under the collar as it stands.'

So then Victor loaded them both in the small front seat of Eddie's little pickup truck, and off they went down the road, disappearing in the wavy lines of heat over the tarmac. And Eddie went back to doing our water pump.

'Why didn't you put paying customers first, Eddie?'

'Your repair is paid.'

'Yeah, but they're paying with real money.'

'Besides,' Eddie said. 'I like to do things one at a time.'

The Desert at Night

Night is my favorite time here. It gets all the way down under 100. Eventually. Not until way after dark, though. Sometimes I take Jax for a little short walk when it's almost dark, and he runs around and lifts his leg on everything. Usually Victor comes along, but tonight he was doing one more job for Eddie.

Eddie had just knocked off work. He finished the water pump and then started getting into the engine of the cherried-out truck so he could tell that poor couple what was what. So then, when he knocked off later than usual, he paid Victor twenty dollars plus gas to drive into Barstow and bring back a pizza from Eddie's favorite pizza place. I was thinking that would have to be a pretty good pizza. It's a long way to drive for an ordinary one.

Anyway, Victor got to drive there in his very own

running car, which made him happy. And since his car didn't have air conditioning, we didn't have to worry that Eddie's pizza would get cold on the long drive home.

Jax and I went for a little walk by ourselves. The moon was up, nearly full, and there was something that was just almost barely like a breeze. It made me glad we decided to stay one more night. I love the desert at night and I hate it in the day, so it would be a shame to spend more days than nights.

I think we'd have been on the road already except for Eddie's pizza, so I liked the pizza idea.

The giant thermometer said 104.

Underneath the giant thermometer, not too far away, there's a big rock. And on the rock there's always this cast-iron skillet with two eggs in it. Somebody around here must put two eggs in it every morning, so people can watch them fry in the sun during the day. They're plenty crispy by this time of night, believe me.

Jax wasn't on a leash, so he sniffed his way over there and ate the eggs. I guess that was OK, because they have to put fresh ones out in the morning anyway. I think if Jax hadn't eaten them the coyotes would come down and get them in the night.

Then I wondered if they were fresh enough, but it was too late. But they didn't make him sick, anyway. He was OK.

So, back to the coyotes. Coyotes are very hungry. So

hungry that we have to keep Jax in the tent with us at night. Even though he's big. Bigger than a coyote. But Eddie says if there are enough coyotes, a whole pack, they'll go after a big dog. Depends on how hungry they are.

But I don't want to get off track.

We turned for home, and . . . That's funny, huh? I just called Eddie's gas station home. We have definitely been here too long. And then Jax and I saw that Victor was back with the pizza, and Jax ran to say hello.

I was tired. So I just walked.

We sat in the back, on our sleeping bags in the dirt, because inside the tent we wouldn't feel that tiny breeze.

Victor got out some trail mix that we were going to have for dinner.

But then all of a sudden Eddie was standing over us, holding the pizza, and we looked up.

'So, who's hungry?' he said.

And Victor said, 'Eddie. You can't pay me twenty dollars to go get a pizza that you're going to turn around and share with us.'

Eddie sat down cross-legged in the dirt without even using his hands. Just sort of folded up and sat.

'Why can't I? Seems to me I can do what I want. So long as nobody gets hurt.'

He put the box between us on the ground and opened the lid. Victor had to hold Jax back.

'He can have a piece,' Eddie said. 'It's a big pizza.'

He was right. It was a big pizza.

We started into the pizza, and it was that really good kind of pizza where you lift up a slice and the cheese drips all down, and it takes some time to gather it all up again. I was really hungry for the first time in as long as I can remember.

'How's that truck?' I asked.

And Eddie frowned.

'Bad. He cracked his block.'

'I don't know what that means.'

'The engine block. That's the whole enchilada. Normally you crack your block on an old car, you just throw the car away. That's what most people would do, anyway, unless it's a valuable car. But this truck. You should see the engine. All chrome. I mean, the valve covers and the air cleaner and stuff are all chrome. It's so clean you could eat your lunch off it. Not a drop of oil leak. It's this guy's baby, I can tell. I hate to call him up and tell him. I figured I'd give him one good night's sleep before I break the news.'

'How long will it take to fix it?'

'Oh, more than a week. If he even has me fix it. Job this big, sometimes people don't. Sometimes they call their brother or their cousin or their buddy to drive out here with a tow bar. Help 'em get the damn thing home. So we'll see. So where are you guys headed in the morning?'

I was glad he asked, because we hadn't decided. We'd been talking about it for a while but then Victor had to go on his pizza run before we figured it out.

Victor said, 'We're trying to decide whether to start at Zion or the Grand Canyon. We were looking at the map to see which is closer. I'm thinking Zion, because then we don't have to backtrack to Barstow to pick up Route 40. And because we figured it would be cooler.'

'Cooler?' Eddie laughed. 'You figured Zion to be cooler? How'd you do your figuring?'

'Well, it's so much farther north.'

'It's also a lot lower in elevation. And a lot hotter. Distance wise, it's more or less a draw. But the Grand Canyon South Rim is around seven thousand feet in elevation, and the North Rim is over eight. High eights in places. So that's your better bet for cool. Plus when you get to about Williams, you have a choice of the Grand Canyon or Sedona. Bout the same amount of drive from there. You could flip a coin.'

Victor and I looked at each other. Jax had finished his slice and was waiting and drooling, hoping for another one.

'Cool?' I asked Victor.

'Cool,' he said.

So that's how we decided that in the morning we would backtrack to Route 40 and head due east.

Then Eddie looked right at me and said, 'How do you remember this place, anyway?'

I tried to look at his face, into his eyes, but it was almost completely dark by then. I could see the tall thermometer behind him, and it was lighted up at 102. I didn't answer at first.

'Was it someplace you went to when you were a kid?'

'No,' I said. 'I never got to go anywhere when I was a kid. I was always too sick.'

He didn't ask any more questions, but I could tell he was waiting. Victor was waiting, too. You see, I never really told Victor how I remembered the place I was looking for, either. I just said it was one of those things that was hard to explain.

'My new heart remembers it,' I said.

'Your new heart . . .' Eddie kind of tailed off. I could tell he wanted to know if I meant that literally. But maybe it was too personal a question.

'After I got my new heart, I remember some things that I think it saw before it knew me. But that I never saw.'

'I heard of that!' Eddie said. Excited now. 'I saw something about that on the news! People who used to be vegetarians, and then all of a sudden they get a transplant and start craving bacon, and then they find out their donor loved bacon. Wow! That's really interesting. I wonder how that would feel. Is it something you can even explain?'

'Not exactly,' I said. 'I mean, it just feels like

remembering. It just feels like any other kind of re-membering. The only difference is that you know you never saw the place you're remembering. You know you couldn't have.'

'Wow!' he said. 'More things in heaven and earth, huh?'

And then we wolfed down the rest of the pizza with-out saying anything.

'Well,' he said. And got to his feet the same way he got down, only in reverse. No hands. He just unfolded and then he was up, holding the empty pizza box. 'I'll let you kids get some sleep. If I don't see you in the morn-ing have a safe trip. Godspeed. And all that.'

He started to walk away, but then I got up and ran the few steps after him. I had to use my hands to get up, though.

I grabbed him from behind and gave him a hug. My arms didn't even go all the way around his big belly.

I said, 'I'll try to come back through and say hi some-time.'

And he said, 'I hope your new heart finds what it's looking for.'

And then I let him go, and he did.

Flipping a Coin in Williams

When we got to Williams, Arizona, we had to sleep in the car. Turns out in the summer, this close to the Grand Canyon, things are a little busy. It's kind of hard to get a camping spot on short notice. Especially since it turned out it was a Saturday night. We didn't know that. What day it was. Victor and I lost track of that a long time ago. Until we tried to get a camping spot. And then we found out it was Saturday night and we'd have to sleep in the car.

Now, sleeping in the car was not the easiest thing in the world to figure out.

Fortunately it was a big car. A big old Oldsmobile, with a solid bench seat up front, thank goodness.

But still.

The only way we could figure to fit Jax into the picture was to let him sleep on the back seat with me, all the way against one of the doors, and then I would have to curl up in a tiny little ball and use him for a pillow.

We tried it for a little while when it first got nearly dark. But it was hard to go to sleep that way.

So I said, 'Victor? Are you asleep?'

He said, 'Nope.'

I said, 'I think I'm going to have to be really tired to sleep in the car.'

'So what do you want to do?'

'You want to take Jax for a little walk?'

'Sure,' he said.

So we got out. And we put on Jax's leash, because Williams was busy with cars. And we walked down a few streets in the nearly dark.

It was a little before nine, and we walked by a place that gave visitor information. It was just closing.

'Hey,' I said. 'Stay here with Jax, OK?'

And I went inside and asked the lady, who seemed sort of nice but tired, if she had some information about the Grand Canyon and Sedona. She laughed in a way that was like snorting. I guess that's mostly what she had.

Anyway, she quick piled up a few brochures, and a little newspaper-type-thing for the Grand Canyon park, and then handed them all over to me and we walked out together. And she put out the closed sign on the way out, and locked the door behind us.

I said to Victor, 'I thought this might help us decide.'

He said, 'I thought we were going to just flip a coin.'

'Well, we can if you want.'

So we stood under a street light, and Victor took out a quarter.

'Heads, Grand Canyon,' he said. 'Tails, Sedona. OK?'

'OK.'

I watched it flip up into the air and fall end over end, and I knew I wanted heads.

'Tails,' Victor said. 'Sedona.'

'OK.'

I guess I wanted Grand Canyon more, but I promised I'd do what the coin said, and, anyway, we could always go to the Grand Canyon later on.

I woke up in the night, and I was stiff, but there was no way to really stretch. I don't know what time it was, because I never wear a watch. But the streets were empty. Not a person or a sound.

We were parked too close to a street light, and I blinked into it, and it was hard to keep my eyes open because it was too bright.

Jax stirred and tried to stretch, but he really couldn't, so then he gave up right away and went back to sleep.

I had somehow knocked down all the brochures. Or Jax had. Before I went to sleep they were on that shelf under the back window, but now they were fallen down all around me. I'd been sleeping with my cheek on one. It was wedged between my face and Jax's side. I guess

I was sweating a little, because I had to peel it off my cheek. It was sort of stuck there.

I looked at it in the light from outside. It was puckered from my sweat. It was a brochure about hiking in the Grand Canyon. I was looking at the back cover.

On the bottom, in big red letters, guess what it said?

'Warning: Do not attempt to hike to the river and back in one day.'

'Victor,' I said. 'Victor. Wake up.'

'What?' he said. I think he said it while he was still asleep.

'I know where we're going now.'

'Sedona.'

'No. Grand Canyon.'

'You said Sedona.'

'You don't get it. I mean, I know now. Where the place is. It's the Grand Canyon that I remember. That's what I'm looking for. That's the place.'

'You mean we don't have to go all those other places?'

'Right.'

'Good.'

We were quiet for a minute, and then I said, 'OK, I guess you can go back to sleep now.'

But he never answered. So I guess he already had.

On My Having a Dream

This is important. This is a big thing.

I finally got back to sleep. It took hours, because I was all excited. I thought I never would get back to sleep, but then hours later, when it was almost getting light outside, I did.

I had a dream.

I dreamed I was standing up above this big stone patio that looks out over the Grand Canyon.

It was right on the edge of the canyon rim, and had this low stone wall so people wouldn't fall right in, and flat stone making up the patio itself, and a bunch of big chairs with arms. Some were big enough for one person and some were big enough for two. Doubles. The chairs were almost all lined up looking toward the edge, facing the low wall. Facing out. So that people could sit there and stare into the Grand Canyon for as long as they wanted.

I stood there in my dream and memorized everything, like I knew even in the dream that I would need it all. That I would need every single detail again.

And then I looked at all the people, and one of them was Richard. But he was younger. A lot younger, like maybe in his twenties. But it was definitely him. There was no doubt about that.

He looked really tired and discouraged.

I started to walk over. To say something to him.

And just then Jax tried to scratch his ear with a back paw and it woke me up.

I tried to get back to sleep to finish the dream, but I never could.

RICHARD

The Grand Canyon

It was a Sunday morning. It was early.

I'd been very deeply asleep. Or very lightly asleep. Does it seem odd that I wouldn't know the difference? Yeah. To me, too. But there's this certain type of dream state that feels different from most. Different how, I can't quite say. It just feels . . . OK, I'm tired of saying different. But any new words I might use to describe it won't seem to flow.

Sometimes this kind of dreaming happens to me at the bottom of a REM cycle, but other times I have oddly vivid dreams when I'm drifting in that no-man's-land of neither awake nor asleep. So there's my confusion about that in a nutshell.

I guess I mentioned that I didn't used to be a person who went on and on about things.

In my dream, I was reliving the story I'd told Connie.

The story of the Grand Canyon, and meeting Lorrie for the first time. Oddly, I seemed to be dreaming not so much of that time itself, but the telling of it. Maybe just because those details were fresh in my mind, freshly unearthed. But I found myself lingering in each section of that experience – the river, the hike, the camp, the lodge – in just about the same time frame and detail as I had in the telling.

Until I got to the part where Connie cut me off.

In the telling of this tale to Connie, after Lorrie sat down and mentioned that she'd seen me on the trail, my dinner conversation had made a sudden forced turn and ended abruptly.

Oddly enough, at this exact same moment in the dream, I woke up.

I lay in bed, the sun just barely glowing through the curtain, letting the moment continue inside me. Enjoying not being pulled off track.

'So, could you just fall over and die?' Lorrie had asked.

And it had taken me a minute to realize she was referring to the hike. Our exhaustion from the hike. Somehow I'd thought she'd meant . . . I was about ready to fall over and die because she'd dropped into my life without warning, and was sharing a seat with me and chatting like we were old friends . . .

Anyway. I was tongue-tied, and didn't answer, so she turned her attention out into the canyon.

And she said, 'We should be sick to death of it, shouldn't we? We should've gotten our fill by now. But here we are. Still staring. It's just so vast and beautiful.'

I sat up in bed.

Vida was looking for the Grand Canyon.

I shook the sleep out of my brain. Rubbed my eyes. Talked myself out of it.

I lay back down.

That was a big jump. That was a bit silly. Just because the words vast and beautiful came up in more than one place.

But then I thought about Vida's postcard. About how she'd asked me if Lorrie was a hiker. She must have remembered something about one of Lorrie's hikes. Which one would likely come through as the most important? That's obvious, right? If she was going to remember one hike, wouldn't the Grand Canyon hike be the one?

I talked myself out of it again. I was only putting things together a certain way because I wanted them that way. I was adding two and two and getting thirty-one.

Except . . . then there was also that postcard she'd left for Abigail. She'd said she was looking for something. And Isabelle, of course, had also said she was looking for something, something that had everything to do with me.

Vida was looking for something vast and beautiful

that had everything to do with me and something to do with hiking.

I sat back up again.

My first coherent thought was this: Boy, are you ever going to feel stupid when you haul all the way out to the Grand Canyon and find out you were only imagining things. That you were being completely delusional.

But, do you notice I said *when*? I didn't say *if*.

There was already no doubt in my mind that, stupid or not, delusional or not, I was going. I had limited options in this situation. Who even knew how many chances I might get? Right or wrong, crazy or sane, I had to take this shot.

I checked my email before I left, in case Vida had emailed. After all, she obviously hadn't called. And she'd sworn I'd be the second to know.

Nothing from Vida.

But, as if life thrived on upping the ante of my profound confusion, I did find a note from Connie.

From: Connie Matsuko
To: Richard Bailey

Sorry this took me so long, I guess I had too many internal tapes playing on the subject of what was going on inside

your head. What you must think of me. I guess it's none of
my business, though, so here it is.

And under that was her phone number.

I quickly hit reply. Maybe it was better that I didn't
have a lot of time to over-think my response.

From: Richard Bailey
To: Connie Matsuko

People who allow themselves to be vulnerable always
amaze me. I don't know how they/you do it. It's perplexing,
but admirable. That's what I think of you.

Then I hit send and got myself out the door.

VIDA

On Calling Richard from Tusayan

We left Sunday morning, and drove for a while, and then I asked Victor if we could stop in Tusayan so I could make a phone call. That's sort of the last stop before the South Rim of the Grand Canyon. He got sulky and quiet and didn't ask any questions, so I guess he figured out who I needed to call.

I'd promised Richard, though. I promised him that when I figured it out, he'd be the second to know.

So we stopped at a gas station, and I gathered up all the change from the ashtray in Victor's car, pretending not to see that he was giving me hurt looks.

I looked at all the change and knew I would have to talk fast.

But in the end it didn't really matter, because Richard wasn't even home.

I left a message on his machine.

I said, 'OK, I figured it out now. I'm going back to where I met you. I mean, to where she met you. Because if I can find the place where she met you, then you have to believe me.' Then I almost hung up, but right before I did, I said, 'Oh. This is Vida. In case you didn't know.'

RICHARD

The Meadow in Question

Not too far north of the Grand Canyon's North Rim is southern Utah. The red-rock desert of Utah. I don't mean to make it sound like it's just a few miles away. Only that there's nothing much in-between. You're in Kanab, Utah, and you head south, and suddenly you're over the border into Arizona. Then there's a little town called Fredonia, and an even smaller one called Jacob Lake, which is hardly even a town by any reasonable standard. Then you're in the Kaibab National Forest, which is closely connected with the North Rim Grand Canyon, but doesn't resemble it in any way.

It all happens very fast.

Why am I bothering to write this down?

Because it was an area full of emotional difficulty for me. Or . . . well, an area full of emotions, let's say. Let's not try to pin down the difficulty of them. Some of them were difficult, others felt welcome. The vast majority seemed to be a combination of the two, leaving me in a state of emotional whiplash.

Here's the issue: it was only the second time I'd ever been to this area. Which caused me to see the two trips as something like a set of bookends, neatly encapsulating the Lorrie era of my life. I came here once just before I met her. Now I'm here again just after losing her. If that's not a set of bookends, what is?

Plain, no-longer-used bookends. Nothing left in-between.

After you get off Route 89A, you have to pick up the little Route 67, which is also called the Grand Canyon Highway. I guess because that's the only place it goes. It starts at the 89A, goes to the North Rim, and ends.

The first time I saw the scenery along this Route 67, I was mainly struck by the extent to which it was not at all what I'd expected.

It's at a very high elevation, parts of it even higher than the rim itself, and it's all green forest. It doesn't resemble the red rock of the canyon, and it doesn't look anything like the image a brain would conjure up to match Arizona landscape. It's just trees. A very green, seemingly endless forest, dotted with these truly lovely high mountain meadows that line the route.

One of these meadows was special. And I was looking for it. Would I know one meadow from another nine years later? I hoped so. Yet I knew in my heart there was guesswork involved.

I pulled off the road and parked at the first one I saw. I remembered the low split-rail fence. Or did they all have that?

I decided I would only drive myself crazy if I tried to find the right meadow all these years later. I should just get out of the car, lie in the meadow at hand, and assume this was either it or close enough.

The sun was nearly down by this time, the weather warm, the sky cloudless. A perfect summer evening. I stretched out on my back in the grass and allowed myself to replay the moment.

After I met Lorrie on the patio of the North Rim Lodge, we talked for a long time, and she told me she'd hiked from the South Rim. Cross-canyon, rim-to-rim, in three days.

'How are you getting back?' I asked. 'Don't tell me you're going to hike it back?'

'No, I'm taking the shuttle,' she said. 'Staying here tonight, and then tomorrow I catch the shuttle that goes around the long way to the South Rim. Back to my car.'

It was an interesting way to put it. The *long way* to the South Rim. By vehicle it was the *only* way. The short way, I had to guess, was the way she had just come.

That's when I lied.

'I'm going to the South Rim tomorrow. Why don't

you let me drive you? The shuttle's kind of expensive.'

I'd looked into the shuttle myself. Thinking it would be cool to keep hiking until I got to the South Rim. But when I found out the price of the ride, I decided I'd spent enough on this little vacation already, and opted instead to just hike down and back. Simpler. Cheaper. I hadn't exactly had money coming out of my ears back then. And I'd been hoping she didn't, either. Because I couldn't think of any other reason for her to say yes.

'That seems like asking a lot,' she said. 'Since you don't even know me.'

But I think she already knew I *wanted* to know her.

'I'm going right to it anyway,' I said. 'How can it be any trouble?'

And she agreed. And since I'm pretty sure she knew by then that I was trying to get to know her, I could only conclude that she must have wanted me to, and I was elated.

I drove from the campground to the lodge at seven o'clock the following morning and she was waiting outside for me, her enormous backpack lying on the tarmac at her feet.

We headed north, up the little Route 67, chatting about something I don't specifically recall. It might have had something to do with a status report on our legs, especially our quadriceps and Achilles tendons. It's a reasonable enough guess, anyway. People who've just hiked the canyon have a tendency to talk about the muscles in their legs. It comes with the territory. Literally.

Then we got to one of those lovely Alpine-type meadows.

'You know,' I said. 'On the way in, I was really tempted to stop and lie spread-eagle in the grass on one of these meadows, like little kids do in the fresh snow. You know. When they're about to make a snow angel.'

'Why didn't you?'

'I don't know. I guess it seemed silly.'

'Stop the car,' she said.

'I don't really want to. It was just a crazy thought.'

'*I* do, though. *I* want to. Stop the car.'

'Too late. We're past it now.'

'So? Back up. There's nobody behind us.'

I braked. Looked in the rear-view mirror. She was right. There wasn't a soul on the road apart from us.

I put my tiny old car in reverse and pulled back several yards and off on to the shoulder, and before I had even come to a full stop she was out of the car and dashing through the grass like a happy little kid.

I followed her, jumping over the low rail fence the way she had, and lying down beside her, close enough that we could talk, but not close enough to make her edgy. After all, we were relative strangers.

It was cold. So cold that the grass was still a little frosty.

'You're not spread-eagle,' she said.

'Oh. Right.' I corrected my mistake. 'I'm not sure why I didn't do this when I first thought of it.'

'Neither am I,' she said. 'Do you usually need a little help being spontaneous?'

'Oh, no,' I said. 'No. Not at all. I usually need a huge amount of help being spontaneous.'

She laughed – giggled actually – and in that laugh was the happy and welcome answer to the question that had rattled in my mind since meeting her. She liked me. I could tell by the laugh. It was overly amused, more so than the situation really called for. Halfway to flirty, though she probably hadn't consciously planned it that way.

Who knows? Who really knows what's going on in somebody else's head? I sure waste a lot of time wondering and worrying about it, though.

We just lay like that for a while. I was watching our breath puff out in steamy clouds, liking the way the morning breeze made the clouds of her breath chase the clouds of mine.

'I have a confession to make,' I said. My lips felt numb, and the words sounded poorly articulated as I spoke them.

'Oh, damn. I knew it. I just knew it. You're a serial murderer. There's always a catch, isn't there? There's no such thing as a free ride.'

'I'm not a serial murderer.'

'OK, what, then?'

'I wasn't really going to the South Rim. Before I found out you were going there, I was headed home. My original plan was just to go home.'

A long silence.

'Well then, it's a good thing we started all the way down at serial murderer. Because, from that vantage point, "little white lie teller" doesn't sound so bad in comparison.'

'OK,' I said. 'Thanks. I think.'

More time lying there in silence. Maybe a second or two. Maybe three.

Then she said, 'Do you honestly think I didn't know that already?'

It's possible that I knew, in that moment, that I would spend my life with her. It's also possible that I only knew I wanted to.

I definitely didn't know that the time I'd be given to share with her wouldn't nearly match the length of my life.

I got up and drove on.

Both then and now.

Only, this time I drove on alone.

I arrived at the front desk of the Grand Canyon Lodge at nearly half past nine Sunday evening.

A very young woman staffed the desk. Very young. She looked about twelve.

'I'm the guy who called three times from the road,' I said.

'I sensed that,' she said. 'So, here's what I have for news. Good news and bad news. The good news is, we got one cancellation. And the really good news for you is that we called all five parties on the wait list, and only one still wanted it. The rest've moved on. So, that's the good news. You're now suddenly number one on the list for a cancellation.'

'And the bad news is, there are no more cancellations.'

'Not at this time, no.'

'And I'm sure the campground is full.'

'I'm sure they have an even longer wait list than we do,' she said.

'OK, thanks. I gave you my cell number, right?'

'Three times. I absolutely promise you, if we get something, you'll be the first to know.'

'Thanks.'

I'm not sure why I had anticipated a miracle as I was driving. Felt one coming, almost. But maybe being number one on the waiting list – at the only lodging on the North Rim, in the middle of the summer – was miracle enough.

In any case, it would have to do for now. It was all I was going to get.

I almost told myself it was too late to go out on the sun porch. Why, I'm not sure. Because it was dark? Yeah.

Maybe. Who wants to sit out there in the pitch dark with no view of the canyon?

But then I stepped out the front door of the lodge into the barely cool late evening, and looked up to see a huge, bright crescent of a waning moon.

Who *wouldn't* want to sit out there and look at the canyon by moonlight?

But maybe it closed at dark.

Then again, maybe not. Probably not. How could the lodge management justify kicking people off the outdoor patio half an hour or an hour after the canyon by sunset morphed into the canyon by moonlight?

No. It must be accessible all night.

I walked around the outside of the lodge toward the rim, fresh out of excuses. The only excuse I had left was the real one. The God's honest truth.

This was going to hurt.

Lorrie and I had originally planned to come to this lodge, to this sun porch, several years ago to celebrate the five-year anniversary of the day we met. But it was also our wedding anniversary, and Myra surprised us with cruise tickets. Then the year after that Lorrie couldn't get away from her teaching for that long, so, for reasons I could no longer recreate, we decided to postpone it for the tenth anniversary of the day, which would have been our eighth wedding anniversary.

That would have been this October. We were going to do this together. The very thing I was about to do now.

Step on to the sun porch at the North Rim Lodge. We were going to do that. Together. Less than three months from now. That had been the plan.

I even had lodge reservations, which I had never thought to cancel.

And, of course, while making these plans, it never once occurred to either one of us that either one of us wouldn't have that long to live. I guess I shouldn't speak for Lorrie. But if she had any prescience of what was to come, she didn't share it with me. I guess it's not the type of thing one shares.

I stood in the grass on the hill just over the sun porch and took in the view in the moonlight. Both the canyon view and the view of the patio itself. Many of the chairs were doubles, like little outdoor love seats for two. And all of the star gazers were couples.

There were no single gazers.

There was no Vida.

There was an empty single chair, but I didn't take it. I couldn't. I couldn't bring myself to go down there.

I sank on to my haunches in the grass, overwhelmed with a sudden fear. Maybe I had missed Vida. Maybe she had already come and gone. Or maybe I was an idiot, and she was never headed in this direction at all.

I rose and walked back to my car, which I'd purposely parked in the more sparsely traveled far end of the parking lot, and curled up in the back seat for the best night's sleep I could manage.

VIDA

On Getting to the South Rim

Victor and Jax and I got stuck in a real long line of cars waiting to get into the park. You had to stop at these little buildings about the size of a toll booth, and the cars got pretty backed up.

It was already getting warm, so we rolled down all the windows. Lucky we just came from days and days in the desert, so whatever kind of warm the Grand Canyon had to throw at us, it was going to be pretty much nothing to us now.

One car moved through and we pulled up a little, and I heard Victor take a big deep breath.

'Holy shit,' he said.

And I said, 'What?'

'It costs twenty-five dollars to get in.'

'Twenty-five dollars? That seems like a lot. Are you sure?'

'Look for yourself.'

So I grabbed hold of the steering wheel and leaned way over his lap, and then I could read the signs. Jax sat up in the back seat and he looked, too. Like he wanted to know what everybody thought was so interesting.

'Yup,' I said. 'Twenty-five dollars. That's a lot.'

'You can say that again.'

'Do we have that much?'

'Barely. After that last tank of gas we have thirty-seven and a little change. No, wait. You used all the change to call that Richard guy. We have thirty-seven.'

'So we have enough.'

'Yeah, and when we get in we'll be down to twelve dollars and a quarter of a tank of gas.'

'Good thing I know this is the place.'

'We still have to get home, you know.'

'Yeah. That's true.' But the extra twenty-five dollars wouldn't get us home.

By now we were up to the little kiosk, and Victor took all of our money out of his pocket and counted out the twenty-five dollars. You could tell it hurt him to do it. There was a nice friendly looking woman in a uniform waiting in the booth, and she took nearly the last of our money, even though I guess she didn't know it was nearly the last, and she smiled at us.

She gave us a nice color brochure about the whole Grand Canyon, and a little park newspaper about the South Rim, and a printed receipt with tape on it to put on the inside of our windshield. She said it was good for a week.

Then we had to do a lot more driving to actually get from the entrance station to the South Rim, and I started to worry a little about gas.

'Thank you,' I said to Victor while we were driving.

'For what?'

'For bringing me here, and for spending almost your last twenty-five dollars so we could get in.'

See, I shouldn't have said he took *our* money out of his pocket. It was really Victor's money. Some of it he had at the start, and some of it he earned working for Eddie. I didn't start out with anything, and I didn't do any work along the way.

'Oh. That's OK. I'm just not sure what we're going to do now.'

'Me neither,' I said. 'So that's why I thought it was even more important to say thank you.'

I spent the whole rest of the day looking for the patio from my dream, and Victor spent the whole rest of the day trying to panhandle for gas money.

Well, Victor did two things, actually. He also hiked a little way down into the canyon to see if there was a sign like the one I thought I remembered. That's the only part of the day that worked out. I didn't do so good finding the patio, and he didn't do so good panhandling gas money.

I couldn't walk as far as a person would have to walk to check the whole South Rim. But there was a free shuttle bus. So I took it from one spot to another. And every time I got off, I'd walk right to the rim and just look out. And every time I looked out I made that noise, like when you pull in your breath because something literally takes your breath away. But there was no one standing near me to hear. I mean, there were always lots of tourists. But they kept to themselves and I don't think they heard.

I knew when I looked into the canyon that I was right. This was the place. I could feel it. I could tell. But the rim part of it was all wrong.

There was this paved trail, called the Rim Trail, and it went all the way along the South Rim. So there was no big hotel with a big outdoor patio that went right up to the rim, because then it would interrupt the Rim Trail. It would get in the way.

I kept looking at the map in my little color brochure, and it seemed pretty clear that the Rim Trail went all the way from one end of the civilized part of the South Rim to the other. No breaks for patios.

But it was important, so I rode the shuttle bus to every single stop and looked for myself. But it was just like the map said.

The place in my dream didn't exist. Not here, anyway.

By the time I got back to where Victor had parked

the car, I was pretty tired, and also discouraged and sad. Victor was sitting on a bench near the visitor center with Jax. He didn't look any better than I felt. I walked over and sat down near him, and Jax started kissing my hands. Like he thought he'd never see me again or something. Or maybe like he didn't want me to be sad. But I was anyway.

Victor took out his digital camera and brought up a photo of the sign and showed it to me on the little screen.

I said, 'Yup. That's the sign all right.'

There were a few extra words about the rim in the sentence, but the drawing of the tired guy and the different languages and all were right on the money. First I was all excited, but then I didn't know what else to say about that.

'How'd you do finding the patio?' Victor asked.

'I didn't find it.'

We just sat quiet for a while.

Then I said, 'How'd *you* do?'

'Pretty bad. I only got six dollars.'

'Maybe it's the economy,' I said. Because I hated to think that people wouldn't be any more helpful than that. 'Maybe they spent all their money on this vacation.'

'Right,' he said. Like he didn't figure that was it.

'Maybe they didn't know it costs twenty-five dollars to get in, either.'

'Maybe *you* need to do this,' he said. 'Maybe people would give money to a sweet-looking girl who weighs about as much as a hummingbird. Maybe they don't like to give money to a six-foot-five Goth guy with a ring in his nose and in his eyebrow. And with a big dog.'

'I would think Jax would be a plus,' I said.

'I think you need to try.'

'I'm not sure I could ask people for money.'

'Well, then I don't know what we're going to do.'

'Are we just giving up and going home?'

'I have no idea, Vida. You tell me.'

He was really tired. I could tell. We both were. It was almost dark, too. It was almost Sunday night. I really thought by now I would have found what I was looking for. I hadn't seen this part coming.

'I still think it's the Grand Canyon. Maybe just some other part of the canyon.'

'Like where?'

'I don't know,' I said. I took out the brochure again. While I was unfolding it, I remembered how Eddie said there was a North Rim, too, and it was higher. 'Maybe there are some more hotels on the North Rim.'

'Maybe,' he said.

But I looked at the brochure, and there was only one. The North Rim Lodge. Just that one. Other than that and a campground, there wasn't much up there.

'There's only one,' I said.

'We can try it if you want.'

I felt something squirrely and scared in my stomach, because I only had that one chance left, and if it wasn't there, then I was wrong. Just plain wrong. Maybe I was crazy. Maybe that dream didn't mean anything. Maybe it was just a dream. Maybe my new heart didn't remember anything. Maybe it was just my old brain playing tricks on me.

Maybe we should just give up and go home.

Except I was right about the sign.

So I said, 'I'll look and see how far it is to drive there.' And I started digging around in the brochure, and in the newspaper. I found what I was looking for, too. It even had a little map. 'Holy shit,' I said. Even though I don't usually swear. I guess that's twice, though.

'What?'

'It's 220 miles. It takes five and a half hours to drive there.'

'Are you serious?'

'It's about ten miles rim to rim. Shortest distance as the crow flies. We could get there in just ten miles if we could fly.'

'But we can't,' he said. 'And we don't have that much gas.'

We just sat like that for a long time. I was feeling the sense of something dark hanging on us. Like it was something I could pick up and put on a scale. If I had a scale. I bet it weighed a lot.

Then after a time, I said, 'I guess I'll have to try it.

I'll have to be able to bring myself to ask people for money.'

'Better hurry up,' he said. 'It's almost dark.'

'You and Jax go wait in the car, OK? I don't want anybody watching this. This is weird enough as it is. OK?'

So they went back to the car and left me alone.

I walked back out to the rim. It's a little longer walk near the visitor center. The rim is not right there. You have to walk a ways. And I was getting pretty tired.

When I got to the rim, the canyon looked redder because the light was on a slant. So I sucked in my breath, even though I'd seen it ten times already today.

It really never looks exactly the same way twice.

I walked along the rim trail for a little while, and I saw lots and lots of people, but I couldn't bring myself to ask any of them for money.

There were some boulders between the paved trail and the rim, and I sat down with my back against one and started to cry. It felt really good. Turned out I'd been holding it in all day. It was a relief to finally let it go. I didn't have any tissues, though, so I had to keep wiping my nose on my sleeve, which I realize is really disgusting. But I don't know what else I was supposed to do.

I saw and felt this sort of shadow, like someone was standing over me, and I looked up and saw this older lady squatting down close. She looked nice.

'You OK, honey?' she asked.

'Kind of sad,' I said.

'Yes, I can see that. What's wrong?'

Now, would you please like to tell me how I was supposed to explain all of this to her?

'It's really nice of you to ask,' I said. 'But it's complicated.'

'I'm not in a hurry.'

'Really complicated,' I said.

She sat down right near me and rummaged around in her big fabric bag and took out a little packet of tissues. And gave me three.

'That's very nice,' I said. 'Thank you.' And I blew my nose, and it was louder than I meant for it to be.

'Anything else I can do that would help?'

'Not unless you're going to the North Rim and can give me a ride.'

'Sorry, no. I'm not. There's a shuttle, though.'

'A free shuttle?'

'No. That one's not free.'

'We have a car,' I said. 'We just don't have money for gas. Or for a shuttle. I guess it doesn't matter anyway. Because I probably wouldn't find what I was looking for there, either. I was so sure it was here, and I was wrong. I'm probably just going to be wrong again. It's probably just as well that we don't have money for gas because it would probably just be a great big waste of a trip.'

Except the back of my head said, The sign. Don't

forget the sign. But I pushed it away again, because I was sad, and that's what I wanted to be right then.

She didn't say anything, so I looked up to see if she was still there. She was. She was digging around in her purse again. I blew my nose one more time, quieter this time, and wiped my eyes on a clean tissue.

'Go try,' she said. And closed my hand around some more tissues. 'Go see.'

Then she got up and walked away.

I sat there for a long time, trying to pull myself together. Then I needed to blow my nose again, so I opened my hand. And I came really, really close to blowing my nose on a fifty-dollar bill. In with the two tissues, she'd left a fifty-dollar bill in my hand.

She was long gone, so I never got to say thank you.

On the Night Before We Drove to the North Rim

We decided not to go all the way to the North Rim till Monday morning. Till the next day. Victor was too tired to go 220 miles all in that same night. So we just drove a little way Sunday night, until we got to a place that was outside the park and we could pull the car over and sleep in it, and maybe if we were lucky nobody would notice.

'What if it's another twenty-five dollars to get into the North Rim?' Victor asked, while we were lying there trying to get to sleep.

'See what the receipt says.'

So he sat up and turned on the overhead light, and it was really glary, because it didn't have one of those plastic covers to go over it. It was just a bare bulb. So I put one hand over my eyes.

Jax looked up to see what was going on, but he

couldn't get up to see, because I was lying on him.

'Oh,' Victor said. 'Good. This receipt says it's good for both rims.'

'Well, there you go, then.'

That was two good breaks in one day.

You have to at least be grateful for that.

It took me hours and hours, but I finally got to sleep. And I had that dream again. Just like before. Or almost just like before.

Only in this dream, Richard wasn't young. He was just the regular age that he is now.

And, also, this time just as I was about to go talk to him I woke *myself* up. I'm not sure why. I just know Jax didn't have anything to do with it at all.

RICHARD

What Life Is, Ultimately

On Monday morning, my back stiff and with a maddening crick in my neck, I got a coffee to go from the deli and found a seat.

Yes, on the sun porch. I just did.

Oddly, it didn't hurt. Somehow my emotional vulnerability of the night before had given way to numbness. Sheer numbness. So I did it simply by putting one foot in front of the other and doing it.

I even took one of the double chairs.

As far as I could tell by feel, it meant little. If anything at all.

The canyon hadn't changed, of course. Canyons never do. At least, not in nine years. Not in a human lifetime. But it looked different to me, so I knew *I* had changed. The red of the rock looked less vibrant, the striations of color less distinct. The way it had taken my breath away when I was a younger man seemed a distant memory at best.

I stayed there all morning. In the sun. After a time I began to feel my skin getting too toasty, so I left my outer shirt on the chair – so I wouldn't return to find all the chairs taken, or even all the chairs closest to the rim – and bought a cheap hat and a tube of sunscreen from the gift shop.

Then I sat there all afternoon.

Hard to imagine I could sit there all those hours without getting bored. Even harder to imagine that I cannot, after the fact, quantify what I was thinking. I'm pretty sure I was not thinking. I'm pretty sure I just sat and stared.

Storm clouds gathered in the afternoon, as storm clouds so often do in the mountains. It felt good to get a break from the sun. Then the clouds let go, and rain splattered the sun porch, and happy couples ran screaming and laughing into the covered, windowed open lobby just to our right.

I stayed.

The rain soaked me through, but I wasn't cold, so I didn't care. I don't know why I didn't care. Normally I would have. But this time I didn't. I just sat. I sat and felt rain soak through the open straw weave of my new hat, and soak my hair and run down my face. I watched it splatter loudly in puddles on the stone all around me, each drop hammering back up into the air like machine-gun fire. I watched webs of lightning crackle in the dark air, framed by their black-cloud background, touching down on the rim forty or fifty miles to the east.

Then, just as quickly as it had come, it blew through again.

First the clouds parted enough to show two or three patches of blue sky. Then it rained a little more but with the sun beating down, lighting up the drops of rain in that odd phenomenon of the sun shower. I hadn't seen one in as long as I could remember. Then it blew away entirely, and people began to reemerge. To tip the water off chairs and look around for something to use to dry them off.

I looked at my watch. It was nearly six. The day was almost gone. I hadn't eaten. Hadn't even felt the empty crampiness of my stomach, though I felt it at that moment. In fact, my numbness dropped away entirely.

Vida hadn't come. I must have missed her. Either that, or she didn't know her way back here after all. I sat a while longer, wondering which explanation I preferred. But it was an unanswerable question. Two equally dismal options.

I folded my arms on the low stone wall and leaned forward, resting my head in that dark safety. I'm not sure how long I remained in that position before I felt a gentle hand on my back.

I jumped, and looked up. Expecting to see Vida.

It was not Vida.

I looked up into the unusually blue eyes of an older woman. A stranger. She wore her gray hair stylishly short. Her silver earrings dangled nearly to her shoulders. I took her to be about seventy.

'I'm sorry to disturb you,' she said. 'Maybe it's none of my business. But I felt I had to ask if you were OK.'

I sat up straighter. Drew in a breath. For the first time in as long as I could remember, I felt a tightening in my throat and a burning behind my eyes. But I didn't let it get any farther than that.

'Thank you,' I said. Careful to keep my lip from quivering. Suddenly I understood that old expression about the stiff upper lip. Although it was my lower lip that seemed to need the most supervision. Still, you have to be careful at a time like that. 'That's very nice of you to ask. I'm . . . Well, I'm not, really. I'm not OK. But I don't really have a problem that anyone can help me with. But thank you, anyway, for asking. I'm just going through a time in my life that's very . . . confusing.'

She sat beside me in the double chair, her eyes soft. One hand on my shoulder. 'You're sure there's nothing you need?'

'Food, actually,' I said. 'I haven't eaten all day. I think I should just get myself up and go over to the deli and get a sandwich or something. Maybe I can just leave my outer shirt here, and maybe my hat on the chair, and then nobody will take my seat. If I ate something maybe I'd be a little more able to cope.'

'I hope so,' she said, and rose, touching my shoulder one last time. 'Be well.'

I watched her walk away.

While waiting inside for my sandwich to be made, my cell phone rang.

I pulled it out of my pocket, suddenly aware that I had let it get drenched. I was lucky it even still worked.

I opened it, and said hello.

'Mr Bailey?'

'Yes.'

'Well, you're in luck,' said a young voice. 'We just had a couple check out three days early. The altitude was getting to the wife. Still looking for a cabin?'

'Yes. Definitely.'

'How many nights do you want it for? All three?'

'Um . . . Is it OK if I don't know right now?'

'How about you come to the desk and we can set you up for the three nights, and then if you need to cancel, we can be flexible about the standard notice, seeing as we already have six more people on a wait list behind you.'

So, there was my miracle. Just when I was sure it was too late to matter. Just when I figured I no longer wanted or needed it.

When I got back to the sun porch with my reservation and my room key and my tuna sandwich and chips and bottle of water, my double seat was still open. On the back was still my wet outer shirt, and on the seat my wet hat. On my wet hat was a single red rose.

I set my sandwich down on the low stone wall and picked up the rose. Someone had carefully wrapped a square of lodge stationery around its stem, and tied it in place with a thin red ribbon. I untied the ribbon and unwound the note.

In amazingly practiced and formal script, it said:

'Life is often confusing, but ultimately worth it.'

I poured a little of my water into the morning's empty coffee cup and placed the stem of the rose in that, so it wouldn't wilt. There was no place to buy flowers at the North Rim, I was fairly sure of that. Had she had flowers with her when she arrived?

One of those mysteries I knew I would never solve.

I flattened and then folded the note, and held it in my hand for a time because I had no dry place to put it. Then I set it on the plastic lid of my takeout container as I ate my sandwich.

I watched the light as it gradually slanted and reddened the red of the red-rock canyon, and I did feel a little better as a result of eating.

I even entertained the notion that I might give Vida one more day.

Probably a waste of time, but I had come so far already.

My mind wouldn't quite settle, though, and I found

myself bouncing back and forth between staying another day or giving up and going home. Could I really bear another day of this? Maybe it was time for this whole ordeal to be over. Maybe it was time to move on.

The best I could manage as far as a decision was this: I would go back to my cabin, get a good sleep, and decide in the morning. Maybe in the morning everything would feel clearer.

I rose to go.

I gathered up the leavings of my meal. Rescued my little note. I tucked it into the pocket of my outer shirt, which was now almost completely dry. Then I changed my mind, opened it, and read it again.

'Life is often confusing, but ultimately worth it.'

I decided I was spending too much time in the confusing part and not enough time in the part that's worth it. So I sat back down, determined to at least watch the sun set over the Grand Canyon one more time.

VIDA

On Having a Real Life

It's Monday morning. (I mention this because I'm starting to pride myself on always knowing what day it is, because we had lost track so completely for so long.) Victor is sleeping really late.

I didn't have the heart to wake him, because I know it's really, really hard for him to sleep in the car. Even though he doesn't have to share his seat with Jax, like I do. But, then again, I'm not six foot five. So he probably didn't sleep for most of the night. So when I woke up and it was pretty well into morning, I just let him keep going. It's not like we're in any special hurry.

I guess for a while there, I felt like I was. Because I had this big, stupid fantasy that Richard would come looking for me. Like he'd get my phone message and come racing to the place Lorrie met him, and then we'd see each other there, and it would be something really special.

But I'm trying to be more realistic. So now I have no idea why I thought that.

Richard didn't even want me around when I was around. He didn't even come see me again when I was in the hospital in San Francisco. Which is less than an hour away from his house. And I could always hear this sort of invisible sigh when I called him on the phone. And even that one time I showed up at his door I knew he didn't really want me there.

So I'm figuring it's time to let that one go.

It's sad. But I guess it's not as sad as holding on to something that was never even true.

I got up and let myself out of the back of the car, and let Jax out so he could pee. I tried to be as quiet as possible so I wouldn't wake Victor up, and it worked. He just kept sleeping.

We were in this nice part of Arizona that's not like a desert at all. It's high up, almost like being in the mountains, but flatter, and there were woods on both sides of the road. Every now and then a car went by, but it was pretty quiet all in all.

Jax lifted his leg on the side of a tree for about an hour. Well, not really, but you know what I mean. For a long time. And then after he was done I figured out that I was going to have to pee in the woods, too. I never did before, but it's not like I had very much choice.

Then after that we just walked around a little. Well, I walked. Jax bounded.

And I felt happy. I felt like I was really out in the world. Not that I wasn't before. I was out in the world in Baker, but I was hot, and worried about the car. Now I was out in the world happier, and figuring this was more how it should feel. You wake up and look around and walk around and think, Hmm. This is what it's like in this new part of the country that I never saw before. It's nice.

And then you pee and brush your teeth and whatever, and then that's your life.

I felt like I actually had a life.

I got my toothbrush out of the trunk, which fortunately doesn't lock. At least, sometimes it's fortunate. Victor just holds it closed with a bungee cord. There were a couple of bottles of water back there, so I used a little to brush my teeth, and then I took my medication and fed Jax some kibble from the big bag in the trunk.

And I got to thinking about how it was my medication that was going to limit this trip. So I counted, and I have fifteen days' worth left. Which means I need to be home and at the pharmacy in two weeks. Or less. This is not negotiable. This is life or death. I could reject the heart without them. And the medications are incredibly expensive, so don't think for a second I could just get them myself out here on the road.

That put a damper on things.

Victor was still sleeping, so we walked down the road a little ways, and then back.

While we were walking back, that's when I noticed that one of the tires on Victor's car had less air in it than the others. The one in the front, on my side. Not the driver side. It wasn't flat exactly. But it looked pretty droopy compared to the others.

Victor slept some more, so it gave me plenty of time to get caught up writing in this book.

About Slow Leaks

After Victor woke up, he looked at the tire with me.

He put his ear really close and listened. I just waited, because if I said anything, I might be talking over whatever he was trying to hear.

Then he straightened up.

So I asked. 'What were you listening to, Victor?'

'I wanted to see if I could actually hear air leaking out.'

'Could you?'

'No.'

'So that's good then, right?'

'Relatively speaking, yes.'

'Do you have a spare tire?'

'Yes. I do.'

'Good.'

'But I don't have a tire iron or a jack.'

'Oh. I don't know what those are.'

'They're things you need to change a tire.'

'Oh.'

'So I guess we just go along as best we can. Maybe it's a slow leak. Maybe it won't change much as we drive. Maybe we'll even see a gas station somewhere along the way.'

'Yeah, maybe,' I said. Because I wanted this day to still be a good one.

'I'm going to have to drive a lot slower, though. It wouldn't be safe to do fifty-five on that.'

'OK,' I said. 'Good thing we're not in any hurry.'

We drove for what seemed like a really long time. Like pretty much all day. It felt more like five hundred miles, but probably just because we were going so slow.

The weather changed, and it got stormy and dark.

Finally there was a gas station. There were two big tour buses stopped, with their engines running, which made it really noisy. Everybody there seemed busy.

I got out and walked Jax around on his leash, and then used their rest room, even though I had to wait in a long line, and while I was in there I washed my face.

When I got back to the car, Victor said the guy wanted twenty-five dollars to patch the leak and fifteen to change the tire. He wouldn't just lend Victor a tire iron and a jack. And he wasn't even sure how long it would take him to get to it.

So instead Victor just put more air in the tire, and we drove on. Medium-slow.

It rained like crazy. The wipers could hardly keep up.

On Finally Getting There

We drove all the way to the end of the road, which ends at the North Rim Lodge. We parked in their parking lot, and it stopped raining pretty much just in time. Victor got out and looked at the tire again. It had more air in it than it did right before he filled it. But less than it did right after.

I could tell he was worried about it, and that it was hard for him to think about anything else.

I was worried about something else entirely.

We started walking toward the rim. The three of us. We had Jax on leash so nobody would tell us he couldn't go.

'You know,' I said. 'If this is not it, then I'm really out of answers. If this isn't it, then I don't know what is.'

'I know,' he said.

I couldn't tell much from the way he said it. I couldn't

tell how much it would bother him if this wasn't it. I only knew how much it would bother me.

Which was bad enough.

'I wonder what time it is?' I asked out loud. I'm not sure why I thought Victor would know.

He looked up at the sun, which seemed to be on a long slant. The biggest part of the day was definitely gone.

'Maybe five thirty,' he said. 'Maybe even six or six thirty. Look. There's a sign that says "Sun Porch". With an arrow. What you're looking for is sort of a porch. Isn't it?'

'Yeah. I think so.'

So we went around the building and came out standing on this little grassy hill, and then all of a sudden there it was. The canyon view, and the stone patio, and the low stone wall to keep people from falling in. The chairs were not just exactly the way I saw them in my dream – more wicker and less wood slats – but I knew they must've gotten new chairs in the past few years, because this was definitely it.

It took me a minute to be able to talk.

'This is it,' I said to Victor. It came out kind of breathy. Like a whisper. I meant to say it in the same loud voice I'd say anything else. But that was all I could manage. 'I found it, Victor. This is what I was looking for, and I found it.'

We stood and stared a while longer. I felt like I had

something big inside me, something that stretched me out, so I had to be bigger than just my actual body to hold it all. I don't guess that makes much sense, but I'm explaining it as best I can.

'So,' Victor said. 'Now that you found it, now what?'

'I have absolutely no idea.'

'You want to go sit out there a while?'

But there were lots of people. In fact, there was only one empty seat, a double, and there was stuff on it, so obviously someone was holding it until they came back.

'I don't think there's a place.'

'We could come back later.'

'Yeah. That would be good.'

'Let's go see if we can find a place in the campground. Probably not, but we can ask.'

'OK,' I said. 'In a minute. I just want to look for one more minute. Look, Victor, somebody left a red rose on that chair.'

'Where?'

'Right there on that empty seat. The one with a shirt on the back. And then there's a straw hat on the seat, see that? And it has a rose on it tied with a ribbon.'

'Oh. Yeah. What about it?'

'I don't know. I just thought it looked nice.'

I could tell he had stuff on his mind and wanted to go.

After a while, he said, 'What did you think you would do when you found it?'

'Do you want me to answer that even if I know you won't like the answer?'

'I guess so. Yeah.'

'I think I sort of had this idea that if Richard knew I was coming here, he would drop everything and come here, too. But I really think that was stupid of me now. But anyway, that's the truth.'

Victor didn't say anything. But it was *the way* he didn't say anything. Not good.

So I said, 'You want to go look at your tire again, huh?'

'I was thinking maybe somebody at the campground might loan me a jack.'

'OK,' I said. 'We'll go see about that.'

We got another nice little break about the campground.

There weren't any spaces. But this nice middle-aged couple who were just checking in heard us asking about one, and they let us set up our tent on part of theirs. They said they came every year, so they knew the campsites were really big, and they were in a little motor home, so really all they needed was just the part of the camping space where you park your motor home.

They were very nice and said if we were quiet we could

park behind them and set up our tent on the other side of their picnic table.

I think it's because they liked Jax. They kept fussing over him and saying he looked just like their Casey, who's gone now.

See? Told you the dog was a plus.

They even loaned Victor a great big wrench – which I guess is something like a tire iron – and a jack, and he changed the tire. Which was good. Because then he could start thinking about something else.

'I think I want to go back there now,' I said.

'OK,' he said. 'Just let me wash my hands.'

They were still dirty from changing the tire.

'Um. Don't take this the wrong way, OK? But I think I just need to do this by myself.'

He took it the wrong way. I could tell.

'In case Richard is there?'

'I don't think he will be. I think that was a stupid idea of mine. But even so. It's the place I remember, and I think I just need to go be alone with it.'

'Fine,' he said. Like it was a cuss word. 'Do whatever you want.'

It was a much longer walk than I realized. And I was out of breath from being so high up in the mountains. And I couldn't go back and ask Victor to drive me because he was pissed off at me. And it was almost sunset, so

I would have to walk back to the campground in the dark.

But I did it anyway.

I had to stop and rest a lot. But it was important. I just knew it was important. I mean, if it hadn't been important, I wouldn't have come such a long way to do this. Right?

Whatever 'this' turned out to be.

RICHARD

Sunset

'Excuse me. Is this seat taken?'

I knew before I looked up. I recognized her voice. I was surprised and not surprised all at the same time.

I looked up into her face, shielding my eyes from the low-angle sun.

'I've been saving it for you,' I said.

'Thanks,' she said. And sat down.

Somewhere in my gut, or in some other cellular location, which might have been every cell in my body for all I knew, I had always believed in at least the chance of Vida's ability to remember. I knew that now, in that retroactive type of knowing that confirms you've known all the time. Only whether or not I *wanted* to believe it – was willing to believe it – had ever been genuinely in question.

She was wearing shorts and sandals, and her legs

looked so thin I thought they must be in constant peril of snapping like matchsticks. And yet they were berry-brown from the sun. I wondered how she did as well as she did out in the world. Better than me, sometimes. Or so it seemed.

'So this is *your* red rose,' she said, touching an outside petal. 'Where did it come from?'

'Some woman I never met before. This older woman. She thought I looked sad, and she left this for me.'

'That's really sweet,' she said. 'So you got my message. I'm really glad you got my message.'

'What message?'

'I left a message on your machine. Sunday morning. Maybe nine or ten.'

'I was already gone.'

'Why did you come here if you didn't get my message?'

'Now that is a very long and complicated story.'

'We don't really need to tell any long stories right now. Do we?'

'I don't think so,' I said.

We watched the sunset without talking for a while. How long a while, I couldn't really say.

I reached into my pocket for the worry stone.

'I think I have something that belongs to you.'

I held out my open hand, the stone resting in my palm. I expected her to take it. Instead she took the

whole hand, and held it, the worry stone pressed between her skin and mine.

We stayed that way for a time, watching the light
change in the canyon.

'I'm sorry about Esther,' I said.

'Thank you,' she said. She didn't ask me how I knew.

After a while I noticed a very tall, skinny young guy
with a big dog standing in the grass above the sun
porch. Maybe it was my imagination, but I could have
sworn he was staring daggers at us.

I indicated him with a flip of my head.

'You know that guy?'

'Oh. Yeah. I do. I better go talk to him.'

She let go of my hand, dropping the worry stone. She
got up and picked it up again, and went after him. The
minute she did, he turned on his heel and stomped
off. She ran to catch up, but was no match for his long
legs. She really only got to the edge of the sun porch
before she gave up. She looked wistfully after him for
a moment.

Then she came back and sat with me again.

'I guess he doesn't want to be talked to,' she said.

'Is he your boyfriend?'

'No.'

'So, I'm a little older. So help me understand. In
modern language, when you're young, does "he's not
my boyfriend" mean that you're having sex with him
but there's no real commitment? I know it's really not

any of my business. I was just curious to know.'

'Richard,' she said. The way you say a kid's name when he's being so silly it strains your patience. 'I'm not having sex with anybody. I never had sex with anybody.'

'Never?'

'When would I have? How? With my mother watching?'

'She hasn't been watching for weeks.'

'But there's nobody I want to have sex with. I mean, you. Just you. Nobody else.'

I had no idea how to react to that. So we said nothing more for a long time. But I had a growing sense of blinders falling away from my eyes. Maybe there was only one way this could end. Maybe the path into it led only one direction, to only one conclusion, and I had been racing down that path for some time, only half oblivious. And maybe the fact that I had not consciously accepted what would happen next would in no way prevent it from happening.

So I stood up, and reached down for her hand, and she gave it to me. And I picked up the rose – not the cup or the water, just the rose – and handed it to her.

And then we went off and found my cabin.

I looked around for her non-boyfriend along the way, but fortunately he was nowhere around.

VIDA

On Richard Trembling

Richard was so scared.

I swear to God if I didn't know better I would think he was a virgin and I wasn't. He actually shook.

It was incredibly sweet. Heartbreakingly sweet, actually. It made my heart hurt to see a big grown-up man be that vulnerable and that fragile and that right on the edge of breaking apart.

Especially this man.

I felt like I had to hold him with just the lightest touch possible. Like when you hold one of those really fine Christmas ornaments or that hand-blown crystal glass that's so incredibly thin. Otherwise he might fly into a thousand pieces, and then not only would he be broken, but I'd cut myself trying to hold him in my hands.

And that's all I'm going to say about that.

You don't just go around writing down in a book a bunch of private things that somebody wouldn't want you to say.

RICHARD

What To Be Sorry For, and What Not To Be

I think I might have dozed briefly. When I woke, Vida's back was pressed up against my chest, and the barest hint of light glowed through the window. Could have been the moon, or the first phase of morning. I really had no way to know.

In my sleep, I'd been allowing the contact with another human being to feel familiar. After all, I'd shared my bed with a woman every night for nine years. And when my eyes flickered open again, the feeling lingered for just a fraction of a second. And then the truth fell on me like the debris of a wall that's been shattered from the outside.

It was her sharp shoulder blades, and the fact that I could feel every knob of her spine against my skin.

I started to cry. All at once. It was outside my jurisdiction. There was nothing I could do to pull it back or rein it in. I didn't sob. It was just a matter of my eyes, and water. They let go like a faucet when you turn the handle from off to all the way on. Part of me knew I should have done this months ago. Another part of me didn't want to do it even now, and would have stopped the process if I could. But it was too late for all that. It was too late.

I thought Vida was asleep until she said, 'Why are you crying?'

'How did you even know I was?'

'I can hear the drops hitting the pillow.'

She rolled over and handed me a tissue.

'I just miss her so much,' I said.

And she tucked her head in close to my chest and held me as tight as she could, and then the tears fell on her instead.

'I think I did a really bad thing,' I said after a while.

'What did you do?'

'I should have told you. When I brought you here. Before . . . Before. I should have told you that I don't see this as being . . . well, you know. Ongoing.'

She took a deep breath, and blew it out in an audible sigh. Like an oddly contented baby before sleep.

'You didn't have to tell me that. I already knew.'

'You did? How did you know? I didn't even know.'

'Because I know who this is really about. And I know I'm not her.'

I cried some more, and she let me, and held me. And handed me another tissue.

'I'm sorry I'm not her.'

'I don't think you need to be sorry for that,' I said.

'OK,' she said. 'But I am.'

To my surprise, she got out of bed and began to dress.

By now there was enough more light coming through the window to signal morning, or what would be morning soon enough.

'I have to go back and talk to Victor,' she said. 'See if he's OK.'

'Are you going to go back home with him?'

'Yeah. I think I should.'

By now she was dressed, and I was afraid she'd slip out before I could stop her, so I held out my hand, and she came close and took it, even though I could tell she didn't know why.

'Could you sit just a second?' I asked.

She did, silently. Waiting.

'This might sound odd, but I'm going to say it anyway. I'm going to try something. I'm going to try to give you the heart again, but maybe better than I did the first time. I kept acting like it was half-mine, which isn't fair. So this time I'm giving it to you the right way, and I'm going to go put my life back together if I can, and I'm going to stay out of yours.'

She smiled at me as though she were the only

grown-up in the room, and I were a child. She brushed a bit of stray hair back off my forehead.

'You know,' she said, 'it's funny. It's just now starting to feel like my heart to me, too. I never told anybody this. They'd think I was crazy. But I think the reason I didn't reject the new heart as much as most patients do is because I let it still be Lorrie's heart. Sounds like it would be the other way around, but I think most people feel like they have to fight something in their body that isn't theirs. But I just accepted that it wasn't mine, and we got along OK.'

'It'll be more yours as time goes by.'

'Think so?'

'Yeah. I do.'

She kissed me on the forehead, and got up to leave. I didn't feel any pull of sentimentality coming from her. I didn't feel like it was hard for her to go. She just seemed done. It stung me a little. No, actually it stung me a lot.

'You might want to go see your mother. I think she might be in therapy.'

'Seriously? My mother? In therapy?'

'She said she'd think about it, and she sounded serious.'

'You think she's in therapy to figure out how to fix *me*?'

'No. I think to figure out how to let go.'

'Wow. Now there's a concept.'

She made it almost to the door, then turned back suddenly.

'Oh. The rose. I almost forgot the rose.' She fetched it from the bathroom, where she had set the base of its stem in a sink partly full of water. 'You did mean for me to take this, didn't you?'

'I did.'

She opened the door and then stood a moment, allowing me to feel the cool breeze of morning and see it glow behind her head.

'We'll still talk, or see each other or something, right?'

'Right. We will.'

'OK, good.'

Then she raced over again, opened my hand and folded something into it. I felt the warm, familiar weight of the worry stone in my palm, and a quick press of her lips on my cheek.

'Here,' she said. 'I think you need this worse than I do.'

Then she let herself out.

I checked out of the lodge just minutes later. I couldn't get away fast enough.

There wasn't much of anyone around at that hour.

The clerk behind the desk was a young woman I had not met before. She looked at me with some slight surprise, and only then did I realize that anyone could see I'd been crying. It was too late to fix that, so I didn't try.

She informed me that my credit card had already been charged, but that the unused nights would be credited back to me. But that it might take as long as three weeks.

I told her I didn't care how long it took.

I walked halfway to the front doors before I remembered, then walked back to the desk.

'I almost forgot. I have reservations for October. I need to cancel them now.'

She pulled it up on the computer while she said, 'Right. Of course. Because you were here now.'

'No. That's not why. Actually. It's because . . . It was supposed to be for my wedding anniversary. But my wife passed away.'

She looked up at me suddenly. I could see her putting two and two together about what she had already observed in me.

'Oh, no. I'm so sorry. That's terrible.'

'Yes,' I said. 'It is. It's terrible. And do you know what else I just found out about it? I just found out it's the goddamn truth, whether I like it or not. And that I can't do a damned thing to change it. Nearly three months later, and I'm just now getting that I have to accept it. How sick is that?'

'It's not sick,' she said. 'We're made that way.'

'Think so?'

'Yeah. I do. We take things on a little at a time because all at once they'd kill us. Anyway, I'll cancel this.'

'No. You know what? Never mind. I changed my mind. Just leave it. Maybe in October I'll come back here all by myself.'

She looked at my face for another minute. I had no idea what she was thinking.

'We only need twenty-four hours' notice if you change your mind.'

'I don't think I will,' I said.

Then I drove home.

VIDA

About What Comes Next

I walked from Richard's little cabin back to the rim. It was just barely light. There was no one around. I guess I beat them all awake.

I could feel all kinds of things I don't think I would have felt before. Not big, dramatic things. Just little ones. The breeze on my face. The bottom of my feet touching my sandals whenever my sandals touched the ground. The stem of the rose in my fingers.

I thought there would be somebody out on the patio, but just for that moment I had it all to myself. Which was nice. Because then I could do this out loud.

Only, you know what? I think I would have done it out loud anyway. But it was nice how there was nobody there to hear me and think I was some kind of loon.

I stood all the way at the edge, near the low stone wall. Looked over the side. It wasn't a straight, sheer drop. I mean, there were some rocks that stuck out a little farther than the patio.

Then I looked up and out. And I cocked my hand back, winding up to throw the rose as high and as far as I could. But I didn't throw it yet.

'I don't think he meant to give this to me,' I said out loud. 'I think he really meant to give this to you. Here. Are you ready? Catch.'

And I let it fly. It sailed up and flew end over end for a couple of turns, but then it looked like it was going to stall. It was so light, I thought maybe it wouldn't go much of anywhere at all. But then a gust of wind came along and took it farther out. It came down on some rocks, but I watched it, and it half-rolled, half-bounced off the edge, and then the wind caught it again, and lofted it farther out into the canyon. And then it fell, and I couldn't see where it went after that.

I'll never know how far down in the canyon it ended up. As far as it needed to go, I guess.

Just before I walked away I said, 'OK, 'bye.' And then I walked a step or two, and then I turned around and said, also, 'Thank you.'

I didn't say specifically for what. I figured she would know.

It was just getting all the way light when I let myself back into the tent with Victor.

I knew he was awake because he quickly rolled over

the other way, so his back was to me. Jax licked me all over my face, like he hadn't seen me for months. It was nice. At least somebody in the tent was still speaking to me.

I lay down on the sleeping bag close behind Victor's back.

'Sorry,' I said.

'You slept with him, didn't you?' He sounded like he was crying. Like he was trying really hard not to cry, but pretty much doing it anyway.

'Yeah, that's what I was just apologizing for.'

'Well, don't apologize. Why should you care? We're just friends, right? I'm nothing to you. You don't care anything about me. Right?'

'Victor,' I said. 'That's so stupid I'm not even going to answer it. I'm going to tell you something else instead.'

I waited. In case he didn't want to hear anything at all from me. In that case, he would have time to tell me so.

'OK, what?'

'It's not going to happen any more anyway.'

Silence. 'You and him?'

'Right.'

'Why? Did he dump you? Did he break your heart? Because if he broke your heart, I'll go kill him. I mean it. I'll go right now.'

'Victor. Relax. He didn't break my heart.'

'So why is it over?'

'Because it wasn't ever really about me. It was always about the heart.'

Nobody said anything for a long time, and then after a while he rolled over, and his eyes were all puffy and red. I thought that was really cool, that he would let me see he'd been crying. I mean, being a guy and all.

I've been hitting the jackpot with that today, haven't I?

'What are you talking about?' he said. 'I have no idea what that means.'

'The heart.'

'What about it?'

'Oh, my God. I didn't tell you?'

'Tell me what?'

'He's the guy who gave me the heart. It used to belong to his wife, but then she died. Did I really not tell you that?'

'You really did not tell me that.'

'Oh. Sorry. I guess I thought I did.'

'So . . . Wow! I think I get it now.' He sounded amazed and sort of . . . reverent. I don't use that word a lot, but it seems to fit here. 'So it was really more about how he feels about his dead wife, and not so much about you.'

'Right. And also how she felt about him.'

'You mean, you sort of remember that, too?'

'Right.'

'Wow. That's weird. I mean . . . I don't mean weird. Just . . . That must be really intense. So, that's it? It's just over now?'

'Kind of. I guess. I mean, we sort of figure the more time goes on the more it'll be really my heart, sort of all the way mine, if you know what I mean.'

'I think so.'

He rolled over on to his back and put his hands behind his head, and looked up at the trees through the open mesh on the top of the tent. He didn't have the rain skirt over the tent because it was so warm and nice.

I put my head down on his chest, and then he put one arm around me.

'I'm sorry you had a bad night,' I said.

'So . . . what about us?'

'What about us?'

'What do we do now?'

'I want to go home and see my mom.'

'Really?'

'Yeah, I think she might be in therapy. So I have to give that a shot. Besides, I promised her. I mean, she *is* my mother and all. She just kind of got stuck in a cycle, I think. I changed so fast she got dizzy trying to keep up. Oh, and I have to pick up Esther's ashes.'

'Then what?'

'Then we could travel some more.'

'Really?'

'Sure. Why not?'

We both looked at the trees for a while, and then Victor said, 'Just friends?'

'I don't know. We'll see. We'll find out, I guess.'

'Where do you want to go?'

'Well, at some point we have to stop and see Eddie again. And then maybe I'd like to go to Germany.'

'Germany? That's an awful long way.'

'Afraid your car'll break down?'

'You're kidding. Right?'

I sat up and punched him hard on the shoulder.

And he said, 'Ow! What was that for?'

'Of course I'm kidding. How stupid do you think I am?'

'Well. You've been shut in a lot.'

'Sick kids study geography too, you know.'

'OK, OK. Sorry.' He rubbed his sore shoulder a little. 'I'd have to get somebody to take care of Jax. But we could go to Germany. I guess. I mean, I don't know *how*. Hell, I don't even know how we're supposed to get home. But we'll figure it out. Somehow. So, how does your heart feel now?'

'Tired,' I said. 'And sad. But it feels like it's just a tiny bit more mine than it was before.'

I put my head back down on his shoulder, and after a while I think we both fell asleep.

I know I did.

*   *   *

Just as we were driving out of the campground, I grabbed Victor's sleeve.

'Ooh,' I said. 'Go that way. OK? Please. Go back to the lodge, OK?'

He'd been just about to turn away from the canyon. You know. Toward home.

'Why? Did you forget something?'

'I have to get a postcard.'

I watched his face fall.

'Vida . . .'

'No, Victor. It's not what you're thinking. It's not for Richard. I have to get a postcard for my mother.'

'Oh. OK.'

He sounded a little confused. Maybe wondering why it was so urgent all of a sudden. But he didn't argue.

He drove us to the parking lot at the lodge, and then he waited in the car while I got out and took that walk toward the rim for what I figured would probably be the last time. Not to sound morbid or anything. Maybe I could come back and see the canyon again someday. It's just that I sort of have it in my head that I want to see new things. Not so much the same ones over and over.

And, also, even though it's nice that this place meant so much to Lorrie, I'm not Lorrie. I'm me.

I halfway wondered while I was walking if Richard was still around here somewhere. Maybe he'd already checked out and gone home. Or maybe I would bump into him any minute. I found myself looking at all the cars, like I could tell whether his car was there or not, which is incredibly stupid, because I wouldn't know Richard's car if I saw it.

I stepped into the gift shop, and there was nobody else there. Which seemed kind of nice. You always expect a crowd near the Grand Canyon, so the fact that I stepped into this little time warp of a lull in traffic seemed . . . well, like I said, nice. Actually it seemed even better than that. It seemed destined. Like I was parting time just by walking through it.

OK. Sorry to sound weird.

The lady behind the desk had gray hair and incredibly blue eyes and she smiled at me with all her front teeth, but not in a fakey way. In this really genuine way, like it made her feel great to see me.

I always think it's really nice to suddenly bump into someone who does that. But I don't want to get too far off track.

'Do you sell stamps?' I asked her.

'I have a few in the drawer,' she said. 'How many do you need?'

'Just one.'

'Oh. That's no problem, then.'

'Oh, shoot. I didn't bring a pen.'

I knew there was at least one in the glove compartment of Victor's car, but it felt like a long round-trip walk. Why hadn't I remembered to bring one with me? I felt a little spacey, like I'd just woken up. And I don't even mean from that nap we had today. More like I'd been asleep the whole time, my whole life up until now. Like I'd just woken up in general. To everything.

'I'll let you use mine. If you just want to write a post-card right now.'

'Yeah,' I said. 'That's what I want. I want to write a postcard right now, and get it in the mail right away. Today. I want it to get home before I do.'

'You can leave it with me, and I'll put it with our out-going mail.'

She handed me the plastic ballpoint pen from behind her ear, where it had been behind her hair, and I hadn't noticed it. I took it, and held it tight in my hand, thinking I was lucky that everything I needed was landing on me. It felt warm on one side, I guess where it had been tucked up against her scalp.

I found a really nice postcard.

They were all pictures of the canyon, of course. But it's funny how you can take a hundred pictures of it and no two of them ever really look the same. I picked one with dramatic lighting. The sky was blackened by weather, with rays of light breaking through on a slant, making the rocks look redder and more volatile. Is that the word I'm searching for? Volatile? It looked almost dangerous. Which you wouldn't think would make it an obvious choice for my mother. But I wanted her to know what an important adventure this had really been.

I didn't want her to think I put her through all this for nothing.

Then I put it on the woman's counter, so my writing would come out neat.

'Dear Mom,' I wrote.

It's funny how this time I knew exactly what I wanted to say. Like the right words had been in there all along, and I just didn't know it.

'Ever notice how kids who get mostly freedom want care and attention, and kids who get a lot of care and attention mostly want freedom? I'm not making excuses for myself, but maybe that's why I forgot to thank you for all the care and attention. I'm coming home now. Let's start over.'

And then I signed it, 'All my love, Vida.'

I stuck a stamp on it, and gave the lady back her pen, and the whole thing came to less than a dollar. I got a few cents change back from my dollar.

And it's interesting, in a way, because that dollar was exactly what I had left over from that nice lady's fifty.

We had almost a full tank of gas, and after that, some figuring to do. Or an adventure, depending on how you want to look at it. But I guessed we'd probably get where we were going. People pretty much always do. One way or another.

Then I suddenly knew I wanted to add a PS, so I borrowed the pen back.

'PS: Did you notice that I wrote something on this

one right away? And mailed it? I'm making progress. Love, V.'

I looked up at the lady when I gave her the card.

'You'll make sure this gets into the mail, right?'

'I promise. It's important, I take it.'

'Yeah, it's for my mom.'

'Yeah. Moms are important. I should know. I am one.'

'I owe my mom. I've been pretty hard on her.'

'I'll see to it that this gets on its way to her, then.'

'Thanks.'

Then I walked out into the sun, into the day, and looked up at the sky one last time. Like maybe there was something more for me to do. Something left over. Some sort of goodbye to say.

But it didn't feel that way. It felt like I was all done here.

So I just walked back to Victor's car and got in and said, 'Let's go home now, OK? I'm totally ready to go home.'

So that's what we did.

RICHARD

Dear Myra,

I'm home now. Back from the last of my fool's errands. For better or for worse I do believe I'm done with all that, and looking more ahead.

I called Roger, and he was very understanding about my previous behavior, and had not yet fired me. So hopefully before too long I'll be giving work another try.

I guess you know there's a summing-up here. I suppose you feel it coming.

You've given me a lot of advice over these months, most of which was welcome, some of which was not, and there is obviously a note left hanging about rightness. Sometimes I felt you were right, other times that you were perhaps too cautious, which is certainly your prerogative.

There's a temptation for me to look back now, having gone down some ill-advised roads, and say you were right all along, and that I should have listened to you. But that's not a hundred per cent of the truth.

Here is the truth, as best I can express it.

You were half-right. You said it would bring me nothing but pain, and you were half right. It brought me pain. But it didn't bring me nothing but.

Still glad for your support, no matter who was right and who was wrong. Mostly we're all walking around being both, I think, at almost all times.

I love you, Myra.

Many thanks,

Your son-in-law (still),

Richard

The Art of Maturation

I haven't picked up this journal for months. I haven't even thought about it. But I had to write this down. After everything else I took the trouble to put down in ink, I needed this last bit to complete the experience.

It's almost like an epilogue. In its own way, it's perfect.

It's now February, near the end of the month, and I just heard from Vida again. There were two postcards in-between. But nothing for several months.

The whole thing went like this:

Connie was visiting for the weekend, and I'd been struck by a brilliant flash of creativity involving scallops, garlic and angel-hair pasta. And then, like many absent-minded professor/mad scientist hybrids, at the last minute I had disastrously forgotten the parmesan cheese.

She was nice enough to run to the store and get some. When she let herself back in, she brought a stack of my mail.

'You never bring in your mail,' she said.

'That's true,' I said. 'I never do.'

'Good thing I'm here, then. You got a Valentine's Day card from Vida.'

'Valentine's Day was weeks ago.'

'Don't know what to tell you about that, ace.'

I was up to my elbows in tomatoes. Peeling, seeding, and dicing. So I didn't tend to it right away.

'What makes you think it's a Valentine's Day card?'

She held it up to face me, flap side out. 'The fact that it says, "Happy Valentine's Day" on the back of the envelope.'

'Strong clue. Admittedly. Maybe it's late because she's traveling. Maybe it had to come a long way. Where's it from?'

'Weimar, Germany.'

'Is that a joke?' I set about washing and drying my hands, to see for myself. 'The postmark says Weimar, Germany?'

'No. The return address says Weimar, Germany. The postmark says Weimar, Deutschland. But I think they boil down to the same thing.'

I threw down the dish towel, retrieved my glasses from the counter, and sat down at the kitchen table with Vida's card. I read the postmark, the return address. Examined the foreign stamps. Wondered what had led her so far from home.

When I opened it, I was taken aback by her artwork. It was a handmade card, with a drawing Vida had done on the front. A drawing of a heart. But not a valentine's heart. A heart. An actual human heart, with red muscle and tissue, and red and blue veins and arteries branching in opposite directions.

I turned it around and showed it to Connie.

'Startlingly realistic,' she said.

I opened it and read.

'Dear Richard,' it read. 'I'm beginning to see that point about love you made when I first met you. Maybe it's less like a valentine heart and more like a real one. Like maybe if you give somebody your heart it's this big gnarly muscle of a thing that's not always too pretty to look at. You know? Enough philosophy. Hope you're OK. Love, Vida.'

I read it twice. Lingered over it a bit. Then looked up at Connie.

'I'll read it to you,' I said.

'Not if it's too personal.'

'It isn't, really. More just a reflection on love in general.'

I read Vida's message out loud, and we sat with that for a beat or two.

'I thought you said she was childlike,' Connie said, tossing me the wedge of parmesan cheese.

'Kids grow up,' I said.

THE END

Author's Note

As I mentioned in my acknowledgments, an amazing opportunity presented itself to me in connection with the writing of this novel. A wonderful and very generous team of cardiac surgeons here on the Central Coast of California – Steve Freyaldenhoven, David Canvasser and Luke Faber – allowed me, with proper permissions from both patient and hospital, to observe a heart surgery in progress. In fact, I was in the operating room, suited in scrubs and shoe covers, masked, standing on a small step platform just behind the patient's head, looking down into the open chest cavity. Witnessing the beating (and repair) of a living heart in a living human.

During some of the quieter moments of this procedure, I was able to exchange a few brief thoughts and hear more information from the surgeons. I found myself mentioning that I'd had a niece, Emily, whose heart had given out when she was only twenty-three. She'd been born with heart defects, nearly died on her first night in the world, and endured a catheterization and two open-heart surgeries across the span of her all-too-brief life. Then one day she went to sleep and did not wake up.

Dr Freyaldenhoven asked me if that had been my reason for writing this book.

I told him I wasn't sure, but that I was about to write an author's note for the novel in question, and so would have to figure that out soon enough.

Here's what I came up with, bearing in mind that imagination is always a hard entity to track with any accuracy.

Like the fictional Richard, I saw an item on the news one day, years ago, suggesting that some transplant recipients seem to experience an odd sense of connection with their donors. A sudden craving for the donor's favorite food seemed to be the most common occurrence. Nothing too amazing on the surface of that, until you learn that the recipients didn't know their donors' favorite foods until after they began craving them.

I remember thinking it was curious, and probably one hundred per cent unexplainable.

But it came to mind again when I began to learn more about quantum theory, a subject which never ceases to fascinate and amaze me. It's almost impossible to imagine that our bodies, which seem so solid and so 'there', are, like all matter, made up almost entirely of empty space. It's also hard to unlock from the old and well-worn idea that our brains are the only conscious organ in our bodies, and that we *are* our brains and nothing more than our brains. But the more I read and learn, the more fascinated I become with the idea that every cell in our body is living, breathing, and – in some unfathomable (at least to me) way – aware of itself and of the whole.

Considering all that, what is a heart when removed from its body? Is it merely a pump, like a spare part you take from a car and put into another car? Most people would say so, and yet it seems to me that their gut emotion betrays their logical thinking. For example, I read about a survey on the subject in which a vast majority of people said they believed that a transplanted heart would carry no traces of the memories or attributes of its donor. Yet, curiously, the majority of those same people said they would not want to receive the heart of a murderer in a transplant.

So maybe it depends on whether one consults one's head or heart in the matter.

Whatever you believe on the subject of cellular memory, and I do not quarrel with whatever you choose to believe, there lies the indisputable truth that the modern miracle of organ transplantation is rich with emotional context. A life is saved because another life is cut short. There is celebration in one family even as there is mourning in another. Often the two families find each other and come together to share the experience, to bond through these complex emotions.

It seemed to me that if I couldn't find a story waiting in that emotional storehouse, it was time to turn in my novelist's hat.

Behind and beyond the fascinations listed above, I was able to weave the layers of this story into a set of circumstances all too familiar to me: a child born with a weak and troubled heart. I knew that pain from close experience.

Maybe I wanted to create a fictional young heart patient and write her a happier ending than my niece Emily was able to have. Hard to say.

But, having said all of that, I do want to thank all the medical professionals who make such happy endings possible in the real world, every day.

Reading Group Guide
for
Second Hand Heart

Can you imagine how you would act in Vida's position;
finding yourself with an unexpected chance to live?

Do you understand the feelings Vida had, or felt she had,
for Richard?

Do you believe it is possible for memory to live on in the
cells of transplanted organs?

How did you view Richard's actions in the novel?
Can you imagine overwhelming grief for a lost one
leading you to act as he did?

Did you think his mother-in-law was right to try to deter
him from making contact with Vida?

Have you ever been touched by any of the issues raised
in this book? What sort of a message do you think
Catherine Ryan Hyde is trying send out?

Do you believe in love at first sight?

Can you imagine a book like *Second Hand Heart*
inspiring people to be more open to organ donation?

How did you feel about the way the novel ended?
Was it as you expected, or would you have preferred a
different outcome?

Here's a teaser from

Catherine Ryan Hyde's wonderful novel

When I Found You

The Day He Found You in the Woods

Nathan McCann stood in his dark kitchen, a good two hours before dawn. He flipped on the overhead light, halfway hoping to see the coffeemaker all set up with water and grounds and waiting to be plugged in and set to percolating. Instead he saw the filter basket lying empty in the dish drain, looking abandoned and bare.

Why he always expected otherwise, he wasn't sure. It had been years since Flora set up coffee for him on these early mornings. Decades since she rose early with him to serve fried eggs and orange juice and toast.

Quietly, so as not to wake her, he took a box of oat flake cereal down from the cupboard, then stood in the cold rush of air from the icebox and poured skim milk into a yellow plastic bowl.

You don't have to be so quiet, he thought to himself. Flora was in her bedroom at the far end of the hall with the door closed. But he *was* quiet, always had been in such situations, and felt unlikely to change his pattern now.

As he sat down at the cool Formica table to eat his cereal, he heard Sadie, his curly-coated retriever, awake and ready to go, excited by the prospect of a light on in the house before sunrise. He sat listening to the periodic ringing of the chain-link of her kennel run as she jumped up and hit it with her front paws. Born and bred for just such a morning as this, Sadie recognized a good duck-hunt at its first visible or audible indication.

He often wished he could bring her into the house with him, Sadie who gave so readily of her time and attention. But Flora would have none of it.

Nathan stood in the cool autumn dark, a moment before sunrise, his shotgun angled up across his shoulder.

He insisted that Sadie obey him.

He called her name again, cross with her for forcing him to break the morning stillness, the very reason he had come. In the six years he'd owned the dog, she had never before refused to come when he called.

Remembering this, he shined his big lantern flashlight on her. In the brief instant before she squinted her eyes and turned her face from the light, he saw something, some look that would do for an explanation. In that instinctive way a man knows his dog and a dog knows her man, she had been able to say something to him. She was not defying his judgment, but asking him to consider, for a moment, her own.

'You must come,' she said by way of her expression. 'You must.'

For the first time in the six years he'd owned her, Nathan obeyed his dog. He came when she called him.

She stood under a tree, digging. But she was not digging in that frantic way dogs do, both front feet flying in rhythm. Instead she gently pushed leaves aside with her muzzle, and occasionally with one front paw.

He couldn't see around her, so he pulled her off by the collar.

'OK, girl. I'm here now. Let me see what you've got.'

He shined the light on the mound of fallen leaves. Jutting out from the pile was an unfathomably small – yet unmistakably human – foot.

'Dear God,' Nathan said, and set the flashlight down.

He scooped underneath the lump with both gloved hands at once, lifted the child up to him, blew leaves off its face. It was wrapped in a sweater – a regular adult-sized sweater – and wore a tiny, well-fitted, multi-colored knit cap. It could not have been more than a day or two old.

He felt he would know more if he could hold the flashlight and the child at the same time.

He pulled off one glove with his teeth and touched

the skin of its face. It felt cool against the backs of his fingers.

'What kind of person would do such a thing?' he said quietly. He looked up to the sky as if God were immediately available to answer that question.

The sky had gone light now, but just a trace. Dawn had not crested the hill but lay beyond the horizon somewhere, informally stating that it planned to come to stay.

He set the child gently on the bed of leaves and looked more closely with the flashlight. The child moved its lips and jaw sluggishly, a dry-mouthed gesture, as if mashing something against its palate, or, in any case, wishing it could.

'Dear God,' Nathan said again.

He had not until that moment considered the possibility that the child might be alive.

He left his shotgun in the nest of leaves, because he needed both hands to steady the child's body against his, hold the head firmly to his chest. He and his dog sprinted for the station wagon.

Behind them, dawn broke across the lake. Ducks flew unmolested. Forgotten.

At the hospital, two emergency-room workers sprang into rapid, jerky motion when they saw what Nathan held. They set the infant on a cart, a speck in the middle of an ocean, and unwrapped the sweater. A boy, Nathan saw. A boy still wearing his umbilical cord, a badge of innocence.

As they ran, rolling the cart alongside, a doctor caught up and pulled off the knit cap. It fell to the linoleum floor unnoticed. Nathan picked it up, stowed it in a zippered pocket of his hunting vest. It was so small, that cap; it wouldn't cover Nathan's palm.

He moved as close to the door of the examining room as he felt would be allowed.

He heard the doctor say, 'Throw him out in the woods on an October night, then give him a nice warm sweater and a little hand-knit hat to hold in his body heat. Now that's ambivalence.'

Nathan walked down the hall and bought a cup of hot coffee from a vending machine. It was indeed hot, but that's all that could be said for it.

He stood for several minutes in front of the coffee machine, gazing into its shiny metal face as if looking at a television set, or out a window. Or into a mirror. Because, in fact, he could see a vague, slightly distorted reflection of himself there.

Nathan was not a man given to eyeing himself for extended moments in mirrors. Shaving was one thing, but to look into his own eyes would cause him to demur, much the way he would if looking into the eyes of another. But the image was just ill-defined enough to cause him no stress or embarrassment.

So he stood for a moment, sipping the dreadful coffee, allowing himself to take in the evidence of his own sentience. Feeling, in a way he could not have explained, that some history was being shaped, the importance of which could not be fully estimated.

Something had been set in motion, he allowed himself to think, that could never, and perhaps should never, be reversed.

When he had finished the coffee, he rinsed out the cup at the water fountain and refilled it with fresh water.

He walked back out to the station wagon to offer Sadie a drink.

Twenty or thirty minutes later the doctor came out of that room.

'Doctor,' Nathan called, and ran down the hall. The doctor looked blank, as if he could not recall where he'd seen Nathan before. 'I'm the man who found that baby in the woods.'

'Ah, yes,' the doctor said. 'So you are. Can you stay a few minutes? The police will want to speak with you. If you have to go, please leave your phone number at the desk. I'm sure you understand. They'll want all the details they can get. To try to find who did this thing.'

'How is the boy?'

'What kind of shape is he in? Bad shape. Will he survive? Maybe. I don't promise, but he's a fighter.

Sometimes they're stronger than you can imagine at that age.'

'I want to adopt that boy,' Nathan said.

He felt more than a little bit stunned to hear himself say those words.

First of all, he had not really known this to be the case. At least, not in words. Not in an identifiable sense. It was as if he had told the doctor and himself in one broad stroke. And, secondly, it was unlike him to share his thoughts easily with others, especially if he had not had sufficient time to mull them over, grow accustomed to them.

It seemed this was a morning of unlimited firsts.

'If he survives, you mean.'

Yes,' Nathan said. Already stung by the gravity of the warning. 'If he survives.'

'I'm sorry,' the doctor said. 'Adoption would not be my department.'

He told the story in earnest detail to the two policemen when they arrived and took his statement, careful to stress that the real hero was sitting out in the back seat of his station wagon.

'Baby'd be dead if it wasn't for you,' the more vocal of the two policemen said. He was a tall, broad-shouldered man, the type who seemed to rely more on brawn than intellect to guide him through this life. Normally Nathan would have been intimidated and repelled by such a man, law officer or not. So it raised a strange and conflicted set of emotions when the policeman spoke to him as a hero.

'And Sadie,' Nathan said. 'My dog. She's a curly-coated retriever. She's a remarkable animal.'

'Right. Look. We know you've got stuff to do, but we need you to show us the exact crime scene.'

'No inconvenience,' Nathan said. 'I was on my way back there now, to retrieve my shotgun.'

They began walking toward the hospital parking lot together.

'I want to adopt that boy,' Nathan said. Not so much to bare his soul, but in hopes of being steered in the right direction. He felt an unfamiliar sense of haste, as if something could slip away from him if he didn't hurry and pin it down.

'We couldn't tell you nothing about that,' the policeman replied.

Nathan wisely resisted the impulse to correct his grammar.

Buy **When I Found You** online
at www.rbooks.co.uk

When I Found You

CATHERINE RYAN HYDE

When Nathan McCann discovers a newborn baby boy half buried in the woods, he assumes he's found a tiny dead body. But then the baby moves and in one remarkable moment, Nathan's life is changed forever.

The baby is sent to grow up with his grandmother, but Nathan is compelled to pay her a visit. He asks for one simple promise – that one day she will introduce the boy to Nathan and tell him, 'This is the man who found you in the woods.'

Years pass and Nathan assumes that the old lady has not kept her promise, until one day an angry, troubled boy arrives on his doorstep with a suitcase . . .

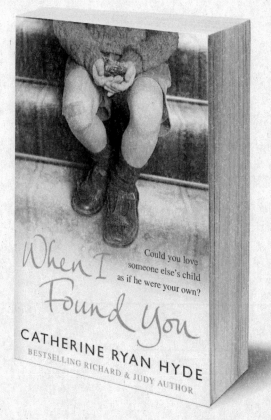

When I Found You

Could you love someone else's child as if he were your own?

CATHERINE RYAN HYDE

BESTSELLING RICHARD & JUDY AUTHOR